COMING HOME

BOOK TWO OF THE FRIENDS & LOVERS SERIES

PE KAVANAGH

BOLD
SOUL
BOOKS

COMING HOME
Copyright © 2018 PE Kavanagh

For information contact: Pascale Kavanagh
www.pekavanagh.com

Cover designed by Olivia Pro Designs and Bliss Designs

E-book ISBN: 978-0-9994679-6-1
Paperback ISBN: 978-0-9994679-7-8

First Edition: May 2018
10 9 8 7 6 5 4 3 2 1

For all of us who had to leave home to discover how much it meant to us.

CHAPTER ONE

A drop of melted Cheddar oozed out between crisp slices of bread, warming the corner of Ramona's mouth. She flicked out her tongue and caught the errant piece of deliciousness. The sharp tang, tempered by something earthy and creamy, pushed a satisfied groan up from the bottom of her belly. This was turning out to be a whole body eating experience.

With one more bite, the first piece was gone. She looked up from the other half of the sandwich, cut into a perfect triangle, crusts removed, to find Lucas' gaze intent on her. "I have to say, your grilled cheese sandwiches are even better than I remember. Even though they were always amazing."

Lucas leaned forward, tanned forearms flexed on the expanse of the stainless steel worktable. "Glad to see my extensive culinary education wasn't a complete waste of time."

She picked up the remaining piece and paused, deciding to exercise the tiniest bit of self-control and not put the whole thing in her mouth. "No. I think you picked right. All this scrumptious food would have been wasted on a bunch of stuffy lawyers."

A shrug accompanied a dimple-enhanced grin. "Except those stuffy lawyers are now my main customers."

"Lucky them." She took one more bite and licked each of her fingers, giving up on manners. After all, this was Lucas, the boy who'd been by her side for the first half of her life. Absence of their hard-earned etiquette wasn't going to offend him. What he was feeding her was much too delicious to hold back.

He pulled a champagne bottle from the industrial-sized refrigerator and refilled her glass. "I still can't believe you're here, in my kitchen. After all this time."

"Gotta thank Connor for that. My brother's been nearly impossible to reach lately, but he made sure I knew how to find your restaurant. I don't do airplane food." Ramona wondered how much her brother had told his best friend, Lucas, about her over the years. Did he know how much time she spent on planes and about her refusal to touch any of that food?

"How come you got in so late? He told me you'd be here by eight or nine."

"Oh, sorry." She gave him what she hoped expressed remorse. When your life depended on air travel, getting anywhere on time was always risky. Besides, she liked having the restaurant, and the chef, all to herself. "There was *weather* in San Francisco, as always. And we hit a bunch of traffic as we approached downtown D.C."

"Did you give your driver the shortcut?"

She shook her head. "How would I know a shortcut?"

He laughed. "Right. I keep forgetting how you never come home anymore."

This hasn't been home for a really long time. "Anyway, I

really appreciate your staying open so late and cooking me all my favorites. I didn't mean to take advantage."

"Mowgli, I can't think of any way I'd rather spend this night than feeding you."

She flattened her palm on the cool steel worktable. His oh-too-sultry smirk generated even more heat in the warm kitchen. "Speaking of which, can you make me another grilled cheese?"

"But you haven't even finished this one. And I have a few more things for you to try tonight."

Ramona shifted on the hard stool. Why did everything he said sound like an innuendo? "It's for tomorrow. For breakfast."

"That's a terrible idea. It's going to be inedible tomorrow." He thrummed his fingers on the counter. "You can just come back and I'll make you a fresh one."

Her eyebrows crinkled in confusion. "Uh, I'm going to be a bit busy tomorrow."

He frowned. "Right. I forgot. Sorry."

She emptied her glass in one gulp. "No worries." She wished she could forget, too.

Lucas pulled a towel from a hook and pivoted to wipe along the edge of the cooktop. His broad shoulders shimmied as he worked a particular spot, sandy brown curls grazing the top of his white chef's jacket.

Ramona sucked in a breath, trying not to ogle the remarkable sight. He definitely didn't look like he'd been partaking of his rich, restaurant food. All the chubby softness of his youth had transformed into a rock solid wall of a man.

He turned as her gaze hovered around his bottom. Her eyes didn't move nearly fast enough to play it off. It was impossible to know if he knew that she was staring. And what she was staring at.

He shook the towel out. "What's up, Mo?"

Something in the sweetness of his voice switched on a memory of a life she had all but tucked away. "It feels like no time has passed. Like we're kids again."

His smile broadened. "Except that instead of being noon, it's midnight."

"And we're in your phenomenal restaurant, instead of my mom's kitchen."

He looked down and swiped a crumb from the counter. "And I've learned how to clean up after myself."

"Looks like you've learned a lot of things. Including how to grow facial hair." *And a super hot bod.*

He stroked his close-cropped goatee. "Yeah, I've had that one down for some time now. Speaking of growing things, I see all those prayers for boobs finally paid off."

Ramona's mouth opened with a dramatic gasp, heat blazing her cheeks, and a laugh threatening to dissolve her efforts at propriety. "That is completely inappropriate."

"Oh, come on, Mo. I was the first one to ever touch them, if you remember."

It wasn't possible to keep a straight face. "There was nothing there to touch."

"Oh, there was plenty. Trust me." He tilted his head and looked up toward the open pipework of the ceiling. "It was the highlight of my boyhood. Maybe of my entire life."

So hard not to check out her own chest, make sure everything was full and lofty. "I would have hoped you'd made some more substantial memories than my non-existent teenage boobs."

"I appreciate your confidence in me, but you seriously underestimate how great they were." He cupped his hands and sighed. "Small, but perfect."

She shook her head and chuckled, keeping her eyes straight ahead. *Don't look down, Ramona.*

"By the way… not small anymore." He wasn't trying to keep his eyes away.

"Okay, you seriously have to stop talking about my breasts." And staring at them. "You're acting like you're fifteen again." She stopped herself from crossing her arms in front of her chest, afraid it would bring even more attention to the area.

"I feel fifteen again, with you here."

Time to regain control of this conversation. "It's great to see you, Baloo. Really great." Too great, maybe. "And I would love if you could get on with making whatever else you intend to feed me. I'm still hungry."

The left side of his mouth quirked upward in the grin she would know anywhere, even though it was on a face she hadn't seen in a very long time. A face, complete with a broad jaw, full lips and a hint of a wrinkle in the corner of his eyes. A manly man's face. "Glad to see the bossiness hasn't changed."

"Haven't quite outgrown that one, I suppose."

He turned on a burner and slid a shiny pan over the flame. "Good."

She scanned the entirety of the bright kitchen, anything to avoid staring at him while he prepared her next goodies. Lusting after her childhood buddy during a quick trip to town was not a smart maneuver. Too many connections would make it impossible to cut-and-run. And when it came to spending time in Virginia, less was more.

He made an almost imperceptible growl in response to whatever was happening on the cooktop. His large hand wiped down the side of his chef pants, highlighting that bottom again. It was useless. She dropped her chin into her palm and just let herself enjoy the view.

Two plates slid toward her, piled with colors as vibrant as the cover of any cookbook. Tart tomato salad and bright green dumplings in a sesame broth brought her closer to satisfaction, but not completely. She looked up from the empty plates with a sheepish grin.

Without a pause, or even a hint of judgment in those hazel eyes, he cleared them away. "Okay, Mo, I've got one more thing."

She was pretty sure he had quite a bit more than *one more thing*. "Great. I need to use the loo, though."

"Use the one in my office." He pointed toward a bowl big enough for her to bathe in. "Just past the mixer and down the hall. I'll bring the final course to you."

"Perfect."

Ramona used the bathroom quickly, averting her eyes from all the mirrors. Thoughts she shouldn't be having made it hard to look at herself. She and Lucas... well, their childhood bond had cracked a long time ago. But the combination of tender nostalgia and sharp desire was making it much too easy to succumb to a very adult fantasy. Besides, Lucas was flirting back. She was sure of it.

She stepped back into the office, large and full, but not messy. No sign of Lucas, so she walked in a slow circle around the space. It was oddly shaped, with almost no parallel walls, several of which were glass, offering a panoramic view of the kitchen. A wide bookcase held ancient-looking cookbooks, and an entire wall, behind a modern white lacquer desk, was graced with framed diplomas, certificates, and letters. She pushed the desk chair aside to examine his awards.

It was impressive. Accolades from two different culinary schools and various specialty programs around the world.

Articles about his first restaurant, and now this newer one. Awards for being named a top young chef three years in a row, and pictures with two presidents. He walked in as she examined the row of five framed letters clearly different than all the rest. They were handwritten and adorned with pencil and crayon drawings, all addressed to Mr. Chef Lucas.

A clang of metal caught her attention. He'd set a large tray on the bench against the back wall, holding another bottle of champagne, as well as several plates with desserts that looked like pieces of art.

As she approached him, her eyes swept over the assortment and her mouth watered. "Wow, Baloo. Is that all for me?"

"For us." He poured a flute of champagne, which made her wonder what had happened to her previous glass. "Start with this."

Slightly bolder than the first bottle, with a hint of peach at the finish. "Spectacular."

"And now this." He put something the color of mocha into her mouth. It melted almost instantly into a sweet, spicy, brandy-tinged bolt of utter mouth happiness.

She walked back over to the desk. "That's a pretty impressive wall over there. Much more so than a silly law degree."

"Says the woman who actually finished law school. And passed the bar."

That seemed so long ago. "Not that I'm practicing law, either."

He swept the hair that had fallen across her forehead over to the side. "You know, I can see that you've been getting proper haircuts, Mo, but it still seems to fall over your eyes."

"Well, it's fashionable now."

He kept his palm on her cheek. "I still can't believe I'm looking at your face. More beautiful than ever."

His finger grazed her jawline and lifted her chin. The perfect start to a kiss, had they been different people.

Ramona turned around to face the award wall, mostly to compose herself and certain she could not hide how very much she wanted him to kiss her. Damn. Indecision sucked, but that's all she could muster.

She pointed to the hand-written letters. "Tell me about those."

He moved directly behind her, his body molded into her back. She placed her palms on the desktop to steady the nearly imperceptible tremor that was developing in response to the pressure of his body on hers.

He exhaled next to her ear. "Oh, my kids." A sweet sigh followed. "They're from Chisholm Elementary, on the south side. I go over there a couple of times a year and do a cooking class, and we talk about healthy food. I love those kids. Sweetest, smartest, most alive people I know. Some of their lives are beyond disastrous. And yet, they are amazing."

He rested his chin on top of her shoulder.

"Looks like they love you back, Mr. Chef Lucas."

A synchronized breath softened her back into his chest. He wrapped his arm around her waist. A lightning-fast analysis of pros and cons played itself out in her head.

Pro: This was Lucas. She'd never been closer to another human being in her life.
Cons: 1 - This was Lucas. They hardly knew each other anymore.
2 - The cause of her return home to Virginia might warrant some decorum.
3 - This wouldn't be a one-night stand she could run away from.
Pro: This was Lucas. The boy with a heart of gold

who'd become a man who was hot as hell. Hotter than hell, probably.

Con: This was-

Fuck it.

In an unprecedented display of boldness, she took his hand and moved it from her hip to her belly, then slowly slid it up, over her ribs, and finally grazing over her left breast, where she kept it.

When his fingers squeezed softly, a scratchy breath escaped him. She placed her palms back on the desk and used the leverage to press her bottom into him, eliminating any space between their bodies. From his chest to his legs, everything behind her was hard as steel.

His hand moved up to her throat, then down again, this time inside the deep opening of her dress. He cupped her breast while the other hand slid down her outer thigh, over her skirt, then back up underneath it. She stepped her legs further apart.

"Ramona..." His fingers slid beneath the front of her thong.

Warm fingers, hot breath, all *yes*. It was increasingly hard to keep up as hands lifted her skirt and pulled her thong down, returning to graze her wetness.

She reached behind her to find the bulge beneath his zipper. Even through his pants, it was evident that there was something significant between his legs and it was rock hard. She clumsily tried to undo his belt buckle while swirling in the sensation of the finger that had just entered her.

He completed the task of removing his pants, evident by the metallic clink of his belt hitting the floor, and then the feel of his cock where his finger had been. He stopped.

"Fuck me, Lucas."

Hesitation gone, he pushed inside her in successive strokes. She willed herself to relax, to take him in, even as her entire body wanted to contract with the craving for him. They moaned in matching octaves. She thought she might burst with the fullness of him, and that would be a perfectly acceptable way to go.

He stopped. Again. "I need to see you."

He pulled out of her and spun her toward him, taking her mouth in a fierce embrace. She perched her bottom on the edge of the desk and opened herself for him. He entered her in a graceful stroke. The wetness dripping from her and having coated him gave him ample lubrication to plunge into her.

She grabbed his neck and molded her mouth to his while he wrapped his arm around her, keeping her from falling back. With each stroke, she groaned louder until that familiar build-up in the deepest part of her belly. The need for a breath pulled her away from his lips and brought her face down to the top of his shoulder, which she bit in matching intensity to the orgasm that cascaded over her.

He slowed as she did.

"Don't stop. Please."

"I'm going to-"

"Yes." Her hands moved to his buttocks and pressed him deeper. His hand slapped the wall when a growl escaped his throat. Each pulse of his orgasm sent a jolt up her spine, and she held on for dear life.

"Holy shit." His body continued shaking as she took his face in her hands.

She ran her tongue along the thick edge of his lower lip and then stuck it in between. The ferocity of their desire gave way to something much more tender and intimate. They kissed like that, as they might have as teenagers, until the cold desk created a shiver up her spine.

She pulled away to catch her breath. He loosened the grasp around her waist and slid out of her.

"Ramona..."

There was nothing she could possibly say.

He stared into her eyes. "Are you okay?"

His semen ran down the inside of her leg. "Yes. Of course."

She wanted to get to the bathroom, but each move sent another trail of cum farther down, now into her shoes. He didn't let go.

She gave him one more kiss before moving him tenderly away.

He helped smooth her dress after he had put his underwear and pants back on. "I now have one less item on my bucket list."

She halted the search for her underwear. Had he really just said... "Fucking someone on your desk?"

"No." He fumbled with the buttons on his jacket. "Being with you."

He really did say it. "Having sex with me was on your bucket list?"

"Since I was eleven." His cheek quivered.

"Wow." Her teenage mind hadn't taken their explorations that far. And this was one hell of a strange postcoital conversation.

"That's not really how I imagined it, though." He grazed her arm. "A bit less fast and furious, maybe."

The room wasn't big enough to contain the enormity of her discomfort. "I need to go clean up. I'll be right back."

She stood in the bathroom for longer than was necessary. This time, there was no avoiding all those mirrors. Eyeliner had smeared across her cheek, and her lips were puffy and red. Her hand shook as she threw cold water on her face. It didn't do anything to still her growing anxiety.

She had just fucked her childhood friend. The boy she thought she'd always love but hadn't seen in fifteen years. It was amazing, no doubt, but wrong. Probably wrong. Maybe not wrong?

Ugh. Either way, she was in no position to address either his confession or their transgression. She tried to wrangle her hair behind her ears, but it was a lost cause. Deep breath in, deep breath out. Maybe it wasn't as bad as she thought. Maybe this night would turn out to be a fun highlight of an otherwise dreadful visit. They could be cool, right? At least long enough for her to do what she needed to do, then get the hell out of town.

Lucas was looking down at his hands when Ramona stepped back into the office. She was not a stranger to sticky situations, but this was a whole different type of challenge. *God, this is awkward.* "It's getting late."

"Let me take you home, Mo."

Anything to not have to keep facing him, hair mussed by her own hand. And not from a rough game of touch football on his front lawn. "Sure, thanks."

They sat silently during the car ride across town. She hoped her father had kept the door unlocked, as she had requested. She didn't want anything delaying a speedy entry into the house.

Lucas took her hand after parking in her father's narrow driveway. "I know this is strange. But it doesn't have to be. It's still just me... Baloo."

"That's what makes it strange." She reached over and gave him a small kiss. "Good night, Lucas."

"See you tomorrow."

The deep smile on his remarkable face was nearly enough to hold down her rising dread about the day that would begin in only a few more hours. The entire reason for her trip.

"Yes. See you tomorrow."

CHAPTER TWO

*R*amona squirmed on the church pew, acutely aware of the tenderness resulting from the previous night's escapades. How embarrassing. Her childhood friend would now think of her as the floozy who fucked him on his desk. Too bad it had felt so damn good. She couldn't even muster a credible level of guilt or repentance. Not for the fun she had the night before and not for the day's solemn event.

Her grandfather certainly knew how to go big, even under these conditions. The largest cathedral in town still wasn't big enough, filled with more old white men than a Rolling Stones concert. Too bad he wasn't there to see it, as he currently resided in the large mahogany box in front of the altar.

Ramona flipped her attention from the ostentatious flowers directly in front of their pew to her father, whose color was fading by the second. He was paler than his dead father. She took his hand and gave it a gentle squeeze.

"It's going to be okay, Dad. You can get through this."

He kept his gaze straight ahead. "I know, pumpkin. As long as you're here."

As per her grandfather's specific requests, they were to have a full Catholic mass prior to the funeral service and celebration banquet. With her father out of commission and her out of the loop for so many years, host duties landed on two much more appropriate people: her brother, Connor, and Lucas' father, Congressman Winston, the son her grandfather wished he'd had.

Thankfully, the Congressman was born for this kind of thing: warm, caring, and likely the only one in the room sad that the old bastard had died. Ramona's grandfather had been hailed the most beloved governor of Virginia, but he was the most awful human being she had ever known. He was the cause of her mother's abrupt departure, her father's descent into addiction, and her own obsession with turning the wheels of power and money toward those who'd been taken advantage of. At least it had set her on a path to a career that she loved, and was damn good at.

Lucas had been nowhere to be found when they'd arrived at the church, which she accepted as a small gift. This day was already enough to handle without having to look in the face of the man who used to race her up and down the block and now sported a rather substantial bite mark on his shoulder.

She used every minute of the mind-numbingly long service to re-enact their fantastic evening, though. Even the memories were enough to create some very interesting sensations between her legs. Lucas had become one hell of a man. She hadn't been seduced like that in... well... maybe ever. It reset all she thought she knew about the boy she hadn't seen in years.

Her brother startled her out of the tenth or twelfth replaying to inform them it was time to go. The eyes behind the black-framed glasses were hardly red. And, of course, in typical Connor fashion, not a single hair was out of place. If only he could figure out how to wear suits that didn't look like he'd stolen them out of his father's closet.

"Let's wait until the church clears out, Con. I don't want Dad standing, waiting to get out, for any longer than he has to."

Ramona waited for a sign from her dad that he wanted to approach the casket, to take a moment alone with his own father, but he made no attempt to stand. Despite his long-term sobriety, he might well have been fantasizing about making his way to the bottom of a very full bottle.

When the entryway cleared, she and her brother each took one of their father's arms and supported him on the brief walk to the limo. They drove slowly to Congressman Winston's house, the location for the next part of the traveling devotional.

The frenzy hit them as soon as they entered the house. Were there even more people than in the church? She could hardly believe this many people cared about the son of a bitch. Maybe they had come just to confirm that he was, in fact, dead.

Her father slumped in her arms moments after Connor got pulled into the crowd. "I think I'm going to be sick, pumpkin."

She scanned the pack of black-clothed bodies for a reasonable opening to squeeze through. "Okay, Dad. Hold on. I'm taking you to the bathroom right now."

A bit rougher than she would have liked, she whisked her father to the larger of the powder rooms on the main floor. Getting him to a more private space would have been optimal, but she had no chance of helping him up the enormous spiral staircase in the center of the house.

She leaned against the wall outside the bathroom and waited for him to finish.

"Mo!"

She snapped her eyes open at the same time she realized she'd closed them.

"I've been looking for you everywhere."

The look on Lucas' face was not what she wanted to see. Urgent, frightened even. She swallowed. "What's wrong?"

"I have to talk to you. It's important."

"It's okay. We don't have to talk about what happened. Especially not today. Let's just let it go for now."

"It's not about that."

Curiosity outranked relief. "It's not?"

"I mean, it's kind of about that. I just need to tell you something."

Her father opened the door to the bathroom, startling them both. "Oh, hello Lucas."

He drew Ramona's father into his arms and held him in a soft hug. "Mr. Barrett. How are you holding up, sir?"

Her father stepped back. "As well as can be expected, I suppose."

"Please tell me if there's anything I can do for you. If you'd like to have a rest upstairs, it's no problem."

"I'm okay for now. Thank you, Lucas."

Ramona began to walk her father back into the center of the house when Lucas grabbed her arm. "I really need to talk to you, Mo. Please."

"In a bit, okay? I'll come find you." Ramona hoped that she could avoid that for the rest of the day. There should be enough people at this event to camouflage her. If all else failed, it wouldn't be the first time she'd hidden out with caterers trying to avoid unwanted attention.

She watched him go left toward the kitchen while she turned the corner to find the next obstacle staring at her. She stopped so abruptly her father nearly toppled over.

"Hey, gorgeous."

The familiar face with a devilish grin felt completely out of context in that room. "Tyler..."

He smirked. "Hmmm. By the look on your face, I'd say you forgot I was coming."

"Oh my God, Tyler. I'm so sorry. I did forget. It's been so crazy..."

"No worries, sweetheart. I'm just glad to see you."

Without asking, he put his arm around her father and walked him the rest of the way toward an open seat. She didn't dare glance back to see if *anyone* was watching.

"You remember Tyler, Dad?"

"Yes, yes," her dad said in a way that Ramona knew meant absolutely not. It didn't matter. Her father had gotten used to getting help from strangers.

As soon as Dad was settled, Tyler wrapped his arms around her. "How you holding up, Robin?"

"Like an umbrella in a thunderstorm."

"Want me to whisk you away from here?"

She broke the embrace. "I can't, Ty. I have to stay, if only for my Dad."

"Where's soon-to-be Senator Connor?"

An eye-roll couldn't be stopped. "Getting his ass kissed, probably, by everyone pretending that he's not the one they really came to see. He'll be lucky if he has a minute to pee. He hasn't even announced his candidacy, and the sucking up has already begun."

"Ah, the benefits of being the one who's going to save the world."

"Yeah, right." Except, her brother thought he just might.

"Any sign of your mother?"

Ramona had completely forgotten about her mother's tendency to show up in the last place anyone expected her to be. "Connor pretty much confirmed she wasn't coming. Not that I'd expect her to, considering her feelings about my grandfather."

"But it is your mother..."

Yes, the last place she would be.

Tyler glanced around the room. "So, this is a huge room full of politicians."

"Yup. And all their servants and sycophants."

"Cool." He quirked an eyebrow in deference. "Such a different scene from our world."

Tyler clearly didn't realize that this *was* her world. Or at least it had been before she walked away from it all.

He steered her from a gawking group of jowly men. "How was the funeral service?"

"Infinitely long and interminably boring. It would have made you grateful to be Jewish."

"Understood. I think heavy drinking is in order. Don't you?"

Now we're talking. "Best idea I've heard all day."

The short line at the bar took no time, and a glass of red wine landed in her very grateful hand. Ramona glanced over to make sure her father was fine. He was mostly left undisturbed. Not a good candidate for ingratiating. She finally exhaled a sigh of relief. It was all going to be fine...

"Ramona Barrett."

The hairs on the back of her neck stood to attention as the other voice that narrated her childhood nightmares spoke her name. There was no need to turn around to know who had addressed her, but she did anyway.

"Mrs. Winston. Lovely to see-"

"Well, look at you. All grown up. I just can't believe how much you kids have changed. It's remarkable." She glanced over at Tyler and likely made the quick assessment about his importance and returned to Ramona.

"You're looking well, Mrs.-"

"Condolences on your loss, Ramona."

"Thank y-"

"Have you seen Lucas yet? Oh my gosh, he might not even recognize you. Let me go get him."

Ramona could have said that they had seen each other. And fucked each other. But she decided against it. Either way, Mrs. Winston had disappeared into the crowd and was on her way back with her son firmly in the steely grip of her hand. *Great.*

As Lucas approached, Ramona noticed that attached to his other arm was a brunette being pulled along like a child on a conga line.

"Lucas, look who I found! It's Ramona! Can you believe it!"

"It's her grandfather's funeral, Mother," he said, with barely restrained contempt.

Mrs. Winston drew a palm across her perfect platinum chignon. "Well, of course."

Ramona took an oversized swig of her wine at the same moment the brunette extended her hand. "Abigail Langley. The future Mrs. Winston."

The contents of Ramona's mouth made an abrupt course change and exited, with impressive velocity, toward the tall, grinning woman in a previously impeccable suit.

Lucas' mother covered her mouth, exclaimed, "Oh my!" and rushed toward the buffet table. Tyler grabbed a handful of napkins from the bar while Lucas stood frozen with wide eyes and a curled lip. Horror.

"I'm so sorry. I don't know what happened. Something must have caught in my throat."

Both men gaped at her, but Tyler reached out to dab at Abigail's collar and sleeve.

Ramona took hold of Abigail's still outstretched hand and shook it. " So sorry about that. I'm Ramona. Nice to meet you. And... sorry... again."

One of the most frightening smiles Ramona had ever seen took over Abigail's face. "Good thing we're all wearing black, isn't it?" A single huff punctured the shocked space.

Abigail's increasingly disturbing reaction temporarily distracted Ramona from what she had just heard. But only briefly.

"Did you say the future Mrs. Winston?"

The creepy smile deepened. "I sure did. Lucas and I are getting married in less than a month. Isn't that right, darling?"

Lucas looked away. "Yes, Abby. That's right."

It took all Ramona's will to manage the contortion that wanted to take over her face, and smile instead. Her heart was beating so hard and so fast she thought she might fall over, and held on to Tyler for balance.

He extended his free hand. "Hi. I'm Tyler. Tyler Diamond."

Abigail's eyes and mouth formed into perfect circles. "*The* Tyler Diamond?"

Tyler put on the humble demeanor that Ramona had witnessed several times, but that the rest of the world didn't know existed.

"Oh, my God. Mr. Diamond, I am such an admirer of yours. I mean your technology has changed millions of lives. Billions probably. Wow. I can't believe I'm at a party with Tyler Diamond."

"We're at a funeral, Abby. Not a party." Lucas spoke to her as if he was scolding a child.

She didn't skip a beat. "Oh, of course, darling. Everyone knows what I meant."

Lucas fixed his gaze on Ramona with a look she could have interpreted as an apology. That is, if she could get her mind to process what was happening.

"Thank you, Abby," Tyler said. "I appreciate that. And congratulations on your engagement."

"Thank you. We're thrilled, aren't we, darling?"

Lucas looked away. He did not attempt to acknowledge or answer Abigail's question.

Tyler cleared his throat. "Well, I guess you can call me the future Mr. Barrett, then."

Lucas and Ramona spoke in almost perfect unison. "What?!"

Abigail laughed, much too loudly. "That's so funny, Mr. Diamond. So you're going to give up your fantastic last name?"

"Well, Diamond is pretty good, sure. But Barrett is the name of legends." Cue million-dollar smile.

Abigail shifted her attention to Ramona as if she was deciding how legendary she thought she was.

Olivia Winston returned at that moment with a cloth napkin, well after they'd all moved on from the spitting incident.

Abigail reached out to pat Olivia's arm. "Thank you, Mama Winston. It's fine."

"So, you've all met. Wonderful!" Olivia beamed at Tyler. Maybe someone had told her who he was. "Did you know that Lucas and Ramona were childhood friends? Inseparable, really. And they had these ridiculous names for each other. Something about animals, wasn't it?" She squinted at her son. "What was it again?"

Ramona answered. "Luc called me Mowgli, and I called him Baloo."

Abby tapped her lip. "Oooh, from that movie. Wait, I know..."

"Jungle Book." Tyler put his arm around Ramona under Lucas' stare. "That's adorable."

Olivia continued. "I have no idea why they would use those odd names. I never did get it."

"That's because Ramona was always climbing trees and playing in the dirt. And her hair was always a mess." Lucas smiled.

"And you were funny and kind-"

"—and fat. Believe it or not, Lucas was a big, round boy, always sneaking food out of the kitchen. You'd never know it now, but I have pictures." She wagged her finger like a good old-fashioned motherly threat.

"That's enough, Mother."

"Speaking of food," Olivia said, with an effortless change of topic, "we have plenty, so don't forget to eat."

They all nodded as the already-was Mrs. Winston gave her best royal wave and walked away.

Abigail returned her focus on Tyler, with a look that Ramona had only ever used while imagining someone naked. "So, how did you two meet?"

"Philanthropy is one of my core values. And Ramona is the best in the world. In fact, we have our pet names for each other, too. I always used to tease her that she was like Robin Hood, if he were brilliant and beautiful. And then she started calling me Bruce, like Bruce Wayne, because... well... mixing mythology."

Lucas' face could not have gotten any tighter. Abigail couldn't get enough. "So, you work together?"

"Not exactly. When I started MindNet, I knew I wanted

to promote as much charitable giving as possible, so I brought Ramona in to create an employee contribution plan. Then she took over the corporate plan for all my companies, and, finally, my personal donations. I feel like one of her makes up for all the greed and destruction of a hundred people. She's amazing."

Ramona smiled in a way that she hoped Tyler understood very clearly. Although she was relieved that Tyler had taken over the conversation, there was going to be a discussion in his near future about their supposed engagement.

"Well, that's wonderful!" Abigail reached out and patted Tyler's shoulder. "Lucas and I met in law school. Which he didn't finish, as you might know, because now he's a world-famous chef. He's cooked for *presidents*." Her head bowed as if she had just spilled state secrets.

Tyler gave her an appreciative nod. "A chef... very cool. Too bad I won't have time to check out the restaurant. I'm headed right back out of town tonight. But next time. Definitely."

"You came all the way from the west coast just for the funeral?" Lucas asked.

"Well, I actually came in from London this morning. But I'm headed to New York right after this."

"I'm headed to New York as well! I'm working on a huge federal case, so I've been spending most of my time there for months. Can't wait till that's over. Anyway, it's a tight squeeze with the last flight out, or I might have to drive."

"Oh, I can take you on my plane if you like."

Abigail looked as if she might start jumping up and down but the precise tailoring of her suit would not permit such movement. "Tyler, that would be wonderful! Are you sure that's alright?"

"Of course. I have plenty of room."

Lucas took one large step forward, closing any gap between himself and Ramona. "While you two sort out the details, I'd like to borrow Ramona for a moment. Have to check the... menu... for our foundation benefit."

No one answered.

The grip on her arm was more intense than she would have liked, as was his stride through the crowded hall. She barely kept up as he pulled her through the center of the room, up the stairs, and into his old bedroom.

She examined the semi-familiar surroundings. It had been re-decorated but still contained hints of when they were kids.

"What the fuck, Ramona?! You're engaged? To Tyler Diamond? I mean, you're not even wearing a ring!"

"First of all, I'm not engaged."

"But he said-"

"Tyler Diamond is like a large child. He likes to play around, tease people. We are not engaged."

His hands flew up to either side of his head. "Why would someone make up something like that?"

She considered how much of the truth to tell. "We used to date. He was joking around. Or maybe he thinks there's a chance..."

"So your internet mogul boyfriend is confused about whether you're engaged or not?"

Although Ramona had hardly practiced law before switching career gears, she could still muster one hell of an argument, when needed. "This would all be fascinating except for the fact that you are *actually* engaged. As evidenced by the excited woman, the enormous diamond, and the wedding scheduled for... what was it... less than a month from now."

"It's not what you think."

"Oh, is Abby a jokester as well? Because she doesn't seem like the type to joke about such things."

"It's complicated."

"Are you kidding me? You pull me into this room ready to accuse me of something when you're the only one who's actually about to be married and neglected to mention that when you were fucking me on your desk!"

And there, the case would have been won.

Lucas stepped back. "I see you're upset. Maybe we should talk about this another time."

One step brought her inches away from him. "Damn straight I'm upset. What did you think? As if it's not bad enough that we... what happened. Now, I'm faced with you being a cheater. This is not who I thought you were. This is not who I wanted you to be." Tears threatened to press through, but Ramona clamped down even harder. She didn't need to cry in front of this hypocrite.

"That's hurtful, Mo." He took a slow breath. "I just need you to trust me that things aren't as they seem. I can't say any more than that. I'm sorry."

"Fuck you, Lucas."

She stormed out of the room and bumped straight into Olivia Winston.

"Everything alright? I heard loud voices up here."

"Yes, Mrs. Winston. Lucas and I were just... reliving old times." She walked several more steps. "Oh, and congratulations on the upcoming wedding."

CHAPTER THREE

*R*amona didn't know if her grandfather had continued his ill deeds from the grave, but someone had turned this dreadful day into a disaster. Coming to his funeral had been a terrible idea. She should have just stuck with her original plan to fly in for the benefit gala in a few days, then fly right out. She'd successfully avoided Lucas during her lightening-quick visits all these years. Clearly, lingering in Virginia was the quickest way to get screwed. In both ways.

She stepped down the stairs, keeping a tight hold on the cool banister. The house was still bursting with bodies, none of whom she gave a shit about. Her father hadn't moved from his spot, his expressionless face breaking into a smile as she approached.

"How are you doing, Dad?"

He swayed his head from side to side. "Not too well, Pumpkin. I think I'd like to go home."

Best news she'd heard all day. "Of course. Let's go."

There was nothing there for her anyway. Tyler would be

leaving any minute, and she couldn't stand to look at Lucas' face. Her brother was nowhere to be found, likely smothered in suits and fake smiles.

Ramona made the executive decision to take the limo back. Connor was resourceful enough to find his own way home.

She supported her father into the house and to his room. His slumped body made her wonder if she should offer to help him get undressed. This was new territory for her and incredibly awkward.

"What can I do for you, Dad? Can I get you some pajamas?"

He lifted his head as if it weighed a hundred pounds. "Oh, no, I'm fine, Pumpkin. I'm just going to sit here for a minute. Gather myself."

It was so hard to see him like this. "Alright... I'm just down the hall if you need anything."

She looked back, fingers gripping the door. "Goodnight, Dad. I love you."

"Oh, sweet girl. I'm so happy you're here with me. It makes everything better." His face brightened the tiniest bit as he smiled. "I love you, too."

The short walk to her room felt like an odyssey. She was done with the crappy day, but her father looked absolutely broken. The mixture of emotions he must have been feeling would have kept her in bed all day.

Before he'd lost himself to booze, her father had taken the brunt of Grandad's cruelty. Maybe what he was feeling was relief. At least she hoped so. A grand helping of relief all around.

Ramona arrived at her door and remembered tiptoeing down that same hallway, like a delinquent teenager, the night before. Except she'd never done anything that courageous as a teenager. Mostly she just hid. Maybe if she'd had a chance to act out more when she was younger, she'd have gotten all this risk-taking out of her system. She'd heed consequences and be less impulsive. She wouldn't find herself in a tizzy about some guy, wasting precious moments she could be spending with her father.

Exhaustion pulled her into the room, longing for rest. She'd hardly slept the night before. How foolish, going to bed all sexed-up and excited. Sure, it had been a night to remember. Scorching hot. Great material to replay during her many nights alone. And wrong, wrong, wrong.

Anger gave her enough of a spurt of energy that her clothes and shoes hit the ground with added velocity. That fucker. Lucas had made a fool of her. No. He made a fool of himself. How had he turned out to be such a louse?

As she looked around the room with bright pink walls, nostalgia weaved itself into the fist of her anger and forced it open. Too many nights had been spent cowering in her bed, wanting to be transported anywhere but there. It was his voice on the other end of her gold princess phone that had helped her calm down. Sometimes even his arms around her while she cried, helping her get to sleep. The boy and the man didn't align. It was all too hard to believe.

She plopped herself onto the large bed, the only item in the room she could tell had been replaced. Even the chair she and her brother had painted with orange polka dots still sat in the corner.

She slid between the cool sheets, so grateful that the day was over. There'd be plenty of time tomorrow to figure out this mess. A good night's sleep would help. Her eyes drifted shut as her body relaxed. Despite her room's history, a sense of safety, the first she'd had all day, wrapped itself around her.

Heavy footsteps sounded through the house. Her initial

startle passed quickly - *it must be Connor coming to check on Dad* - but the sound continued getting louder and closer to her room. Maybe something had happened and he wanted to talk. He opened the door and she squinted at the silhouette. Something was different about the frame of the body, the line of the hair. Her eyes snapped open. It wasn't Connor. It was Lucas.

"What the hell are you doing here? How did you get in?"

He stepped over her clothes and shoes, strewn across the carpet, and walked over to her bed. "Because your father has yet to ever lock the side door."

She sat up, trying her best to cover what was not being sufficiently concealed by her skimpy nightgown. "What do you want, Lucas? I've really had enough. Today was..."

"I know. It was a spectacularly shitty day for you. And I didn't help things by coming after you that way. I wasn't being rational. So, I'm here to apologize."

"Really? You couldn't just send me a text or apologize tomorrow?"

"No." He took off his suit jacket and unbuttoned his shirt, dropping them both on the back of the chair. "Because I also came here to do this."

Ramona watched, mesmerized, as he stripped down to his shorts and slid into bed with her. The shock of it stole her ability to respond. It was all déja vu, although instead of sneaking into her room through the window, he had walked down the hall. And instead of her house burning with the rage of her parents, the inferno was happening inside her own body.

He turned her away from him and enveloped her in his body. He had always been bigger than her, but the size difference had magnified. His breath brushed against the top of her shoulder as he held the pressure that forced her to soften into him. Tension and anger gave way to grief. She closed her eyes and let the tears flow.

"I'm sorry, Mo. I'm sorry about your grandfather. I'm sorry about your father. I'm sorry about what happened today. I'm sorry you got blind-sided. I'm sorry that I didn't get to talk to you about last night. I'm sorry that I didn't tell you how much I loved being with you."

With each statement, he touched his lips to her shoulder or her hair or the edge of her ear. She fell asleep to the poem of his apologies.

The pressure of a warm body behind her and the rumble of breath in her ear startled her from sleep. "Baloo." She wiggled her body. "Baloo. Are you awake?"

He pressed his hips into her back and sighed.

"Lucas! Wake up."

The breathing stopped. "What's wrong? Are you okay?"

"I'm okay. I'm awake."

She rolled over to face him.

He squeezed his eyes shut and then blinked several times. "You want an awake friend."

His job. To talk to her when she couldn't sleep. To ease her back into safety. "Yes."

His face softened. "I'm here. Talk to me."

"I'm worried about my Dad. He looks so weak, like he's just going to break any minute. I mean it's just not fair, now that he's finally getting his life together, he's sober, he's painting again, he even has a girlfriend, then his body decides to give out. It's not fair."

"It's definitely not fair. Is the dialysis helping?"

"It's keeping him alive, but I don't know for how long. That's where he met his girlfriend, you know. She's the receptionist at the dialysis place. They see each other three days a week, whenever he goes there. And Connor says she stays over some weekends. They're so cute together. She looks like Mom, but she's super fiery. Brazilian, I think. He always smiles when he talks about her."

"I've met Leni - she's wonderful. And I'm so happy for him. Maybe this is his slice of happiness."

"He deserves more. I deserve to have more. I finally have a dad who's not drunk and angry all the time, and I don't know how long..."

He ran his thumb over her cheek, catching the tears before they tumbled over her nose. "I'm sorry. But he seems happy. Like he's lived through so much physical pain that this medical stuff is nothing. Let him have this time knowing how much you love him, not how much you've missed."

And that's what he did best. Listen, support, bring a sense of perspective to her scary thoughts. Nothing but compassion shone in his eyes.

As if it was the most natural thing in the world, she reached forward and kissed him. He pulled away.

Reality punched her in the gut. "Shit. I'm sorry. You're not-"

Her sentence was stopped by his lips, much more insistent than her delicate kiss. His hand wrapped around the back of her head, gripping, while her leg slid over his hip, pinning his bottom half to her. She ground into him, pressing the length of his erection between her legs, bare under her nightgown. Resistance could not survive the heat of her desire.

In one move, she was on her back, with him on top of her and her hands pushing his shorts down. The tip of his cock pressed against her, reigniting the cascade of sensations from the previous night. The delightful sense of being pushed open as he slid himself into her. It couldn't have been more than a few minutes before the rhythm of his stroking, the fierceness of his mouth on hers, and the squeeze of her nipple in his hand tore a moan from her throat. He plunged into her and joined in the cries of delight.

She fell asleep much more deeply after that, but awoke, once again, to surprise at the man in her bed and a desire to be taken by him. She lifted herself above him and dangled a breast into his mouth. He sucked fiercely while she placed him inside her. Crouched over him, she let his hands guide her hips, not just over his length, but in small circles. He finally slid a finger over her clit and kept it there as she rode him to another orgasm.

Before she could recover, he placed her on her knees and entered her in one firm stroke. Her legs nearly gave way as the tremble became an explosive series of pulses voiced with a repeated call of her name.

They collapsed into sleep for the final time.

He was already awake, looking at her, when she opened her eyes. Before she could speak, he pressed his mouth to hers and left it there. She moved away to take a breath.

"Good morning," he whispered.

That seemed an insufficient greeting after the past twenty-four hours. Her own flinch of realization was interrupted by his look of concern.

He gave his head a brisk shake. "I just can't believe my eyes. What I see and what I feel aren't making sense."

She wanted his words to make sense. They didn't. "I don't understand what you're saying."

"When I look at you, I see this remarkable, stunning woman. But it's someone I don't completely recognize. It's all new to me – how you look, how you sound, how you feel in my hands, on my body."

She didn't like where this was going.

"But then, on the inside, it feels like us. Like Mowgli and Baloo and nothing has changed. You're still the person I love most in the world. You just happen to-"

"You can't say that, Luc." Like an old-fashioned alarm clock, the blaring mistake of his words brought her just short of panic.

A crease formed between his brows. "Why not? It's true."

"Because we don't know each other... like that... anymore." All the goodness had drained from her awareness. "And frankly, I don't think you're in a position to say those things to me."

He scanned down to her breasts. "A position? Are you being ironic?"

She pulled the blanket up higher. "No, I'm not being ironic. I'm being realistic. This situation is not going to be about... that."

"Now I don't understand what you're saying." He spoke in full voice. The sexy whispers were gone.

"I'm asking you not to go there. It's too hard, already." It hardly made sense in her head, but she hoped he understood. Or even that she might understand.

"So it's okay to have sex, but not okay to have feelings?"

"No. None of it is okay, Luc. That's the point!"

He opened his mouth several times, as if to speak, and stopped.

"Do you have something to say?" Each word bit more sharply.

He worked his jaw. "I... I'm sorry, Mo. I can't."

She sat up. "I'm getting up now. It's probably time for you to go."

He took a firm grip on her shoulders. "We're not going to do that, Ramona. We're not going to spoil this amazing time together with bad feelings. I'm going to respect your request. I won't talk about... feelings. But being with me and hating yourself isn't going to work."

Damn. She couldn't even be pleased that he had deciphered her jumble of thoughts. He shouldn't have known she was hating herself. Guilt burned at her throat and filled her mouth with bitterness.

She looked away as he got dressed, afraid that the sight of him would force her to pull him back into the bed and confess that her heart was bursting as much as her body was burning. But none of that was possible. He wasn't her Baloo anymore. He belonged to someone else.

The clink of his belt was followed by the sound of a zipper. "What are you doing today?"

She didn't want to tell him about her day. She didn't want to make small talk. Her first choice would have been to pack up all her stuff and get the hell out of Virginia. It was just as toxic as she remembered. Barring that, she would have wanted to force Lucas to tell the truth about Abigail. About his engagement. About why he had spent the night in her bed and not with his fiancée.

She couldn't leave - had the foundation benefit in three days. And she didn't want to hear the whole story, either. The truth was almost certainly going to make things much, much worse. At least now she could pretend that there was a perfectly good explanation for all of it. She could live in a fantasy that made her actions free from consequence and something she could easily walk away from. Ignorance was the price she would pay to stave off the admission that she had repeatedly done the most terrible thing, ever.

"Ramona, please don't shut me out. I know you can tell what's real and what's not."

It was impossible to not look at him. He pulled his jacket

off the back of the spotted chair and slipped it on. That arm had just been around her. That chest beneath her. Those fingers inside her.

"You agreed you wouldn't talk about it." Besides, she had no idea what was real.

He did not make a move toward the door. "All right. So tell me about your day."

A sigh rattled out of her. "I'm taking Dad to dialysis, then Connor and I are going to get started on packing up Grand-dad's house. That is, unless our cousins have already looted it."

"Good luck with that. The Governor wasn't short on possessions."

"Tell me about it." This small talk wasn't so bad. "What are you up to today?"

"It's paperwork day. Light at the restaurant on Mondays and Tuesdays so I catch up on all the administrative stuff. I actually like it, the business side of things."

She stood up. *I can do this.* "And that's why you're the hottest chef in town."

He wrapped his arms around her. "Am I? And by hot do you mean sexy?"

That mouth.... No. She pushed out of his grip. "I actually meant award-winning, acclaimed restaurant kind of hot."

He frowned. "Oh."

He kissed her lightly on each cheek, then on her lips. "Have a great day, Mowgli. I'll talk to you later."

She held herself together long enough to watch him walk out of her bedroom, and then fell back onto the bed, exhausted. So much for a good night's sleep making it all better. Which, of course, she hadn't gotten because she decided that screwing him - twice! - was a better idea.

Fuck. She'd managed to make the horrible situation even worse. Maybe she wasn't that different from old Grandad after all.

CHAPTER FOUR

*R*amona stared at the knee-high piles of books in the middle of her grandfather's library. She and Connor had agreed to take only the books they cared about, leaving the rest for donation. There were already more than she expected.

A first edition Darwin sat on the top of her pile. Her brother had claimed the entire collection of classical political books, including de Tocqueville, Locke, Plato, and Machiavelli. Thank goodness her cousins were too stupid to understand that some of the most precious items in this house were on these shelves.

Whatever else her grandfather was, he did prize knowledge and the power of language. That might have been the only thing she shared with the man who'd been the most powerful antagonistic force in her life. The bastard whose tyrannical hold on his family had left most of them scared, drunk, or on the run.

Connor, perched on a tall ladder, pulled a small dark book from one of the topmost shelves and handed it to her. A Carnegie joined the pile.

He reached his arm across to pull another book out. She flinched at the thought of him losing balance. "You sure you don't want me to take a turn up there? You're going to get a cramp in your neck. Or maybe kill yourself."

Connor examined the spine of a book with a dull green cover. "It's fine, sis. You can take over when I finish this wall."

Ramona reached her arms up, then bent forward in a stretch. Everything ached. The combination of sleep deprivation, emotional turmoil and... extracurriculars... had left her a tight, sore, ball of tension. Maybe if they finished up early enough, she'd try to find a yoga class.

Her back cracked and popped as she slowly stood up. Yes, yoga sounded like exactly the right thing to address both her physical and mental distress. "Hey, do you know any good yoga studios around here?"

The carved lines of her brother's face grew even sharper. "Kidding, right?"

"No, I'm not kidding. Yoga would be great for you. Maybe loosen you up a bit."

"Here, catch." He vaulted a hefty brown book with gold lettering toward her. "Nope. But you're welcome to come to Crossfit with Lucas and me. We go at five thirty."

That didn't make sense. That would be peak restaurant time. "Five thirty? Aren't you both working?"

"AM, Mo. Morning time."

Gruesome. And she knew exactly where Lucas was at five thirty that morning. "That's a hard no from me. Thanks, anyway."

It was good that Connor had found an outlet for all his energy. He'd always been tightly wound, so a vigorous workout might have been the only time he let loose. The idea of Crossfit made her shudder, but it appeared to be working for her brother. She had to admit, he looked better than she'd seen him in a long time. His lean frame had filled out, no longer so gangly. As for his workout buddy, that physique was created by nothing less than the gods. And that thought was like taking a huge shovel to the already bottomless hole she was in.

For the second time in twenty-four hours, the sound of footsteps preceded the appearance of the very last person she expected to see. Except for the lustful thoughts she was having just seconds before he appeared.

"Anybody order dinner?" Lucas stood in the doorway, large brown bags hanging from his hands and a broad smile on his face.

"Dude! I was just about to pass out from hunger." Connor jumped off the ladder and greeted the new arrival, giving his sister a curious look as he passed. Ramona paused with a book dangling from her hand as if she had been frozen.

Lucas put the bags down and took a step toward her. "Ramona..."

The book dropped onto the floor, creating a much louder crash than she anticipated. "What are you doing here?"

"Haven't you heard? I'm your brother's personal meal delivery service."

Connor chuckled before rummaging in one of the bags and pulling out a green bean. "You *offered* to come help. And bring dinner."

She clenched her jaw before willing her face to relax. "Oh..."

Lucas did not make another move toward her. She shifted her gaze from one man to the other. This was much more upsetting than she wanted or expected it to be. Merely being in the same room as him had turned her into a bumbling mess. Or a fawning schoolgirl. She needed to pull herself together.

"I'll take these down," Connor said, as he picked up the

bags. "We'll eat in the nook by the kitchen. Luc, grab a pile of books when you head down."

Connor strutted out of the room. Neither of them budged until his footsteps changed from the tap on the wooden staircase to the silence of the carpeted hallway.

In a few steps, Lucas had reached her, slid his hand behind her neck and kissed her in the type of greeting that might have been predicted considering their very recent activities. It took more than a beat for her to push him away. And every ounce of willpower. He really didn't need to be such a great kisser.

She steadied herself. "Why are you here, Lucas?"

"Your brother-"

"You can't do this. Not here." *Not anywhere, actually.* She flitted her eyes at her grandfather's enormous portrait. Evil motherfucker.

"Okay, Mo." He bent down to pick up the largest stack of books, balancing it on his chest and nearly blocking his view. "I'll see you downstairs."

The men had set the table and opened each of the containers by the time Ramona came down carrying her own pile. She plastered a fake grin on her face, determined not to allow her discomfort to seep into her mannerisms.

"What do we have here?" She peered into the boxes, filled with colorful salads, a rice dish, a stew of some kind, and something, off to the side, that made her inhale sharply.

"What's up with the grilled cheese sandwiches, Mo? Lucas told me I'm not allowed to touch them."

She stared at Lucas, unable to prevent the feeling of gratitude for his thoughtfulness.

He placed one of the three sandwiches, crusts removed, cut into perfect triangles, on a plate. "They're specially made for Ramona."

"Is there some secret story about those sandwiches?" asked her curious brother.

Lucas shook his head. "It's just something from way back."

They ate in silence. Well, Ramona ate in silence as the two men spoke in a shorthand she'd forgotten they used. She got up from the table with several of the now empty boxes.

"So what's happening with the house? Who's going to be taking care of it?" Lucas asked.

Connor answered. "He left it to Mo."

There was no additional response for so long that Ramona wondered if the guys had left the room. She looked behind her to check.

Lucas shifted his stare from Connor to her, then back to Connor. "No way."

Her brother grabbed a piece of broccoli from one of the boxes. "Right? He gives the most personal item in his estate to the one who left. Funny."

She dropped the containers into the garbage and returned to the table.

Lucas slapped his forehead. "Are you telling me he left this house to you?"

She cocked her head, wondering about his incredulity. "Yes."

"Holy shit. The cousins must be furious. And how about you, Con?"

"To be frank, the rest of us received significant inheritances. Arguably, much more valuable than this one house. I got the Lake House, and almost all of his business interests."

Lucas huffed out a breath. "That old man... always defying expectation."

About the only thing her mother and grandfather had in

common was a pathological need to never do what was expected. "Yup."

Connor shrugged. "He respected you the most. I think he saw you as most similar to him, except that all your energy was pointed in the opposite direction. Think about it, Mo. You're the only one who ever stood up to him-"

"-and suffered the consequences." Which were frequent and plentiful.

"True enough." Connor nodded. "But I think it's clear that you were the only one he trusted with the thing dearest to him. This house."

Ramona gave her brother her best scowl.

"Damn. I'm totally shocked. What are your plans for the house?"

That was easy. "Clean it up. Sell it."

Lucas paused for a beat. "But it's not just any house. It's part of American history. I mean, you could do so many amazing things. Build a school, or a library, or a shelter..."

The scowl remained. Its direction shifted. "I'm not going to move back here to take care of this, if that's what you mean."

"It's not. I was just-"

"It's one more thing that doesn't really belong to me that I'd have to take care of. No, thank you." She crashed the plates together and walked them over to the sink.

"Take it easy there, Mo. No need to get so snippy about it."

She didn't look back to address her brother and his ignorant statement.

Lucas answered. "It's okay. It's none of my business, anyway."

Ramona excused herself, mumbling something about the bathroom. She stepped into one of the many tucked-in spaces in that enormous house and leaned against the wall. She tried to muster her yoga teacher's calming voice, instructing her to breathe deeply. Moments later, the men crossed the foyer and headed upstairs to the library. Two of a kind, they were. Born days apart. If not for Connor's sleek black hair and Lucas' curls, they might have been twins. Evil twins.

She'd had quite enough of her brother's odd looks and Lucas' stupid ideas. He clearly had forgotten how far away her life was from all of this. A life she couldn't wait to get back to. Sure, that house was a part of history, but it wasn't going to be her burden. Someone else would have to pick up that mantle. In just a few days, she would be far away from all that disarray.

She paced in the large foyer, heels clicking on the checkerboard marble floor. Being emotionally out of control sucked. So did pretending it had anything to do with the damn house. It was guilt.

For so much of the last two days, she'd felt herself sliding into the warm wonderfulness that was Lucas Winston only to be reminded of the brunette calling herself his future wife. How could this be happening? Ramona didn't do messy, tangled, or fraught. She got her needs met and mostly avoided anything hinting at complex intimacy. Her history and her mother had made it perfectly clear that that never ended well. Lucas, had he been a stranger, would have been the best one night stand ever. But she'd already had two nights and wanted many more.

Footsteps on the upstairs landing sent her scurrying into the kitchen. She didn't want to see either of them. She was too confused, too frustrated, too ashamed. If hiding were an option, she would have taken it.

· · ·

Connor appeared in the kitchen after the front door closed with a resounding thud. She fiddled with the few food containers still sitting on the table.

"What the hell is going on with you and Lucas?" His tone was not full of brotherly love.

Ramona cringed, praying that he meant anything other than what was in front of all their faces.

"Are you mad at him or something? You were really shitty to him."

"I-"

"And when he showed up, it was like you had seen a ghost. Did something happen?"

All she could do was nod. And hope that her brother would magically hear what she was terrified to say out loud. "Yeah, something happened. Something bad..."

"What could possibly have happened? You've only been here for two days. And you guys haven't seen each other in more than ten years. How could you already..."

Ramona kept her gaze steady as she watched realization dawn on her brother.

"Mo... Did you..."

"We... went too far."

He opened his mouth wider than she'd ever seen. "No..."

"I know. It's bad. And I'm not handling it well, as you can see."

"You know he's engaged-"

"Clearly. Hence the problem."

Connor sat down and ran his hand through his hair. Same as Ramona's but somehow never managed to be unruly or have a single hair out of place. Ever.

A quiver began near her chin. She swallowed hard to not start crying.

"I can't believe it. The two of you... I mean on one level

it's completely obvious. Maybe even destined. But after all this time, and with the situation. There's nothing good about this."

She kept her attention on her shaking hands. "I've never been this kind of person, Con. I don't want to start now. He's getting married. But something seems really wrong about the whole thing."

It never crossed her mind that Connor would know the secret, so she didn't ask. Her straight-laced, excessively logical brother didn't dally in such drama. She prepared herself for some stern words. He might even call her crazy.

"You're right."

She jerked up. "What? Do you know something?"

"Luc and I are like brothers. Have been our whole lives. Didn't even tell me he was *thinking* about getting engaged. They hadn't dated since law school. Then he shows up one day and tells me they're getting married."

"I don't understand." She really didn't.

"Me neither. There's something going on, and he can't or won't talk about it. I'm pretty sure she's not pregnant. But they never even see each other. She's been living in New York for years. They're only together for public appearances. Maybe she's blackmailing him... I can't make sense of it."

"Do you know her at all?"

"Not really. Her firm was involved in a case I worked on years ago. Before she went to New York. We interacted professionally, but nothing stands out. She seemed just like all the over-ambitious lawyers in town."

"The whole thing is crazy."

He pulled his glasses off and let them dangle from his fingers. "You know how our families can be. Nothing is ever simple. Everything is a coverup or a conspiracy or some intricate plan. All I know is there's something deeply wrong with them."

"It looks real enough to me." God, that moment Abigail had stuck out her hand, complete with enormous diamond, to introduce herself, had turned into a brain tattoo.

"No way. But it doesn't matter. You need to stay away. The last place you want to be is in the middle of this, whatever it is. Do you hear me, Ramona?"

She nodded, stunned by the rare appearance of her actual name.

He continued. "You haven't been around for a while, but I'm sure you remember how messy things can get. You're only here for a week. Don't get yourself caught up in something that's going to blow up into the rest of your life."

Yes. One week. "I'm trying."

"I don't understand how..." Connor's expression went from concern to recognition. "Wait! You saw him on Saturday night."

"You're the one who told me to go to his restaurant. We ended up... well... you get it. Then last night he came to the house." It only crossed her mind after all the words had tumbled out that her brother might not want to hear about her sexual exploits. Oh, well.

Connor's eyes darted back and forth. "Dad was right. He told me he saw Luc's car, but I thought he was dreaming. Not cool, Mo."

"I'm fucked. Never in my life have I aspired to be *the other woman*." A wave of nausea forced her to gasp. "It needs to stop."

"Damn straight. Cut it off now." Connor's tone lost any hint of compassion. "No more."

She nodded while her brother patted her back. It was clear. The first step to taking command of her feelings for

Lucas was squashing her own emotional storm. No more anger, guilt, or blame. Then she needed to *manage* him like she did her skittish clients. Be the grownup in the room. Yes, Connor was right.

He looked down at his watch. "Sorry to do this, Mo, but I've gotta go. Have to be across town for a meeting."

"No prob. Thanks for your help today. Love you."

He kissed her on the forehead. "Love you. Be good."

With each step up the stairs, Ramona reasserted the solidity of her plan. She could rein in the chaos. She could salvage the last few days of her visit. But first, an apology was due.

CHAPTER FIVE

*R*amona stood at Lucas's front door for long enough after ringing the doorbell that a wide range of doubts crossed her mind. She had gotten the address wrong. He wasn't home. Or worse, he *was* home and didn't want to see her. She reached her hand to try the bell one last time when the door opened.

"Mowgli!" Surprise sparkled in his eyes.

"Hey." She held out one of the large cups in her hand. "I brought you a peace offering."

He narrowed his eyes. "Is that..."

"A green juice."

He took it from her and lifted it to examine the brownish-green color. "Come in."

She made it as far as the edge of a lovely sitting area. "It's really good, Luc. Healthy."

He twisted his lips to the side. "If this is what you bring in peace, I'd hate to see what you give someone you're mad at."

"Just try it, you big baby."

He drew up from the straw and let it linger in his mouth.

He nodded. "Okay, not bad. I like the lemon. And the cucumber cuts some of the bitterness."

"Good. Now drink up. It's good for you. Packed with vitamins and anti-oxidants."

"You came here to make sure I got my essential nutrients for the day?"

She took a sip of her own drink. "No. I came here to apologize for being a bitch last night. You didn't deserve that. I'm just-"

"You've never been a bitch to me, Mo. I was intruding. It wasn't my place to tell you what to do with the mansion."

She looked past him, toward a portrait of his family, hanging above a simple stone fireplace. "We need to stop... It's not good for either of us."

He stepped into her line of sight and narrowed his eyes. "I thought we were talking about the house."

"It's all related, don't you think?"

He shook his head. "No, I don't."

She sighed. Why was he making this so hard? "In any case, it's best if we cool it. Whatever's going on with you - it feels like something else than what it appears to be - I just don't want to get involved. That's why I moved as far away from my family as I could. I'm just not built for this level of drama."

He put down the drink, still half full, and took her hand. "Come. Let me show you around the house."

The fact that he had brushed aside her concerns did not go unnoticed, but she enjoyed the warmth of his hand and the pull of his arm, and followed him into the living room. Ramona-the-intrepid had become Mo-the-marshmallow.

"This whole area wasn't even here. I added it on," he said indicating a sunken lounge that looked like a modern version of a room in their parents' houses. He described the floor tiles and built-in cabinets while she looked around, a boyish pride keeping a wide grin across his face.

He whisked her from one room to another, stopping to give her the details about interesting pieces of wood, or the directions of the windows, or any of a hundred particulars about the house. A full circle led them back toward the kitchen. She'd hardly kept up with his technical explanations, but the excitement in his voice brought a smile to her face.

He pointed through the large windows providing a nearly panoramic view of the dense woods behind his property. She followed his finger to the far right, to a structure covered in cedar that looked like something from the Far East. Slats of rust-colored wood perfectly aligned under a flat roof, wide doors taking up nearly the entire expanse of one side.

"What's that?"

"A ryokan. Traditional Japanese house. It's got a sauna and bath."

Her gaze followed the winding stone path that connected the main house to the structure. "That's fantastic, Luc. It's lovely."

He faced her, beaming. "I built it."

"You what?"

"After I finished the house, I needed something else to do. You know how I don't like to be idle. So I built it. Took almost a whole year."

Realization dawned slowly. "What do you mean finished the house?"

"I built most of this as well. It was a terrible, run-down mess. But I loved the neighborhood and the property, so I decided to remodel it myself."

Ramona flashed to his childhood obsession with building blocks. This man couldn't get any more impressive. "I can't find a reasonable thing to say. It just feels incredible. Impossible, really."

He wrapped his arm around her waist and led her outside. The sharp tang of cedar tickled her nose well before they'd arrived at the ryokan. It was even more beautiful up close.

She ran her hand along the vertical post carved with Japanese characters. "What does this say?"

"Where the heart dwells."

Instead of lingering on the sensations around her own heart, she stepped into the large room. The same vertical slats lined the interior, tatami mats covering the small patch of floor not taken up by the large square bath. It looked like a Japanese travel brochure.

"Would you like to bathe with me?"

His voice startled her out of the examination of a woodblock print she recognized. "What? No. I mean, we can't."

He stepped toward her and cupped her cheek. "We can."

Resolve and certainty drained out of her body. She glanced at the paneled bath, imagining how wonderful it would feel to step into the hot water. To watch him come to her. To be with him in this sanctuary.

She pulled away. "I feel like you're not listening to me, Lucas. I'm not going to deny that something is happening. I mean, something happened. But I'm not interested in this arrangement. I've never aspired to being someone's mistress."

He walked over to the tub and put his hand on the dark green cover. "What if I told you it wasn't at all what you think? What if you knew that you are the only woman I would invite here?"

"It can't be..."

"It is." He folded the cover in half and then removed it. Steam slithered up from a large open tub.

In slow motion, she watched him unbutton his shirt. No

amount of composure could stand the sight of a half-undressed Lucas Winston. Much less a fully naked one. She stared at his particularly fine ass as he climbed the two steps and entered the tub. Free from the pesky foam and bubbles of jacuzzis and hot tubs, this bath allowed a clear view of everything. Everything.

As if in a daze, she slipped off her t-shirt and jeans. Then her underwear. His eyes burned into her so intensely that the water almost felt cool on her skin. She sat across from him.

He did not move toward her. Just kept staring. "Are you comfortable?"

"Yes, I am." It was true. The combination of the water and the setting felt like a salve to her frayed nerves.

"Good. I don't want you to think that I invited you in here just to get you undressed. I'll stay on this side if that's what you want."

She dropped down so she was immersed up to her lower lip. How delightful it would be to go under.

He spread his arms along the edge of the tub, the top of his carved chest peering out of the water. It didn't matter that she knew better.

Her body was on his in less than a breath. She pressed against him and groaned into the arms that wrapped around her.

"It's so confusing, Lucas," she pleaded, hoping he would say something to make it all better.

He tightened his hold on her. "I'm sorry, Mo. I wish I could make it easier. I just can't explain. Yet."

A chill prickled her skin. She was so desperate to rationalize her behavior, to be with him, she would have taken anything. Any explanation. Even the *yet* that hung on the air felt like a lifeboat. She clenched her jaw to prevent herself from asking. They'd agreed. If only there wasn't this unrelenting voice telling her that this was exactly where she was supposed to be. And if only it wasn't loud enough to drown out the resolve that had brought her to his house.

She leaned against the back of the tub and dropped her head onto his arm. There they sat, unspeaking.

"Are you ready to get out?"

He'd read her mind. Instead of experiencing the serenity of the situation, she was growing more and more agitated by desire and confusion. "Yes."

He moved toward the edge and stepped out. She'd never tire of that view.

He opened a door that she thought was just a wall and pulled out a plush towel. He held it out for her to step into and then wrapped it around her.

She looked up at him as he rubbed her dry. "Thanks for keeping your word."

"You didn't believe that I wouldn't make a move on you, did you?"

"I suppose..."

She pulled him in for a hug, becoming acutely aware that the towel separating their bodies wasn't nearly enough. The situation just got harder. And so did he.

He pulled away and glanced down. "Sorry. That was... involuntary."

She turned away and stifled a chuckle.

"Okay, coast is clear."

He'd wrapped himself in a towel, but there was still too much sexy flesh to keep things cool. She focused on a stone etched with Kanji.

"Will you sit with me for a few more minutes? I'm not ready to leave here yet." Lucas slid open another secret panel and pulled out a cream-colored pad, and unrolled it onto the mat. He adjusted the falling towel and laid down.

Ramona tentatively stepped toward him, tightening the hold on her own towel, and feeling immediately foolish for doing so. It's not like he hadn't already seen everything. And had everything. Ugh.

She snuggled into his shoulder, resting her arm along his side. Clouds passed slowly overhead, visible through the large glass panel on the ceiling. So much to learn from those clouds. "This spot is amazing."

"I come in here after work and have a bath. Then I lay here and look at the stars. Sometimes I even sleep in here. I love everything about it."

"I can see why." She couldn't understand how he had created this life for himself. "I have to say, Luc, I never would have predicted what a homey guy you'd turn out to be. I mean, building this whole structure, as well as your beautiful house. I imagine you here with a wife, a couple of kids, some dogs. That's the kind of house you've built. It's not what I would have imagined for a young, hot bachelor."

Only after the words came out of her mouth did she remember that he was, in fact, not going to be a bachelor for much longer. It made her stomach lurch and she bolted up.

He sat up, put his arms around her and led her back down to lay on his chest. He stroked her hair. "Don't go there, Mo. It's really not relevant."

She swallowed. "But-"

"I built this place, guided by something unconscious. I wasn't thinking about creating a family homestead. I just wanted something that would feel good every time I came home. Something that would be beautiful and serene and comfortable. You know, basically the opposite of how either of us grew up."

She started to relax, immersing herself in the current conversation instead of the terrible thoughts. "I can understand that. And I applaud you for making it happen. I'm sure it's a wonderful place to come home to."

"Actually, it's never felt more like that than now, with you here." He took a long, slow breath. "You're the first person who's been in here with me."

She bit her tongue, hard, to hold back yet another question. Why hadn't his fiancée spent time in his house?

"How about you, Mo? Tell me about where you live."

She laughed. "Imagine the complete opposite of this," she waved her hand around the room, "and you'll be spot on."

"What do you mean?"

"I basically live in the residential wing of a hotel in downtown San Francisco. I spend so much time traveling, I didn't think it was worthwhile to put down firm roots. And it's easier with someone taking care of all the maintenance. I don't have to worry about anything."

He wrapped his fingers around her hand and squeezed. "I'm sure it's beautiful."

"Yes. Modern, immaculate, with a great view. Everything's top-notch, including the service. They've been great to me."

"But?"

She wove her fingers in and out of his. "It's not what I would consider home. It's more like a place to keep my stuff, and somewhere to sleep when I'm in town."

"Hmmm..."

"Are you judging me?" She poked him in the ribs.

"Not at all. And I can see how that would make sense for your lifestyle and given your past. We didn't have great role models for home and family and peaceful spaces. But don't you want something more?"

She had to think about it. "My semi-nomadic lifestyle suits me. It works."

"Maybe that's because that's all you've known. Ever since your mother took you and fled to California, you've been moving. Then-"

"At least I came back, even for short visits. My mother has just kept running."

"Is she still in the jungle?"

Ramona shrugged. "I couldn't even tell you. She calls me once a month, usually from some untraceable satellite phone in a village without running water."

"Wow. I can't imagine."

"She's deliriously happy, though. She gets to be the kind of doctor she always wanted - part medicine, part magic - and can pick up and move to the next thing at any moment. No tethers, no binds, no connections she can't cut whenever she wants. Compared to her, I'm downright sedentary." And much more sane, hopefully.

"Well, you did pick a career that has you trotting around the globe. And a lifestyle with no roots."

She stiffened, evaluating the offense.

"Trust me, I get it. I just wonder if it's what you really need."

And there it was. "It's pretty presumptuous for you to think you know what I need. You hardly know me."

"Don't get offended, Mo." He kissed her forehead. "I feel like I *do* know you. But maybe all that is outdated. No longer relevant."

"Maybe." It was more likely that he knew her too well.

They laid in silence until the sun beat down from directly above them. It was nice to have let go of some of her worry, even for a short time.

She sat up. "This was nice. Thanks."

She stood up, and he followed her. They gathered their

clothes. "I appreciate you keeping your word. About not... trying anything."

He held her face in his hands but didn't speak.

She pulled away. "I need to get dressed and get going." Or else she would be the one crossing her own line.

They walked to the house in silence. Lucas' beautiful house in a sprawling neighborhood of beautiful houses. Everything she looked at, touched, exuded care. And he matched it better than she'd ever imagined a person and a house could.

She drove away from his house, glancing at her rearview mirror to see him waving goodbye. Families strolled on the wide sidewalk, everyone smiling as if they were in a commercial. This neighborhood was like an ad for domesticity.

How had they begun their lives in such similar settings and settled on these versions of home that couldn't have been more different? Admitting that he'd been right, that she'd grown tired of running, was not a possibility. At least not until all of Virginia was in her rearview mirror.

CHAPTER SIX

*I*t was the wrong thing to do, and she knew it.

The driver turned off the main road and wove through a part of town populated by the mansions Ramona recognized from her youth. Much more ostentatious than Lucas' lovely neighborhood. She checked the GPS in the center of the dashboard to make sure they were headed to the right place. She didn't know about this shortcut, which wasn't unexpected, considering that she hadn't lived there since she was a teenager.

She sat back in her seat and tried to calm her pounding heart. Meeting Lucas and his friends for chef's night at his restaurant was not a smart move. His invitation earlier that day had been sincere, no doubt. They'd left on good terms. He'd proven he could keep his word and that maybe they might be able to rebuild a friendship. If she survived his marrying another woman, that is.

It was all so strange. She'd been running away from Lucas Winston for most of her adult life. Now, for the second time that day, she couldn't get back to him fast enough. They had tried to stay friends after she moved across the country, but every time she heard his voice, it hurt more. It was too hard to watch his life grow and blossom while hers, with her isolationist mother, grew smaller and tighter. Her mother's demands to cut all ties eventually overpowered any desire she had to stay connected.

The part of her life with Lucas in it had been the scariest, with her father's drinking and her grandfather's rage, but also the sweetest. The part of her life without him was lonelier, but she'd learned to be strong and independent. Just as her mother had taught her.

The car merged back onto the main road, bringing the bright sign for Winston's into view. Maybe it wasn't too late to ask the driver to turn back and take her home. What was she thinking? Tempting fate, that's what.

Ramona stepped into the bustling restaurant and scanned the expansive seating area. All of the noise and activity emerged from the bar, teeming with men in black. She stood, moving her gaze slowly from one young, handsome face to another, allowing herself a chuckle at the preponderance of hot guys and the absence of any women.

She'd spent her whole life around men grasping for power or already in possession of it. She could navigate this scene with one hand tied behind her back, and for that moment, while she smiled to herself, she nearly forgot about the one man who could effortlessly crumble all her confidence.

As if they could sense her presence, the heads turned one by one to watch as she walked toward them. Eyes landed on cleavage, which she might not have chosen to feature so prominently, on her legs, elongated by stiletto boots, and on her face, framed by ebony waves.

Lucas was one of the last to notice her, but gave her the least subtle reaction. He did nothing to hide both his surprise and his delight at her appearance.

"You came," he said through a wide smile.

"Yup. Crashing the all-male chef party, I see."

Someone had taken her hand. "Allo, Ramona. I 'ave heard so much about you," an enticing French accent was attached to the warm hand that held hers. "My name is Henri." He touched his lips to her knuckles.

Lucas scowled. Openly. "Let me introduce you around." He raised his arm, which silenced the group. "Gentlemen, this is Ramona Barrett. My childhood best friend."

Rounds of greetings, including a few hugs and kisses, kept her occupied for several minutes while Lucas stepped back. His gaze never left her, even as her body was jostled by the boisterous attention.

She addressed the small, rapt audience. "So, what happened to all the women?"

Henri tilted his head. "What women?"

"All the women chefs. Were they not invited to this gathering?"

Mumbles filled the space.

A different man, with a long, blond ponytail, answered. "Oh, they're invited." His southern twang made her smile. "They're just not comin'."

"I don't see why not," she said, allowing a hint of sarcasm to flavor her words.

A grip she recognized tugged at her arm, pulling her from the cluster of men. "Have a seat, Mo." Lucas brought her to an open bar chair. "What would you like to drink?"

She scanned the impressive collection behind the bar. "Belvedere martini. Olives. Thanks." The young man behind the bar nodded his approval and got to work. She wondered if Lucas knew or employed anyone who wasn't ridiculously attractive.

His arm cupped her shoulder as he bent to whisper in her

ear. "I'm so glad you came. You had me wondering..."

He lingered there, up against her ear, for much longer than it took to speak those few words.

Heat rose from her chest to her cheeks. She pulled away when her drink arrived, grateful for the ice-cold glass. "What are you drinking?"

"Nothing." Lucas shook his head. "I'm driving."

"Oh..."

She stared blankly at the meticulously organized bottles and the sparking lights behind the bar, being careful to avoid the patch of mirror that would reflect her discomfort. Within two sips of her perfect martini, Lucas had been pulled away for a discussion on cheese.

Henri wasted no time taking his place much too close to her. "Lovely Ramona. Tell me... 'ow long will you stay here?"

"Only until Sunday. I came to town for a death in the family."

"Ah, tes, of course, I know your grandfazer has died. I am so sorry." He took her hands and looked down, frowning.

"Thank you." It wasn't even a burden anymore to hold her tongue about what a raging bastard he'd been.

"You must come dine wiss me. I will make myself available whenever you are free."

Well, that was direct. "I appreciate the offer, Henri, but I'm afraid I am completely booked with family obligations for the rest of the week."

"No, it cannot be! You must allow me ze pleasure of your company. Zere must be a time-"

"I think I heard her say no." The booming voice resounded behind her, as if from nowhere and everywhere at the same time. She did not turn around. Didn't need to.

The Frenchman laughed too hard. "Ha! Are you keeping her calendar now?"

Ramona stood up. "No. He's not. But Luc is concerned about the benefit gala we are throwing for the foundation we run." She glanced back, but not long enough to catch his eye. "Don't worry. I'll get everything done."

Lucas responded. "I'm not worried-"

"Good!" Henri's whole face lit up. "It is settled. When would you like to meet?"

Ramona reached into the purse hanging from her shoulder and pulled out a business card. "Why don't you give me a call? Maybe we can find a time."

As she turned to walk away, Henri held firmly onto her hand. Too firmly. Then, with the grace of an old-fashioned charmer, he brought her knuckles to his lips.

Unsure what to say or do, Ramona slid her hand out of his, more concerned about the dark eyes watching her from a few feet away, then the man in front of her. "I'll be right back."

It wasn't a long walk to the ladies' room, but each step felt like more eyes were burning into her back.

Sure, it might not have been the coolest thing to give another man her number while the man who'd been in her bed days before stood and watched. She reminded herself that he was engaged to another woman. He had no right to feel slighted. Unfortunately, this did not help the bad feeling in her stomach one bit.

She was glad to see the two men were on opposite ends of the bar when she returned from the bathroom. Instead of picking one side or the other, she headed toward the group in the middle, and effortlessly slid into their conversation.

Despite the absence of women, Ramona found very little pickup action among the group. Conversation flowed easily about her infamous family, about Lucas' childhood, and even occasionally about food. The final martini - she'd lost count of how many had been handed to her - hit hard enough that she knew heading home would be a good idea. She had the tolerance of a giant truck driver, but having yet to get a good night's sleep was making her more susceptible. She pulled out her phone and opened a ride-sharing app.

"Lovely, Ramona." Smooth French cream was pouring into her ear. "How eez your night going?"

"It's been great. You all are a very fun bunch." Her fingers kept hitting the wrong keys.

"Why don't we sit and 'ave one last drink togezer?"

"Oh, Henri, I'm actually heading home now. Thank you, though." Why wasn't the locator on the app showing up with the correct address?

"Oh, even better. Let me take you 'ome. Zen we can fuck in ze car."

She paused the tapping on her phone to look up at him, disbelieving what she'd just heard. "Excuse me?"

"I will drive you home. Zen we can talk."

Right. Talk. Not fuck. She exhaled a laugh.

"That's very nice of you, Henri. But I wouldn't want to pull you away from the festivities. I think the party has just begun." The area was even more crowded than when she arrived, chefs showing up after their restaurants closed. Or so she assumed. Regardless, it was much later than she was used to being out.

"It is no party here wissout you. I see zees ugly faces all ze time. Yours, 'oweverrr, eez a very special experience."

Wow. This guy could charm a statue into a date. She smiled at him. Maybe dinner with a fine, charming Frenchman wouldn't be such a bad idea.

"I'll take her home."

That voice again. How was it that he was always hovering nearby but never in her sight?

"Oh, Luc. *Ce n'est pas nécessaire!* Zis is your party. You cannot leave!"

"Watch me."

He took her arm and, leaving no room for discussion, strode out of his own restaurant.

There had been fewer than a handful of occasions in Ramona's life where she had felt so overpowered that it left her speechless. Most of them involved her grandfather.

She pulled her arm out of Lucas' grip but continued to follow him through the dining room, kitchen, offices, and out to his car.

"What the hell was that?"

As if he were reporting the weather, he answered, "I heard you needed a ride home. I'm glad to take you."

She sat a bit too heavily, slammed the car door a bit too loudly, and exhaled with a huff, but said not a single word. She wished she hadn't had that last martini, which she blamed for the absence of a coherent response. Anger mingled with confusion in a swirling mess.

They wove through the same neighborhood she'd passed earlier, now completely desolate. Not even a street light or house light was on. They arrived at the stop sign on the other side, where Lucas stopped for too long. There were no cars coming in any direction, and he could have easily merged into traffic.

Finally, he turned right. But her father's house was to the left.

"You went the wrong way," she muttered.

"What?" he snapped.

"To get to my dad's, you were supposed to turn left."

He veered to the small shoulder on the side of the road and slammed on the brakes. "Oh, now you choose to say something?"

Much too slowly, she understood where he was heading. "I don't know what's going on, Lucas."

He stared straight out the windshield. "Do you want me to turn around?"

All her wooziness snapped into unwelcome sobriety. This was her chance to make a different choice. The right choice.

"Please answer me, Ramona." Something created a tremble in his voice, but she didn't know if it was anger or sadness.

"No."

He pulled smoothly out onto the main road and drove the remaining miles to his house.

Not a single look or word was exchanged until they had both entered the house. He disappeared into the dark kitchen and re-emerged with a tall glass of water.

"Please drink this."

"It's just water, right?"

"With vitamin C. To counter all those martinis."

Within the first few sips, she understood the depth of her thirst and wiped out the whole glass. Her head was crystal clear. Now, if only she could rationalize the folly of that evening.

"What you did tonight..." She shook her head, unable to continue.

"Which part, exactly? Saving you from Henri, who's fucked everything in a skirt? Or maybe safely getting you home?"

"I'm not home." That should have been obvious.

He nodded, but the disgust never left his expression. "Yes, of course. You're at my house."

"Why Lucas? Why did you bring me here?" *Why did you*

want me to come home with you?

He leaned against the archway separating the living room from the hallway and kitchen. "I thought you chose to come here."

She put the glass down too hard, and the sound made both of them jump. "I see. You're not going to answer, is that right?"

He stepped toward her. "Do you want me to say that it drove me crazy to see you flirting with Henri? That I couldn't stand one more minute of sharing you? Would that adequately explain my behavior?"

He continued to step forward, and she stumbled back, both craving and unprepared for that level of honesty.

"You can't..."

"You keep saying that, but you must realize that I can. And I do."

She stepped behind the recliner, creating a physical barrier between his approaching body and her trembling one. The pull between her mind, her body, and her heart was threatening to tear her apart. "Dammit, Lucas. I thought we'd come to an understanding today. This morning. It was going so well."

"Was it?"

"Okay, I'm sick and fucking tired of your responses. You're clearly trying to make a point. But you have no standing here. You have no rights or claims as far as I'm concerned. None."

He raised one arm as if to make a point, then let it drop by his side. "What if I was trying to protect you?"

"Well, that's both unnecessary and presumptuous. Do I look like someone who needs protecting? And if I did, why would it be you?"

She didn't move away as he stepped next to her and

gently took her hand. "Because I want it to be."

She wanted him to proclaim his love, to deny his engage-ment, to erase the reality of their situation. The right words would have sent her running into his arms. Instead, she made do with a sliver of honesty and the pull of her own desire.

As he walked her through the living room, down the hall, and into the bedroom, she gave him no resistance. He sat her on the edge of the bed, kneeled in front of her and removed each of her shoes. Light kisses on each of her kneecaps preceded his standing and pulling her shirt over her head. Without being asked, she laid back on the bed, where he crawled and took off her jeans.

His fingers grazed over the top of her thong before sliding under the waistband and easing them down her thighs. Her breath caught as he slid an arm underneath her back and lifted her up just a few inches before putting her back down in the center of the bed.

He shifted forward, depositing a line of kisses from the top of her abdomen, down the center, and then burying his face between her legs.

Her first orgasm crashed into her like a freight train, pulling a howl that resonated throughout the empty house. The next ones rolled over her more gradually but no less intensely. There he stayed, with his mouth and his hands between her legs, giving her only just enough time to recover before returning.

It was only after he'd placed her exhausted body under the covers, taken off all the clothes she'd forgotten he was still wearing, and lay down next to her that she had a moment to process what had just happened. Ramona was no stranger to fantastic claims of power and ownership, but in those hours, in that bed, transpired the clearest act of possession she'd ever witnessed.

CHAPTER SEVEN

$\mathcal{R}$amona awoke to light brightening the dark beneath her lids and the sound of rushing water. She rolled away from the direction of the annoying brightness and was immediately reminded of the previous night's activities. It felt as if she'd had an overly vigorous workout - abdomen, back, and thighs aching. She curled into a ball and pulled the covers around her. Was there such a thing as an orgasm hangover? Even her throat was sore.

A few blinks brought the room into view, including the line directly into the bathroom where Lucas stood immobile in a glass-enclosed shower. She squeezed her eyes shut and then opened them again, just to make sure she was not, in fact, dreaming. His chest rose and fell with a deep breath as he braced himself with a hand against the wall. He did not look real. More like something out of a highly photoshopped ad. And certainly not anything like the boy she had known so long ago.

The pull drew her out of bed, each step reinforcing how thoroughly used her body had been. A flash of memory stopped her steps as she relived his fingers inside her, his lips pulling on her clit, her nails digging into the skin of his shoulders as her body heaved and pulsed. Before she had even caught her breath, he was on her again. And again. The whole night. Not once had she touched him. Or done anything but receive him. And come.

He lifted his head and smiled. But it was not a friendly smile. It was a smile of a man who'd accomplished what he'd intended. Who'd proven a point. Over and over again.

She stepped into the shower, the warm water electrifying her tender skin, and brought her mouth to his before he could say anything. Their bodies pressed together, heat and steam and desire everywhere.

She pulled away to look at him, then blinked to force her thoughts into line. She ran her finger across his collarbone, skimming the red finger-shaped marks that dotted his shoulder. "It's you. But it's not you."

As if he knew what her cryptic words meant, he answered. "It's only me. It's always me."

"You were the boy I loved." Her hand skimmed across the hard muscles of his chest.

"And now?"

She spoke as if in a daze. "This man... I don't know..."

"You do know. It's still me. Don't doubt what you feel."

Her hand dropped down and wrapped around his raging erection. He groaned.

He'd probably had no release or relief after hours and hours of pleasing her.

She dropped down to her knees. His body began to shake and she feared he might come before she had a chance to put his glorious cock in her mouth.

He proved to be much stronger than she expected. The warm water showered the back of her body, keeping her warm, while she enjoyed every inch of him. Whenever she would sense his approach to release, she would loosen her grip, move him away from the back of her throat, pause.

She looked up at him while she caught her breath, which nearly made her gasp. His hair dripped into his wide-open eyes, his face flushed and every muscle in his body flexed as if to give her something even more stunning to appreciate. She flicked her tongue along the ridge of his head until one of his hands slammed against the glass wall. He wouldn't last much longer, so she enveloped him with her mouth, nearly gagging as he filled to the back of her throat.

The rumble began so low in his body she felt it before she heard it. And then all she knew was the warmth streaming down her throat, the extreme contractions in his cock and the near crumbling of his formidable body.

Still holding on to him, she stood up and kissed him.

"Fuck..." he whispered into her mouth.

He stepped both of their bodies back to place her under the spray of the shower. She tilted her head back and went under. She opened her eyes and watched him creating suds in his hands, which he then rubbed over her body. With the same meticulous attention to detail he had demonstrated in cracking the code of her orgasm with his mouth, he bathed her. Taking time with her long hair, kneeling to wash her feet and tenderly touching between her legs, free from claim or desire, but full of tenderness and care.

She didn't even wait until drying off before walking back into the bedroom and laying on the bed. Her eyes drifted closed with the sensation of his lips touching hers.

Delicious scents mingled in her awareness, bringing her from dreaming to waking, no less disoriented than when she'd fallen asleep.

She opened her eyes to an empty bed for the second time that day but didn't bother searching in the bathroom. She knew exactly where Lucas was and what he was doing. Still feeling the tenderness in her muscles, she scanned the room for something to wear.

The shirt he'd worn the night before lay draped on the overstuffed chair in the corner. She picked it up and dropped her face into it, taking a deep breath. Yes, that was his intoxicating scent, like fresh bread and the ocean.

She slipped it on but didn't bother to close any of the buttons. An unexpected sense of comfort accompanied her on the short walk to the kitchen, free from any worry about milling around his house barely covered.

His concentration turned to delight as he saw her. "Good morning, sleeping beauty."

"Mmmm... that was probably the best nap I've ever had. Thanks for letting me sleep."

"I'm not sure I could've kept you awake even if I wanted to." He stopped moving the frypan across the burner to give her a smolder.

"I'm awake now."

He turned off the stovetop and upended the contents of the pan onto a large oval plate. She wrapped his large shirt around herself. "Can I help?"

He stopped on his way to bringing the platters over to the table. "I'd love if you didn't cover yourself."

She dropped her arms to the sides, allowing the shirt to fall open, giving him full access to her naked body.

He returned, slid his hands around her waist and pulled her into him. His teeth grazed the edge of her jaw, sending goosebumps across her skin. He stepped back, scanned her body, and exhaled a deep sigh. There was no question what that look meant.

He filled two large mugs with coffee, served the beautiful breakfast onto their plates and held her chair out to sit.

Ramona gave herself a moment to appreciate the perfection of the meal in front of her. Omelets, sausage, roasted vegetables, something that looked like a custard in a large ramekin.

"I'm sorry, no green juice. If you'd slept a bit longer I would have gone out to buy one for you."

She placed her hand on his thigh. "This breakfast couldn't be improved. Even with a green juice." Her hand pressed into the muscle and squeezed.

Her stomach grumbled.

"Please... eat."

Everything was as delicious as expected. Maybe even more so as her hunger blossomed. He'd already finished when she began on her second helpings. The custard ended up being the creamiest, most exquisite bread pudding and she considered picking up the whole container and licking it.

She caught him beaming at her. "I feel like you're waiting for me to finish."

"I am."

The answer surprised her. "Why?"

"Because as soon as I'm done feeding you, I'm going to be fucking you."

The spoon that was halfway up to her mouth dropped out of her hand, clanged on the side of her plate, thunked on the edge of her chair, then landed with a crash on the stone floor. Neither of them moved to pick it up. Instead, she stood up, popped a piece of sausage into her mouth, and strode down the hallway into the bedroom.

By the time he arrived, her shirt was on the floor, and she was leaning back on her arms in the center of the bed. His t-shirt and bottoms joined hers on the floor and then he was on top of her. All of him, hovering, holding, just above her but not any closer.

She tried to use her strength to get him to drop down, to eliminate any space between them. He stayed up on his straightened arms.

"I see you as clearly as I ever have. Not as a woman who's separate from the girl I loved. The one I knew I would never stop loving." He stared into her eyes. "But it's not different for me. It's all you and always you."

Finally, he lowered himself, easing her thighs open with his own. He pressed into her, everything heightened by the tenderness from the previous night's activities. With each stroke, he pushed in a bit further and she willed herself to relax, to stay present, to take him in. What began as a slow build escalated quickly into a frenzied reach to grasp and hold everything that was him. She could not get enough of his mouth on hers, his body in her arms, his cock inside her. She wanted all of him, leaving nothing for anyone else.

He slowed down, and she took his face in her hands. It was so hard to keep her eyes open as the waves of pleasure built with each stroke. He never broke contact.

"Kiss me," she whispered.

With excruciating slowness, he brought his full lips to hers, the weight of his body pressing into her. She pulled him tighter, closer, fuller. Her breath quickened, her hips bucked against him.

"Ramona... Tell me what you want. How can I please you?"

That question, from that man, a hair's breath away from her flesh, created a pulling in her lower belly. A recognizable contraction before release. There was nothing left but to let him love her.

Still feeling the pulses from the orgasm that washed over

her, she watched as his expression transformed from a focused intensity to the ecstasy of release. She cried out with him, everything dissolving into the song of their unity. He continued to pulse inside her for much longer than she'd ever experienced. She pulled him in tighter, wrapping her arms around his broad back, never wanting to let him go.

Their bodies dropped heavily onto the messy bed, sheets and pillows unnecessary in the tangle of bodies. As the minutes passed, her eyes stayed open just a sliver, breathing timed to the gentle stroke of his fingertips up and down her arm. He might have been drifting off to sleep. She kissed the tip of his nose and his eyes opened wide.

"I thought you were sleeping," he said, through a drowsy smile.

"I don't want to sleep anymore." Her fingers skimmed down his chest and belly, landing on the ever-hardening situation between his legs.

The amber of his eyes flashed as he rolled her on top of him. "Me neither."

The morning drifted into afternoon in a steady stream of sex and sleep, punctuated by another luscious meal, leaving Ramona more relaxed than she'd been in a very long time. Their bodies molded, with a perfect seal, to each other.

"I love the way we fit together," he rumbled into her ear.

Like a lock and key. Like friends who became lovers. That gap of so many years now meaningless. It all of a sudden struck Ramona as odd. Perhaps not relative to the greater issue, but odd nonetheless.

Of all the women he could have easily had, why was she the one in his bed? "I have a question."

He didn't even try to hide the stiffening of his body. "Okay..."

"Why did you want to be with me?"

"Ramona." Her name sounded more like a growl than a word.

"Please. I want to better understand what we're doing. Or at least why."

A deep sigh lifted and lowered his chest. And then another. She bit her lower lip. Maybe he couldn't answer this question, either. Maybe-

"You are the bravest person I know."

Now, that she didn't expect.

He cleared his throat. "You stood up to the scariest person I've ever met-"

"The Governor."

"Yeah. It was amazing to watch you. Bold, fearless, with the ability to outsmart anyone. Even him." He pressed a kiss just above her ear.

"I'm not sure I felt bold or courageous or any of that. It just felt like... survival." The arm around her tightened its grip.

"I've never told you this, but even after we fell out of touch, you were always my inspiration whenever I needed some courage. When I left law school, when I had to confront my parents, all the degradation I was subjected to in culinary school and the apprenticeships. I would picture you, hair all over the place, pointing your tiny finger at your grandfather and letting him know what was what."

"That's pretty funny." It was, but not the answer she was looking for. "But how about now, as we are? What makes you want to be with me?"

He laughed. "I see. You mean other than your pussy makes me believe in God?"

She spun around, eyes blazing. Surprise splashed into a hint of self-consciousness.

"Oh, you're being serious." He lowered his dark lashes. "Sorry. Alright, I'll tell you why you're here."

He shifted their bodies, bringing himself face-to-face with her. Their eyes connected across the pillow. "You're smart, one of the smartest people I know, but you never use it as a weapon. You're committed to helping others while being surrounded by people who only ever want to take. You curse better than anyone I know. When you're sleepy, you make a sound like a cat purring. You think about what you say and do before saying and doing anything. You-"

"Okay. Thank you." Maybe this was more than she could handle.

His eyes narrowed. "Excuse me. I am not done."

She nodded because, frankly, what else could she do?

"Let's see, where was I?" He rubbed his chin. "It's as if you're made of steel and stone and bulletproof glass. But in reality, you're like molten gold. Or melted cheese. Just so warm and wonderful. You're who I'd want to be, if I weren't me."

Holy Mother of God. There was no point in even trying to keep herself together. She had to tell him...

He burrowed into her gaze. "Is that what you were asking?"

"Yes. I mean, no. I mean..." She ran her palm across his cheek, the stubble waking all her nerve endings. "Aren't you going to ask me?"

"Ask you?"

"Why I'm with you."

He put his hand on hers, then slid her palm to his mouth. His soft lips, warm breath, steady pressure raised the temperature of the room by several degrees. He placed both of their hands on the center of his chest. "No, love. I'm not going to ask you."

Her spine straightened as if it had been animated by some outside force. "Why not?"

"Because I know you're struggling. And conflicted. I don't need you to declare your feelings under these conditions. I'm already asking too much of you."

Reality pressed at the base of her throat, stealing her breath and her words. He *was* asking too much of her. How had she forgotten all of that? All those beautiful words he said did not make up for the fact that he still hadn't told her the truth. And yet, something, maybe the fact that she was sex drunk, kept telling her not to run. Not to get lost in a story she didn't know. If she could see this through, maybe something wonderful would be waiting at the other end. Or maybe something devastatingly awful.

She left him splayed out on the bed to head to the bathroom. She couldn't remember ever being this sore. A glance at the clock glowing on the nightstand nearly made her trip as she tiptoed back to bed. It was three pm.

As quietly as possible, she gathered her clothes scattered around the room, each piece evoking a memory and its very own aftershock. Her body had clearly been rewired for orgasm, and even the thought of him gave her a lovely jolt. Fully dressed, she took in the sleeping vision. Who could imagine the most wonderful boy would have filled into a man that looked like that?

He fluttered his eyes open as she zipped up her jeans. His smile dropped as he bolted up. "What are you doing?"

"I have to go, Luc. It's the middle of the afternoon. I'm

surprised my family hasn't sent a search party. I was supposed to be home hours ago."

He rubbed his palms over his face then swung his legs around and stood up. His naked body nearly made her forget why she was leaving.

So tenderly, as if they hadn't spent the entire day fucking, he ran his finger across her cheek and kissed her. She dropped the jacket that had been in her hands and wrapped her arms around him.

"I don't ever want you to leave," he whispered.

She held the breath that wanted to rush from her lungs and the tremor that rose up her spine.

"Is that too much for you to hear?"

All she wanted was to drown in the amber of his eyes. "You already know the answer."

He nodded, a sad smile spreading across his face. She released her embrace and he stepped away, then began pulling pieces of clothing out of drawers.

"It's okay, Luc, you don't have to get up or get dressed. You relax."

"I'm driving you home."

"You really don't-"

He stopped zipping his jeans. "I'm driving you home." He softened his tone. "Please. I want to."

She halted her movement toward the bedroom door. "Okay. Thanks."

As she stepped into the hallway a sensation that might have been mistaken for a heart attack gripped her. Leaving that room, that house, that man, was exactly the wrong thing. It didn't matter anymore what it looked like. It didn't matter that a huge secret filled the space between them. All that mattered was being with him. Whatever situation had forced him into this engagement, she could help him. She could free him. They would figure this out together.

"Ready?" He put his hands in his pockets.

"Yes, I'm ready."

But that conversation would have to wait. She had to get home.

CHAPTER EIGHT

*T*he mid-afternoon heat was no match for the warmth that enveloped Ramona. Even as the sights whizzed by on their drive across town, she couldn't stop staring at Lucas. Couldn't stop wondering how fifteen years apart had completely disappeared. Forced to admit he was the one she always wanted by her side.

He parked in the driveway of her father's house and turned to her.

What to say or do after the time they'd spent together? "Thanks for everything. I..." She struggled to find the words. "I have no idea what to say. Everything feels incomplete or inappropriate."

"You don't have to say anything, darling Mo. I-"

Three honks of a horn caused them both to jump. A car pulled next to them in the driveway. Her father and his girl-friend waved and smiled. Yes, they would just be returning from his dialysis appointment.

She looked over at Lucas, panic quickening her breath.

He stroked her hair. "It's okay, baby. I'm just going to say hello to your dad."

She nodded even though it was the last thing she wanted to happen. Going public was one step too far.

The two men met in front of the garage doors with a deep hug.

"Lucas, it's always a pleasure to see you!" Her dad gave Lucas a pat on the cheek. "You remember Leni, right?"

"Of course." Lucas gave her a kiss on the cheek. "*Muito abrigado.*"

She beamed. "Oh, Lucas, you are too charming for your own good!"

And too handsome. And too smart. And too...

Leni swatted his arm. "Ramona didn't tell me you were coming to family dinner. What a wonderful surprise!"

"Well, I... uh..." Luc's too wide eyes met Ramona's. She shrugged.

"I think it's wonderful," Mr. Barrett said, holding on to Lucas as he walked toward the house. "You have always been family."

Ramona tried desperately to remove the shocked look from her face before facing Leni, who was pulling grocery bags out of the trunk. The men were almost at the door, her father leaning into Lucas' strong frame.

"Can I help you, Leni?"

"Oh, that would be nice. Thank you."

Out of the corner of her eye, Ramona watched Lucas pick her father up and carry him the rest of the way into the house.

Leni touched her hand. "I'm glad Lucas was here to help."

Ramona stacked two bags in each arm. "How was it today?"

"Oh, your father did very well. Everyone loves him so much at the center. The hardest part is getting him to sit still and relax. He just wants to tell jokes and visit with everyone."

"He looks tired."

"Yes, well, it's a bit draining. He'll rest for a couple of hours and by the time we are ready for dinner, he will be back to himself."

They walked straight into the kitchen, deposited their groceries, and began to sort through the items. Leni hummed something lovely while she moved things around in the fridge. It must have been Brazilian.

Her father really couldn't be accused of straying from a type. This woman could have easily been her mother's sister. They looked and acted so much alike. That is, if her mother had been happy and her father had been sober.

Ramona followed in step with Leni's instructions, taking the produce to the sink for a rinse.

Heavy footsteps caught her attention.

"Okay, ladies. Put me to work. What can I do?"

Leni put her hand on her hip and turned straight to Ramona. "Ramona, dear, please tell your fancy chef boyfriend he is not allowed in here. I don't want him upstaging me."

Both Ramona and Lucas began stuttering over themselves.

"Oh, we're not-"

"I don't mind-"

"I wouldn't think of-"

"It's no problem-"

The lovely older woman turned her head from one to the other, back and forth. "I think both of you need to leave my kitchen. I can't have all this craziness around the food. Now shoo!"

Startled by Leni's tone, Ramona chuckled and dropped the vegetables.

Lucas put his hands up and started backing out of the kitchen. "Okay, okay, I'm leaving."

"But Leni," Ramona responded, "it's not fair that you should do all the cooking for us. We can help. We'd love to."

She wagged her finger at both of them. "No! Your father requested this specific meal - it's his favorite - and only I know how to make it. So you will have to busy yourselves with something else." She pursed her lips to hide a smile. "Anyway, there will be plenty of work to do cleaning up after dinner." She winked.

Lucas wrapped his arm around Ramona's waist and led her out of the kitchen and into the sitting area.

The sound of muted drums underneath a lilting voice emanated from the kitchen. Leni must have put on some music. It was lovely.

Lucas pulled her in and held their bodies together, a gentle beat creating a sway. "Will you dance with me?"

She reached around his neck and lay her head on his chest. "I'd love to."

Moving only enough to stay with the music, Ramona relaxed in his arms. The silliness of it, dancing in her father's sitting room, to music they could barely hear, was nothing compared to the tenderness of it. He moved her, he held her, he hummed into her hair.

"So, I guess you're staying for family dinner."

He jerked both of their bodies to a stop. "I don't have to, Mo. I'm not trying to intrude. I'd love to spend some time with your dad, but it doesn't have to be tonight. I can excuse myself if you don't-"

She squeezed him tighter. "I'd like you to stay."

His chest softened. "I was hoping you'd say that. Whatever Leni's making is going to be epic. Seriously."

"Oh, really?" She looked up at him with narrowed eyes. "That's why you want to stay? Brazilian food?"

"That's just a bonus. We both know why I'm here."

He touched his lips to hers. What started out as a gentle kiss grew to a crash of mouths and a flurry of hands. Ramona pulled away, breathless. It was too weird to be making out with him in the middle of her father's house. Like some ridiculous time-travel age-switching TV movie.

Something heavy clanged on the stovetop. She snuggled back into his arms.

"I'm feeling... happy. Really happy," he said.

She pressed her lips to his neck. "Tell me more."

"I'm generally a happy person. But this, with you, is something else entirely. It's like happy squared. Happy stuffed in a grilled cheese sandwich."

She closed her eyes, wanting to paint that moment into her permanent memories. Such a simple thing, but it had never made so much sense as right then. "I want you to be happy, Lucas."

"Thanks. I appreciate you saying that."

The muted sounds from the kitchen shifted to a country beat, a fast strumming guitar wafting over them. Leni had interesting taste in music.

Ramona reluctantly pulled out of their embrace. "I need to change. I've been wearing these clothes since last night."

"Well, mostly *not* wearing those clothes." His left eyebrow perked up.

"Okay, then, Mr. Happy, I'll be right back."

She arrived at her messy room, pulled off her clothes and deposited them in the ever-expanding mound in the corner. She rummaged through her suitcase, the choices slim. A light blue blouse over a white peasant skirt would have to do.

Happiness. Had she ever thought of herself in those terms? Probably not. She was a driven person, a decisive person, maybe even a demanding person. But a happy person? It had never crossed her mind to use that trait to define herself. Maybe that's what sat in the middle of all those intense emotions she'd been feeling that week. From desire to guilt, anger to ecstasy, confusion to clarity. Batted around like a tennis ball. Monkey mind, as her yoga teacher would say. But right in the middle, if she let herself be there, was this sweet, simple satisfaction. Maybe she should have listened more to all those exhortations to enjoy the moment.

Ramona plopped onto the couch next to Lucas and took his hand.

He ran his other hand over hers. "You look lovely."

Why did each of his compliments make her feel like a blushing schoolgirl? "Thanks."

"Where's the Con-man?"

She frowned, remembering her brother's admonition to stay away from Lucas. "He'll be here. Late, I assume."

"More exploratory meetings?"

"Yup. I think he's actually going to run for office. All the advisors are telling him it's feasible. Sounds impossible to me. A young, inexperienced upstart running against the beloved incumbent. And why would he want to? Makes no sense." She shook her head.

"He's not just an upstart. He's a Barrett. That's gold in this state. And he's got hugely powerful allies-"

"Like your father."

"Yes, like my father. But many more. I'm really proud of him. Senator Connor Barrett. Doesn't that sound great?"

She couldn't share in the enjoyment. "I'm not thrilled. You know how I feel about all of this." Her dorky brother was stepping back into the dirty family business.

She dropped her head onto his shoulder and closed her

eyes, wondering what it was going to take to talk Connor out of this foolish idea.

"Hey! What's up, people?"

At her brother's voice, Ramona bolted upright, pulling her hand out of Lucas'. "Connor!"

"Hey, Con-man."

"Hey, Lu-ser."

Ramona rolled her eyes. "I'm not sure if you guys got the memo, but you're grown men. You don't have to use those childish names anymore."

"Oh, really Mowgli?" her brother added.

Both men laughed at her.

"Well, I'm not calling *myself* Mowgli." She stood up and gave her brother a hug. "Anyway, nice to see you."

"Smells amazing in here. Where's Dad?"

"Still napping, I think." Thank goodness her father hadn't witnessed what had just taken place. "Why don't you go wake him up?"

Connor strode down the hallway toward their father's room.

Ramona exhaled relief at the ease of interacting with her brother. He hadn't appeared to suspect anything. One look at Lucas, however, brought concern front and center. "What's up?"

His expression soured. "Did you tell your brother anything? About us?"

She slowly nodded. He sprung to his feet. "He might not understand."

"He doesn't. But that makes two of us."

"Baby, I'll be able to tell you everything. I just need a little more time."

God, how she wanted to believe him.

. . .

Lucas and Connor pushed their chairs back from the table and rubbed their bellies in unison, like twins. Ramona turned from one to the other and then to her father, beaming at Leni. Those three men formed the triangle of home and family and love. She stood, noticing the fullness in her belly as well. Dinner was delicious, but she remembered their promise to take care of cleaning up.

Lucas hopped up and picked up a plate in each hand. He nodded at Ramona. "Let's do this."

They marched into the kitchen, where Lucas opened the dishwasher, and Ramona turned on the faucet. She flicked her finger under the stream, waiting for the water to heat up enough to rinse the plates. Lucas held a plate in midair.

"Were you just looking at my ass?"

His face erupted into a wide grin. "You caught me. I was remembering something..."

He slid the plate into an open slot in the dishwasher, wiped his hands on his jeans, gripped her shoulders and pressed her body against the sink and his lips to hers. Her still wet hands wove through his hair. It felt as if the steam rising up behind them was being created by their bodies.

"What the fuck?"

Lucas flew off of her and they both stared at Connor, fuming in the doorway.

"Con, don't freak out," Ramona said.

He ignored his sister and glared at Lucas. "Listen, man, I can't figure out what's going on with you, and you won't tell me. Fine. But I won't let you fuck with my sister. This is the kind of bullshit our families would pull."

Lucas took one step toward him. "I'm not fucking with her. I love her. Always have. Always will."

If Ramona hadn't already been pressed against the kitchen counter and cabinets, she would most certainly have fallen several steps back. Her fingers gripped the edge of the counter to still the quake in her body.

Lucas put his arm out, reaching for his friend. "You know that, Con."

Connor shook his head as if he was trying to dislodge something. "What I know is that Abigail Langley thinks you're going to marry her in a few weeks."

"It's not..."

Both Ramona and Connor pitched forward, awaiting his next words. None came.

Connor raised his arm and pointed toward the front door. "You need to go, Luc."

Lucas turned to Ramona and nodded, then strode through the kitchen. She heard him say goodbye to her father and Leni, then leave.

She was still gripping the counter when her brother freed her hands. "You didn't have to do that, Con."

"We swore we would never be like our parents. Remember that, Mo? This... this is something out of their playbook. I just can't have it."

She exhaled, sense coming back into her hands and her mind. "You're mad at him."

"I'm furious. I can't believe he would hide something this big from me. He's like my brother. We don't keep secrets, much less something this important. And you... Have you been sneaking around all week? I thought we agreed it was going to end."

Her whole body drooped. "I'm sorry. I lost my bearings. He's... We're... I forgot that we're not those people. I'm not that kind of person."

Connor rubbed the back of his neck. "He said he loved you, Mo. What are you going to do about that?"

She wasn't going to forget that anytime soon. "I don't

know. But I'll figure something out." She turned back to the sink and picked up a plate. "Don't worry."

For the remainder of the evening, everyone skillfully pretended that nothing strange or bad had happened. The meal was as incredible as expected, and it was wonderful to see her father so happy. Leni treated him like a king, which he deserved.

Most of the conversation revolved around Connor. Him being Mayor was innocuous enough, but Senator meant being in the thick of it. The whole grubby game of politics. And she hoped to never be around that again. Unfortunately, her brother had caught the bug and didn't appear to be letting it go. At least it had given everyone else something else to think about. Too bad it left a very unpleasant taste in her mouth.

By the time Ramona slipped into bed, the path forward with Lucas had started to emerge. A few changes to her plans for the rest of the week clarified them even more. It was about time that decisive Ramona stepped up to the plate.

She almost didn't answer the phone when she saw Lucas' name flash across the screen, but curiosity got the best of her. It would be a test of her resolve.

"Hey."

"Mo."

She listened to him breathe through the crystal clear line. "What's up, Lucas?"

He exhaled. "I don't know what to say about today. I didn't mean to ruin your family dinner. It was never my intention to-"

"You didn't ruin it."

"Are you angry with me, too?" His suffering crawled through the phone line and wrapped itself around her.

"I'm not angry. But I can't do this. It's not who I want to be."

"It's not what it seems, Mo. I wish-"

"I hear what you're saying, but until I know what's going on, I can't continue. You have to understand."

"What about what I said? About how I feel?"

She couldn't respond. All those words he'd said had been ringing in her head all night, and she desperately wanted them to stop.

"Maybe I can come by tomorrow, before we go to the benefit. We can talk."

"I'm going with Tyler. He's on his way back into town."

"No, Ramona. Please don't do this. I promise you, it can all be explained."

"Okay, then explain." She counted to ten. And then ten again, her heart breaking with every round.

"I told you-"

"That's my minimum requirement, Lucas. If you can't tell me what's really going on, I don't want anything else."

The quiet hush of his long breaths filled the phone line.

"I see. Well, then, goodnight." She touched the red dot and put the phone down.

After tossing and turning for most of the night, visions of Lucas' wedding intermingling with his professions of love to her, Ramona gave up trying to sleep. She padded out to the kitchen and was surprised to see her father already sitting at the table.

"Dad, what are you doing up so early?"

"Good morning, pumpkin. Leni had an early shift, so I just got up with her."

She looked at his dark eyes and drawn expression. "Why don't you go back to bed? Get some more rest?"

"Agh, all I do is rest. I'm tired of resting."

They both laughed. "I don't think that's a thing, Dad."

"It is now."

"How about I make us some coffee?"

"That sounds perfect."

She could hardly find her way around the kitchen, which had been reorganized by Leni, but she did know how to access the all-important coffee-making supplies. The coffeemaker began its bubbling while she watched the blinking lights of the small red clock.

"I heard what happened last night."

She spun around to face her father. "What?"

"I heard what happened between you and your brother. And Lucas."

She swallowed, afraid and embarrassed at the same time. "I'm sorry, Dad. That was completely inappropriate, I know..."

He shrugged. "I wasn't surprised. I knew something was going on."

This was likely the most humiliating moment she'd had with her father since the dreaded birds and bees talk. "I don't know what to say."

He waved her over to him, then wrapped his thin hand around hers. She looked down at the veins and bones so evident underneath his loose skin. "I'm ashamed of what I did. It's wrong."

"It's complicated, that I can agree with. I'm not so sure about wrong."

Her eyes opened wide to make sure those words had come out of her father's mouth. Sure, he was no moral authority, but he had always had a strong sense of keeping appearances. "I'm surprised to hear you say that, Dad."

His head lolled to the side. "Love is a different game than anything else we do. We can't pick who we love or when it appears for us. I think life is too short to give those moments away."

"He's engaged to someone else."

He shrugged again. "I'm an old man. But I hear things. And I know things. What's clear to me is that he's telling the truth about always having loved you. And he's telling a lie about the engagement. I don't know why, but you and I both know that in this town that sort of behavior is pretty normal."

"But we're not in the game. He's not playing politics."

"Maybe his fiancée is."

A small beep pulled her attention to the coffeemaker. It took all her willpower to still the tremble in her hands as she poured the coffee into two colorful mugs.

She'd never considered that this scheme might have been driven by Abigail. Not that she had any idea what the scheme was. The whole thing was indecipherable.

Her father wrapped his hands around the warm mug and smiled at her. "Your mother was the love of my life. I didn't think I would survive her leaving me. Not that I blamed her."

Ramona swallowed a gulp of the too hot coffee, uncomfortable with the turn of the conversation.

"I was resigned to be alone. I mean, who was going to love this dried-up drunk?"

"Don't say that, Dad."

"But it's true. And then the most amazing thing happened." His eyes brightened. "This gorgeous woman, who'd always been extra nice to me, even in my worst days in the hospital, fell in love with me. I mean, I thought I was the last person on the planet to deserve another chance. After all I'd done. But I got one."

Her eyes filled with tears. She'd never had this intimate a conversation with her father and to see him speak so honestly warmed her heart. "Leni is wonderful. I love the two of you together. It makes me happy, Dad."

"Yes, me too." He grinned. "But my point is that love is like magic. It doesn't follow the rules or predictable patterns. It just comes when it comes. Leni was my second chance. I think Lucas is yours."

"But how? It doesn't make sense."

"That's the problem, pumpkin. You're trying to make it make sense."

She wiped a tear away.

"I always wondered what would have happened if you'd stayed here. If your mother hadn't had to take you kids away. I always thought you and Lucas would have gotten married young and had a bunch of babies by now. But seeing you together now, as adults, I'm starting to doubt my assumption. As kids, I don't think you were ready for how big it would be. But I think you're ready now."

"But he's engaged." She felt like a broken record.

"Fair enough. But don't discount your feelings just because they don't look quite right. Trust your heart, pumpkin. It's always led you where you needed to be."

She got up from her seat and squeezed her father. "I love you, Dad. More than you'll ever know."

CHAPTER NINE

*R*amona smoothed the crease that kept forming around her hips. She'd have to stay standing if she didn't want her dress to look awful by the end of the night. Maybe the mulberry silk hadn't been the right choice. But it was lovely.

If she'd been wearing a watch, she would have checked it. Tyler was late.

The black car stopped in front of her driveway just as she unlocked her phone to text him.

She watched through the living room windows as he jumped out and ran up to the front door, which she opened. He stepped into the house, out of breath. "I'm so sorry I'm late! The traffic here is brutal. I almost got back on the plane and flew to your neighborhood."

"It's okay. We'll be fine."

He held her arms. "You look gorgeous, Robin. Like a dream."

"Does it make you want to give me money?"

He squinted. "Giving you money isn't the first thing that comes to mind, but, sure."

She slapped his chest. "Don't be crude, Ty. All that matters is buffing up the foundation. We've been under-funded for too many years now. Time to turn that around."

"If anyone can do it, you can."

As expected, Ramona and Tyler made a grand entrance, reporters huddled around the entrance to the reception hall. There were several she didn't recognize. Perhaps an appearance by the world-famous Tyler Diamond had increased their exposure. She gave the photographers her best smile and said a silent thank you to her friend for supporting her in so many ways.

The first sight of Lucas, with Abigail on his arm, wiped the smile right off her face. They looked like they belonged on a celebrity red carpet, complete with tuxedo, designer gown, and bright white smiles.

Tyler moved his arm behind her with a tight grip. "Don't worry, Robin. I've got you."

Abigail's expression moved along a matching spectrum, from beaming smile to unmistakable disgust, as if she had taken a whiff of something very bad.

The two couples approached each other. Everything moved in excruciating slow motion. Had Lucas told her that Abigail was coming? She didn't think so.

They stood staring at each other for longer than Ramona could stomach. She dipped her head in acknowledgment. "Lucas. Abigail. Nice to see you."

"And you too, Ramona." Abigail gawked at Tyler's arm around Ramona's waist. "Tyler. I didn't realize you'd be attending the benefit. I thought you were in Europe."

"I wouldn't miss it. Anything to support Ramona."

Fear that Abigail had found out about her dalliances with

Lucas sent a flash of terror down Ramona's spine. Her smile pulled the tightened skin of her cheeks. She swallowed.

Lucas reached his hand out to Tyler. "Thanks for coming, Tyler. Your support is so important to us."

Tyler chuckled. "You bet."

Lucas turned his confused glance to Ramona. "I need a few minutes of your time, if you don't mind. The caterer isn't clear on the timing for all the speeches and dinner service."

Tyler gripped her waist a bit tighter. She appreciated it but had to pull away. "Excuse me, Ty. I'll be right back."

Ramona increased her pace across the main hall, through the first prep area, to the caterer's kitchen, staying out of the reach of Lucas' arm.

She looked around the bustling back room, filled with chefs and servers. "Where is the catering manager?"

Lucas pressed his lips together. "I made that up."

She turned on her heel to meet his concerned gaze. "You did what?"

"I just needed to talk to you. Before we got too immersed in the evening's activities. You look beautiful, by the way."

Anger tickled behind her eyes. "You pulled me back here to tell me that?"

"No. Not only that."

"This is ridiculous, Lucas. We've got important work to do tonight. Please don't make this about our situation. I need to focus on the foundation."

He touched her cheek, and she had a fleeting impulse to grab his hand and run out of the building together. She moved his hand away.

"We're good together, Ramona. Look me in the eye and tell me we aren't."

"No. I'm not going to do this. You know my terms, Lucas.

I need the truth." She took two long steps away from him, stopped and turned back. "But not tonight."

Cocktail hour passed too quickly for Ramona. The large room, full of potential donors - big ones - needed to be worked hard. It looked like Lucas was too busy following her every move to do his fair share of schmoozing. At least he remembered to do her intro.

The crowd quieted within moments of him standing on the small platform in the center of the room. He'd mastered the smile-and-wave while waiting for the crowd's attention.

"Good evening, everyone! I'm so taken back by the response to tonight's event. We've already achieved over half of our donation goal just from pledges made here. As you know, the Barrett Winston Foundation is the culmination of two families' commitment to making the world a better place. Your participation is deeply appreciated, and your support is critical." A small round of applause kept him from continuing. "Folks, as you know, I'm just the warm-up act. The person you really want to hear from is my much more beautiful, talented, and engaging partner-in-crime. So, please give a warm welcome to the indomitable Ramona Barrett."

They hugged as she stepped onto the small elevated area. He lingered a bit too long handing her the microphone. She avoided his eyes, knowing what she *didn't* need was to get the Lucas Winston butterflies.

"Thank you, everyone. We come together on the tail of a tragic event - the death of my grandfather - but we have a chance here, tonight, to make the vision he shared more than fifty years ago with his best friend Kenneth Winston blossom into something earth-changing. Something exponentially bigger than anything they could have imagined. But we can't do it alone. We need your help."

She paused to connect with the rapt audience. Tyler winked at her. "I encourage you to take a look at the plans we have detailed in the prospectus. I welcome your suggestions and comments. In fact, Lucas and I, as co chair of the foundation, would love to have conversations with each and every one of you. As you know, I've devoted my life to the refinement of charitable giving, but nothing is as important, or as personal, as this particular foundation.

"There are so many problems in the world that we can't address. But there are enough that can be remediated or rectified with your help.

"We - those who can - are charged with helping those who can't. It's part of the privilege of being in the positions we find ourselves. I thank you again for your attendance tonight, for your kind words of condolence, and for honoring my grandfather with the support of his foundation. Please enjoy the wonderful food and music."

Applause continued well after she'd moved from the center of the room. She was buffeted with greetings, compliments, and hugs as she made her way to Tyler, who was beaming by the main bar.

"If you didn't already work for me, I'd hire you. Right on the spot. You're damned impressive, Robin. Might have just added another zero to my donation."

She ran her palms down the lapels of his tuxedo. "Now, *that's* what I want to hear."

"You're such a good speaker, Ramona!"

That voice caused her to jump back. She turned slowly, not really wanting to share the moment with that particular woman. Or her date. "Thank you, Abigail. Kind of you to say."

"If I ever need to raise some money, consider yourself hired!"

Ramona wondered how much venom was evident in her polite laughter. There was not enough money in the universe for her to want that job. She grabbed a glass of champagne from the passing waiter and took too large a gulp.

"Careful, now! Remember what happened last time when you drank too much."

Lucas pulled on his date's arm. "Abigail! That's so rude!"

Ramona kept her gaze locked on the woman. She didn't want to see even one part of him. "Oh, that's okay. And she's probably right. It's best to be careful in these situations. I wouldn't want to cause another stain."

Tyler's laugh got buried in a series of coughs. He was a terrible actor.

Lucas hardly waited for the coughing man to regain his bearings. "Tyler, I know you were interested in coming to the restaurant. We're having a special wine pairing dinner this weekend. I'd love to invite you as my guest."

"Oh, that sounds great. But Robin - I mean Ramona - and I are headed out in the morning."

Lucas' face fell. "Headed out?"

"Yeah, I need to get back to London and Ramona's coming with me. We're working on a tech education initiative with a British company. The timing just happened to work out perfectly."

Lucas' eyes bored into her. She was not going to engage.

He tilted his head and squinted. "I wasn't aware you were leaving so soon."

She desperately wanted to be out of that conversation.

Tyler touched her arm. "Well, I was going to take the meeting by myself, because I thought she'd be tied up with family, but she's ready to go, I guess."

"Yes, I am."

"Next time, Lucas." Tyler clasped his shoulder. "I really am dying to try your restaurant. It's the talk of the town."

Lucas lifted his chest. "Yes, next time."

Ramona pretended to wave at someone in the crowd and walked away.

She could almost feel Lucas' body behind her as she wove her way through the crowd. Every step forward was halted by someone wanting a handshake or a chat. She cut to the left, hoping to lose him, and found herself on a straight trajectory toward his mother. She was trapped.

He closed the space between them, to the point that his jacket brushed against her bare shoulders. "You were just going to sneak out of town and not tell me? What is going on with you, Ramona?"

She turned around slowly. "It's time for me to go back to work. I don't live here, remember?"

He shook his head, incredulous. "I understand you're struggling with what happened... with what's happening... but what you're doing is... unlike you."

"Maybe you don't know me quite as well as you think, Lucas."

"I guess not, "he said, his voice trailing away as she walked farther and farther from him.

The numbers indicated they had done well, exceeding Ramona's monetary goal for the night. Too bad all she felt was sadness. That situation with Lucas had ended as badly as her worst fears. What a complete mess. She tossed and turned in her bed - the same one he'd been in just days ago - before giving up on the idea of sleep.

She tiptoed down the hall and into the next room, then burst out laughing. The sight of the man who she'd only ever seen in the most plush environments sitting on a small bed in a small room, surrounded by art supplies and teenage boy paraphernalia, was too much. It looked like he was trying to sleep in a time-warped storage closet.

"Sorry about the conditions, Ty. I guess Dad didn't try very hard to convert this room after Connor left home."

"It's fine. I kinda like it. Definitely a change of pace and a million times more comfortable than the Ritz-Carlton. And you know I'm no snob." He patted the small space next to him and scooted over the few inches available to him. "Come sit with me for a minute."

She did so without hesitation. He took her hand. "Tonight was hard for you, wasn't it?"

A ball of tears made its way up her throat. She swallowed and nodded. He pulled her into his arms. "I'm sorry, Robin." He stroked her hair while she softly cried into his shoulder.

A deep breath helped her pull herself together. "I'm sorry, Ty. This is inappropriate. You don't need to see my crying over some guy."

He flashed her the trademark Tyler Diamond smile. "Although I would have happily accepted you sneaking into my bedroom for another reason, I knew you wanted to talk about tonight."

"I don't know that there's anything to talk about."

"You love him."

The answer came out before she could stop it. "Yes."

"And he loves you."

"N-"

"That wasn't a question. I was letting you know that I

knew." Otherwise known as a *Diamond* question, a technique he had perfected in his business dealings, and which drove her crazy.

She huffed. "Whatever you think about who loves whom doesn't matter. He's getting married in two weeks. That's the reality."

He nodded and smirked, adding to her impulse to want to strangle him. "About that..."

Her gaze snapped to his. He knew something. "What? What is it? What do you know?"

He gently stroked her hand, which was their particular shorthand for slow down, take a breath.

"You remember that I gave Abigail a ride to New York after the funeral?"

"Yes."

"I noticed a few things."

She sat, keeping her expression calm and her breathing slow. He wouldn't continue unless she was in control. Hysterical women did not get any of Tyler's attention. She nodded slowly.

"I definitely can't claim to be an expert on women."

She continued to nod and gave him what she hoped was a compassionate, knowing smile.

"But having three sisters taught me a few things. A woman who's about to get married thinks about one thing and one thing only."

That was easy. "Her wedding."

"Exactly. Although Abigail spoke freely, even voluminously, she did not once bring up her engagement, her fiancé, or her wedding. For the four or so hours we were together. It was obvious enough that even I noticed."

Ramona pulled her bottom lip between her teeth. She wasn't sold on the fact that this was incontrovertible evidence that the engagement was a sham. Odd, certainly. But Abigail was odd. "Maybe she's not one of those girls who's all wedding crazy."

"Except for the fact that when we were in public, it's the first thing she brought up. Remember?"

"That's true." Ramona furrowed her brow. "You're right."

Her mind got busy sorting all the conflicting information, hoping for it to fall into orderly piles, which would make sense.

"There's something else, too." Tyler interrupted her sorting with a peculiar look.

She tilted her head from side to side. She knew Tyler well enough that there was no question where this was going. "You didn't."

He grimaced. "Not strictly speaking, no."

"But?"

"*She* might have. Actually, she did." He gave her an awkward smile as if to say look at how funny I am.

Ramona's mouth dropped open. Before a stream of expletives flew out of it - including a particularly scathing *cheating bitch* - she flashed to a scene just one day before of her on her knees with Lucas' cock pounding against the back of her throat. No matter how much she wanted it to be true, two wrongs did not make it right.

"Are you saying-"

"She gave me a blow job. Enthusiastically."

Ramona dropped her head in her hands. "Ugh." Hearing it explicitly made it even worse.

"Are you disgusted with me?"

She looked up at his worried face. "I wish I could be. But I've done much worse. For likely the first and only time in our lives, I've crossed the moral line a hundred times farther than you."

"You slept with him." Tyler never spoke about her and other men. It was a clear boundary.

"You don't want to hear about this, Ty."

"Yes, you're right. It's hard for me. But I'm your friend, first and foremost. The other stuff is my issue to deal with." She was probably the only person in the world who could see the hint of sadness in his smile.

She leaned back into his shoulder. "You're such a good guy."

"Don't tell anyone."

She laughed. "No one would believe me, anyway. Thank you for being there for me this week. You were a lifesaver."

"Anything for you, Robin. Even if it means sorting out your guy trouble."

Tyler was one helluva man. They might have been good together if she'd given him a chance. But all that was irrelevant now that Lucas was back in her life. No matter how great Tyler was, she couldn't see him as more than a friend. And no matter how much trouble Lucas was turning out to be, he'd taken hold of her heart. Again.

CHAPTER TEN

Two weeks later

Before Ramona's eyes opened, the pounding in her head reminded her of the previous night's events. She pulled her stiff body to sitting and rolled her head. Passing out on the couch had left a painful crick in her neck, as evidenced by the loud pops and clicks with every move. It had been a really long time since she'd drunk so much that she'd been unable to make it to her own bed.

She narrowed her eyes at the large white clock across the room and did a quick calculation. Everyone would be on their way to the church right now, if not already there. Lucas and Abigail's wedding day had finally arrived. Ramona had spent the previous two weeks up to her eyebrows in work, flying across the globe, attending meeting after meeting. Anything to take her mind off that day. She kept waiting for him to call and tell her the wedding was a sham. He wasn't going to marry Abigail. He only loved her. But no call came. Even a night drinking and crying hadn't purged the torment from her body.

Several blinks brought the rest of the room into view. The spare, bright space, typically pristine, was strewn with bottles, plates, and congealed slices of pizza. A glance confirmed the apartment was empty. She didn't remember saying goodbye to her friends.

One of the consequences of constantly being on the road was having no friends in her own town. She'd had this place in San Francisco for five years, but she might as well have been a visitor. When she needed a couple of girlfriends to help her drink it out, she called on some new friends: Camille and Jenna, both connected to a long-ago ex-boyfriend, Jackson King. He'd wanted to come over too - they'd been close friends for years now - but considering it was his cousin she was crying about, she kindly asked him not to.

Even Tyler volunteered to help her drown her sorrows, but she knew better than to accept. Their entanglements were a bit too tricky. He'd been pushing hard for her to take an assignment in London for a year. It was probably the most prestigious offer she'd ever had - which may or may not have involved some royals - and would have kept her far away and distracted from the Lucas situation. But she didn't want it. No more running away for this gal. Her plan included heading directly into the pain. After her one night of inebriated avoidance, of course.

Standing up created a wave of dizziness. Nausea, too. Food, water, and bed might be her only hope. Maybe she wouldn't wake up until the next day. At least then, everything would be done. There'd be no more hoping and wishing and waiting.

She opened the refrigerator to retrieve the water pitcher and saw her phone sitting on top of a block of cheese. *What the...?* A spotty memory of someone taking it from her when she insisted on calling him. At least they hadn't hidden it somewhere harder to find.

As soon as she picked up the cold device, texts and missed calls filled the screen, covering up the picture of her and her dad. She wiped the fogged-up glass on her leg. Her brother's name was on most of the message bubbles. The adrenaline of panic forced any bit of intoxication away. Something had happened to her father. She touched the button on the most recent voicemail and put the phone to her ear. It chilled her entire body.

"Hey, Mo, where are you? You better-"

The phone beeped with a new call. Her brother again. She picked up.

"What the fuck, Ramona!"

She moved the phone, and her brother's booming voice, away from her ear. Too much sound for her state. "Connor, please stop screaming. What's going on? How's Dad?"

"Dad? Dad's fine. Why are you asking me about Dad?"

"You called me a million times. I thought..." She looked at the clock again. "Wait a minute. Aren't you supposed to be best man at a wedding right now?"

"That's what I'm calling about! Dammit, Mo, you don't have a lot of time. I need you to focus and listen to me."

She walked over to the kitchen table and sat down heavily in a padded chair. A fresh wave of fatigue hit her. Why didn't she have a lot of time?

"Are you there? Are you listening?"

"Yes, Con, I'm listening. What is going on?"

"He's not getting married today. And I know why."

She waited for him to continue. And for the pounding of her heart to stop being deafening. "God, can you please say something?"

She heard him take a deep breath. "It's hard to know

where to start. He came to my house really early this morning and told me the whole thing. Abigail is running for Congress. But everyone hates her."

No surprise there.

"Anyway, apparently, Lucas owed her a favor. And getting engaged was him paying her back."

"What? That makes no sense. What kind of favor would require someone to marry you?"

"Well, that's the thing. The favor was not to marry her. It was to dump her at the altar."

She wondered if her brother was inebriated. Or having some sort of mental breakdown. "I don't think I'm awake enough for this conversation. You're making no sense. Why don't we talk later?"

"No!"

She pulled the phone away from her ear again. Why was he yelling?

"We don't have time, Mo. I really need you to pay attention. She wants to get elected, but everyone hates her. Thinks she's too perfect. Untouchable. Some advisor told her that she needed some big tragedy in her life to get people to feel bad for her. She devised this grand plan to pretend to be engaged and then get dumped. It's been going on for almost a year."

Ramona was surprised the chair still held her up considering how heavy her head felt. Thoughts swirled and swished just outside her grasp. "Why didn't he tell anyone?"

"Hardcore NDA, apparently. Couldn't even tell me, until this morning, when the gag order ended. I guess she didn't want to take any chances that the scheme would get out."

"Holy shit, Connor. I'm having trouble keeping up. This is really twisted."

"You're going to have to. I've been calling you since he left here hours ago. He's going to be there any minute, Mo."

"Be where? What are you talking about?"

He groaned. "Are you drunk? You're being really slow. Yes, he's on his way to your place. Went straight to the airport after leaving my house. The only thing on his mind is seeing you."

"Oh, my God." She wanted to have something else to say, but nothing came. Could this really be happening?

"Listen, Mo, I'm really sorry for the shitty things I said to you. I should have trusted you knew what you were doing. I was just so angry with him."

"It's okay, Con. I had no idea what I was doing." Shit. "What am I supposed to do now? I haven't spoken to him since I left Virginia."

"From what he said to me, he's serious, sis. He loves you, which we already knew. He wants to be with you."

She took in the disaster that currently filled her apartment. It was in no condition to receive a visitor. She looked down at the pizza stains on her crumpled tee shirt. Neither was she.

She got up, tucked the phone under her ear, and picked up a sponge. "Okay. I gotta go. I'm a mess."

"Wait. Are you going to tell him?"

That stopped her in her tracks. Yes. It wouldn't have to be a secret anymore. "I suppose. But I really gotta go."

"Alright. Love you, sis. Good luck."

"Love you. I'll let you know what happens."

She moved in double time, like a turbo-charged cleaning robot. Everything hauled into the garbage, bottles thrown into the recycling, couch reassembled into reasonable shape. She wished she had a better sense of his ETA. Was there time for a shower? What would he do if she wasn't available to answer the door? In that moment, logistics was much more within her capabilities than emotions.

Ramona stripped down as the water heated up. It would have been great to linger in the hot shower, but she couldn't risk it. She pulled her soaking wet hair into a bun on top of her head, threw on clean jeans and a sweater and walked back into the living room. She almost expected him to already be in her apartment, sitting on the couch waiting for her. Would security stop him at the front desk? Had Connor given him all the details of how to find her place? Damn, why had she destroyed so many brain cells with all that Tequila?

She looked down to see she was wringing her hands. How foolish. What was there to be nervous about?

Coffee. She needed coffee.

She paced across the compact kitchen to the drip of the coffee maker. She didn't want to be planning out her response to an undefined question. *What did Connor mean about wanting to be with me?* Did he tell Lucas about her ideas? Would she really do it?

The knock on the door startled her enough to slosh the hot coffee onto her fingers. She grabbed a towel to wrap around her hand and then stood at her front door. She counted four breaths before answering.

The man who appeared on the other side of the door was in many ways familiar, but at that moment, like a creature she did not understand even one bit.

"Hi, Ramona." His eyes looked tired and bright at the same time.

She stepped to the side. "Hi. Come in."

He held eye contact. "I'm taking by the look on your face that you knew I was coming."

She nodded. "Connor..."

"Good. I'm glad. I wouldn't have wanted to barge in like this without you being a little bit prepared."

"Doesn't mean I'm prepared. I'm struggling to understand what's going on."

"I get it, and I'm here to answer all your questions. Would now be an okay time to talk?"

She walked toward the sitting area when his hand caught her arm. In one move, she was pressed against his body, enveloped in his arms, feeling the vibration of his chest as he spoke her name. She tilted her head up and touched her lips to his. Everything felt better.

He slowly pulled away. "I'm glad you feel that way about my being here. I wasn't sure what to expect."

She stepped back, out of his arms, all the confusion and self-consciousness returning. "Can I get you something? Coffee? Water? Food?"

"Water, for now, thanks."

He was sitting on the edge of the couch, perched forward, when she returned. She sat down next to him, and he took her hand instead of the water.

"I'm so happy to see you, Mo. You have no idea."

"I... I don't understand what's going on, Luc. Connor tried to explain it to me but..."

"Yeah. It probably makes no sense." He shifted his seat to face her. "Let me explain..."

She grabbed a pillow and wrapped her arms around it, suddenly uncomfortable and unprepared to hear the truth from his own lips. She'd been waiting for weeks, but now that the moment had arrived, she wanted to run away. Or throw up.

He tilted his head. "Are you okay? You look like you're not feeling well."

"I had a rough night."

His eyes widened. "Because you thought I was getting married today?"

She considered her response. He'd flown across the country to see her. Admitted he loved her. Maybe hiding and pretending were no longer necessary. "I kept waiting for you to call me and tell me it wasn't going to happen. But I didn't hear anything from you. What else could I have thought?"

"I couldn't say anything. The NDA was solid, up until midnight last night."

That didn't make sense. "Last night?"

"Well, technically, it's still in effect, but the friends and family waiver kicked in. Finally."

She appreciated the relief on his face. Despite the fact that his words were far from comprehensible.

"Mo, when I signed it, I had no idea it was going to matter that much. Then you showed up at my restaurant. I tried my damnedest to get Abigail to modify the terms, but she wouldn't. Even though she liked the idea of us being together - it would add to the horror of her situation. Fiancé dumps her for another woman is apparently great political fodder. And a great headline."

She wanted to laugh with him. Even to smile. But the sickness and the resultant grimace wouldn't budge.

"Maybe I should start at the beginning. Abigail and I were in law school together, as you might remember. We dated for a while but it never got serious, and we stayed friends. Then everything fell apart when I decided to drop out. My family was up in arms, my mother wouldn't even speak to me, most of my friends abandoned me. It was an eye-opener. I never realized how many people around me were only interested in my family. I felt like a naive ass."

That period of time was a distant memory for Ramona. And not a pleasant one. She'd been so mad at him for going to law school, for following in his family's footsteps even though he knew it wasn't right. She'd called him a coward and a sellout.

"I'm sorry, Lucas." She dropped her head and took a ragged breath. "I was probably the shittiest of all your friends. I didn't care that you decided to change courses. I'd never forgiven you for starting out on the path you did."

She picked up the glass of water and took several gulps. Only after putting it down did she remember that she'd brought it for him. "Oh! Sorry! That was your water. I'll get you a new one."

He pulled her back down when she tried to stand up. "It's okay. We can share it." He took a sip. "I don't blame you, Mo. I understand how frustrated you were with me. I didn't have my head screwed on right. It was a really hard time."

She lightly touched his arm, then couldn't decide what else to do. Squeeze his shoulder? Take his hand? She dropped her hand back onto her own lap.

"Abigail was the only one who stood by me. She even mediated with my family. The whole thing was very surprising, even now, knowing her and her personality. So, by the time I got back on my feet, I was immensely grateful to her. I made her a promise - if there was anything she needed, I would do my best to help her."

Ramona shook her head. This is where the story fell apart for her. "So she asked you to fake marry her?"

"Sort of. About a year ago, she was advised that she had no chance of winning a popular vote. Her *perfection* made her really unlikable and also invisible. She needed a scandal. Something that would make people pay attention."

Ramona squinted. "Didn't you think it was crazy?"

"Absolutely. I wanted nothing to do with it. I'd worked so hard to keep myself outside of my family's games. This was exactly what I'd upended my life trying to avoid. Then she reminded me of the promise I made. She broke me down, and I ended up agreeing."

"Luc... it all just seems so preposterous."

"I know. But I didn't imagine I'd... well... get into a conflicting situation. I wasn't seeing anyone. I was focusing all my energy on the restaurant and my house. We were hardly ever together. It wasn't going to be such a great imposition. But then..."

Ramona held her breath.

"You. You ruined the plan. Sent me running to Abigail desperate to get out of the contract. Or at least renegotiate."

"She refused."

"Yeah. I think she didn't realize how being connected to my family would also give her a boost. It was working even better than she hoped."

"And now?"

"I'm sure there's a video of her breakdown at the altar all over the internet. Lucas-the-cheater is probably a trending hashtag. I know it's going to be a media circus for a while. That's okay. It's done now."

"Aren't you worried about your reputation? How about the restaurant?"

"For better or worse, Mo, my customers love this type of drama. I would imagine that it's going to be impossible to get a reservation at Winston's for many months. That was never my intention, but I was prepared. That town thrives on scandal."

"Wow. That's quite a story. I can hardly believe it."

He slid over toward her. "I was actually thinking about disappearing for a week or two. Maybe spending some time... away."

There was no need to ask for further details. She knew exactly what he meant. "I..."

"So now that you know. Now that I'm free, can we talk about us?"

Ramona swallowed. The problem was not that she didn't know what to say. It was that there was too much. "I'm not sure what to say. This is all so..."

"I love you. I want to be with you. I'm willing to do anything to make that happen. But I have no idea what you want. That's what I'm here to find out."

She dropped her head, which had become unbearably heavy, into her palms. One breath. Two breaths. Three breaths. Four-

"I don't mean to rush you. If you need time to process what I've told you, time to think about how you feel, I'm happy to give it to you. I can clear out of here, go to my favorite cafe in the North End. I'm not in a hurry. You've always been worth waiting for."

She hadn't realized she'd been crying until the wetness soaked her hands. She looked up to see the softness in his expression, the earnestness in his eyes. "I don't need time. I know what I want."

He looked at her as if he wasn't sure if what she'd just said was good news or not. She could swear he braced himself.

"Do you remember our conversation about home?"

He closed his eyes. Hopefully, he was imagining the same scene she was referring to, when they lay on the tatami mat in his bathhouse. Barely dressed and open-hearted. "Of course. I loved being in there with you."

"You said something that bothered me. That maybe avoiding home wasn't serving me anymore. Maybe I needed something more."

"I guess..."

"In so many ways, I love my life. The freedom, the lack of anyone depending on me. I get to help lots of people, but no one gets to ask anything of me. And still, even though my life is everything I wanted it to be, there's something missing." She studied his face, waiting for a reaction that didn't come. "I don't even know what that is, specifically, but I feel its absence. Does that make sense?"

"I think so, Mo. I think I understand what you mean." He didn't look like he did.

"So, this feeling got mixed in with my heartbreak about you, and some new ideas started filling my head. Things I hadn't let myself feel or think for a really long time. And then I met this amazing woman - actually, it's Jackson's girlfriend-"

"My cousin, Jackson? The legendary playboy?"

Unless she'd seen it with her own eyes, believing Jackson had a legitimate girlfriend would've been impossible for her, too. "Not anymore. He's head over heels. Anyway, Camille, that's her name, was desperate for a way to make right on something terrible that happened to her family. And she's got a lot of money to throw at it. I've been talking to her about my grandfather's house and maybe doing something with it. Together."

His eyes widened. That was the conversation they'd had that ended in a very unpleasant fight.

"She loved the idea. I think it's going to happen."

"You're going to do something with the mansion? Wow. That's amazing, Mo."

"I know I got angry when you first suggested it. I'm sorry about that."

"If I remember correctly, I got that delicious green juice as an apology." He smirked. "But seriously, that's great news."

She smiled, satisfied that she'd been able to say it out loud. "So, that's it."

"Wait... what's it?"

She gave him her best *are you daf*t expression. "The decision I made."

Too much was going on in his face. As if he was trying to solve a really hard puzzle. "What are you saying, Ramona?"

She sighed, exasperated with his lack of comprehension. "I'm saying that it's going to be much easier than you thought."

He slid forward in his seat. "Why?"

"I'm coming home."

CHAPTER ELEVEN

*R*amona had no desire to cry. In fact, she didn't even feel sad. She stared out of the picture windows of her apartment, eight flights up, at the scene below her in the loading area. Lucas and his cousin, Jackson, took turns pointing into the moving truck. She imagined them debating the exact orientation of her meager belongings for the safest trip across the country.

Jackson and Camille had come to help, but it was unnecessary. No one realized how little Ramona owned. Nearly all the boxes were filled with clothes and shoes. A few boxes of books, some files and mementos, and a couple paintings barely filled the small truck. She only had two significant pieces of furniture: a red lacquer cabinet she bought in Bali and a wooden totem that her mother had sent her from the Amazon. The *actual* Amazon. It was supposed to bless her with health and purpose. It seemed to be working.

Camille stepped out from the kitchen and stood next to her, looking out the window. Their friendship had deepened quickly. Ramona let herself receive the small hug from her new friend, who hadn't been able to hide a worried look all day.

Everyone expected Ramona to be emotional. They hadn't gotten it quite right, though.

At least it wasn't an emotion she recognized. A strange emptiness filled her abdomen. The act of leaving someone or something was as familiar as her right hand. But the act of going toward something was akin to a trip to Mars. Not only foreign, but nearly unrecognizable. It had been such an easy decision to make. Leave this place - she could hardly call it home - and move with the man she loved toward the family she wanted to be around. But now that it was happening, some of that clarity, certainty, and anticipation was turning into an upset stomach and a small voice relentlessly saying *NO*.

"Should we go downstairs and see if the guys need any help?" Camille offered.

Maybe getting out of the apartment, into the warm, sunny day, would be smart. At least something other than staring down at the streets and growing increasingly worried about her choice. Being a good daughter and a good girlfriend required skills she hadn't acquired but would be needed immediately. "Yes. Good idea."

The two women walked out of the apartment and into the elevator.

"I know I've mentioned it a million times, but I'm so happy for you, Ramona. It's a miracle how things ended up. I mean, after that night..."

Yes, that night, when she'd drunk herself into a stupor imagining that Lucas was going to marry another woman. "I'm pretty embarrassed about the whole thing, actually. What a drama queen I was!"

"Please don't say that. Heartbreak has no protocol."

Ramona squinted and started laughing. "That's a Jackson-ism, isn't it?"

"Yeah. Sorry." Camille spoke through a chuckle she couldn't cover. "He's getting to me."

Jackson had an endless supply of wisdom nuggets. Everyone around him was well acquainted with *Dr. King, psychologist to the stars.* "That's okay. Trust me, I understand."

Camille's face shifted just enough to remind Ramona that bringing up her experience with Jackson in front of his current girlfriend probably wasn't the most tactful thing to do. "Shit! I'm sorry, that sounded totally wrong."

Camille slapped her arm. "You know, normal was never my thing. Being friends with my boyfriend's ex-girlfriend is going to have an occasional awkward moment. Especially now that she's dating his cousin."

"Wow, when you say it like that, it sounds so twisted. Let's not turn into a daytime drama, okay?"

"Deal."

The two women shook hands before stepping out of the elevator.

Lucas and Jackson, sporting matching broad smiles, turned in unison as the women stepped outside. Camille threaded her arm through Ramona's as they walked toward the truck. It definitely appeared as if Ramona's days of being a loner were in her past and she might have to add *being a good friend* to her long list of things to master.

"How's it going up there?" Jackson asked.

Ramona shrugged. "We're done, I think. Anything else will be yours to deal with."

"I just can't believe the timing of all of this." Lucas clasped his cousin. "The fact that you need a place to stay at the same time that Mo is about to break her lease is pretty miraculous, don't you think?"

Jackson tilted his head up to the blue sky. "It's a sign."

The women flitted eyes at each other.

"Of what?" Ramona asked.

"Dare I say, fate?"

Everyone groaned. Jackson, or rather Dr. King, had definitely mastered the art of bullshit.

"Well, I'm with Jackson. I can't think of anything better than what's happening." Lucas pulled Ramona into him and pressed an extended kiss onto her surprised mouth.

For just a few seconds longer than she would have normally lingered, in public and all, Ramona let herself be kissed. Really, really well. She gazed into his eyes after their lips had separated. Everything she needed to know was right there. Relief from any anxiety she hadn't admitted washed over her.

"You all right, baby?" Lucas whispered.

"I'm great." And she wanted to mean it.

By the time Ramona turned her attention to the other couple, they had begun their own smooching session. It didn't matter that there was a whole web of entanglements between the four of them. Ramona had never had couple friends before, and this was fun.

She was honestly happy for Jackson. To find a woman who could tolerate his eccentric personality was surprising. To find one who was as awesome as Camille was nothing short of miraculous. They made her feel hopeful. As if all those terrible marriages and shattered families she'd witnessed in her life could be erased by a single instance of true love. Their success as a couple could mean-

"What are you thinking about?" Lucas startled her out of the wonderful daydream.

"Oh, nothing. Fairytales."

"Really? I was wondering if it was weird to see Jackson... like this... I mean you two... dated."

"Ugh. I wish everyone would stop referring to ancient history. Jackson has been a friend, and nothing more, for a really long time." She looked up at Lucas. "It's not weird for you, is it?"

"Well..." Lucas gave her a small smile. "I'm not going to let it be. How's that?"

She nodded in acknowledgment. "And lest we forget your recent situation. AKA the Abigail incident."

He grimaced. "Okay. I won't ever bring up your dating Jackson if you promise to not bring up... the incident."

"You got it." Ramona almost found it effortless to pretend that was really going to happen.

"So, what's next?" Jackson asked.

"We're done, guys," Ramona said. "You've been awesome. Thanks so much for your help."

"Then, we're going to head out. Have to clean up before dinner."

"Dinner?" Lucas' brows wrinkled. "I was going to take you out. My favorite teacher runs one of the best restaurants in the world. And it's in this neighborhood."

Jackson squinted. "That sounds great, but we're all expected at my parents' house for family dinner. All of us."

An invitation from Jackson's parents, Lucas' aunt and uncle, was not to be taken lightly. "Aaah, I see," Lucas said.

Goodbyes were brief, now that everyone knew they were on a strict schedule. There was no tolerance for showing up late to the King household.

Stepping back into Ramona's now empty apartment was

surreal. Not because it no longer felt like home, but because of the realization that it had never felt like home. Empty or half full, it was all the same.

"Are you sure you're alright?" Lucas stared at her with his soft hazel eyes. "It's okay to feel nostalgic. Or sad. Or nervous. You don't have to hold it together on my account."

"I know, Luc. It's just... I'm not really sure how I feel. Maybe overwhelmed."

He moved the hair that was always falling into her eyes behind her ear. "I know this is a big deal for you. For us. I don't take it lightly."

"It's not that big a deal." She gave him her best convincing smile. "Really."

He responded with a shake of the head. "It's me, Mo. You know I can read you, right?"

She dropped her head.

"I'm not trying to push you to feel or say anything." He tilted her chin up to face him. "I just want to make sure you know that I'm here, to hold you, to catch you, to listen. You're not doing this on your own."

What an unusual idea. She'd done everything on her own.

"I love you, Ramona."

"Love you, too." If only her voice hadn't shaken quite so much.

By the time they were in the car, on the way to Elena and Jonathan King's house, Ramona had grown to appreciate the surprise plan. It was a good idea to be surrounded by a large, boisterous family instead of her quiet, empty apartment, her flurry of thoughts, and a curious Lucas. And she looked forward to seeing everyone.

Her childhood had been spent intermingled with the

Kings and the Winstons. She and her brother had been included in all the shared activities of the two families. There'd been so much crossover, she had always presumed she was also related. It all fell apart when her mother finally escaped the death grip of her grandfather and took her and Connor to California.

That's probably when Ramona's sense of separateness was born. Her mother's most prized character trait was her independence, followed closely by righteous indignation. Cecilia Barrett had cut all ties to not only family, but also to their friends. She'd wanted nothing to do with any of those people whom she considered all part of the same evil that had destroyed her husband and her marriage.

Ramona didn't enjoy those memories, the heartbreak she'd felt at leaving the life she knew. The most difficult had been leaving Lucas. Without him, she was sure she'd be alone forever - misunderstood and unloved. It took everything she had not to lose her way. At least she had Connor, but only for a few years before he went back to the East Coast for college. And then she was as alone as she'd ever been.

The sun had begun to dip below the horizon, painting the sky in bright pinks and oranges. This was prime time in the Bay Area, when the weather finally warmed and days were perfect. They'd arrive at the King's in a few minutes.

Ramona touched her hand to Lucas' arm. Despite an upbringing that would have crushed a lesser man, he'd turned out to be a wonderful person. Strong, loyal, forgiving. Devoted to a fault. Her heart flooded with love. He was everything she'd ever wanted. Even when she'd had to force herself to forget him.

"Hey, love. What's going on in that brilliant mind of yours?"

"Thinking about the Kings." It would have been too hard

to explain the intense jumble of thoughts she was having about him. "It's been a while since I've seen them."

He took her hand and brought it to his lips. "I really appreciate your being such a good sport about all of this. I would've been happy to tell them we couldn't make it."

"No, I'm happy to go." She was.

They were the last to arrive, which caused Ramona to cringe with embarrassment. Preparing for a scolding from Jonathan King, all she received was a warm hug.

"Ramona Barrett. Well, look at you." He held her arms and beamed. "I remember you running around the yard with all the kids, no higher than my hip."

"Yes, Uncle Jonathan, it's been a long time."

"And I just heard you've been living in the Bay Area all these years. Why haven't we seen you?"

"Well..."

Jackson interjected. "Dad, she may have had a place here, but her travel schedule makes me look like a homebody in comparison."

"Either way, I'm glad to see you. My condolences on the Governor's passing, by the way."

"Thank you, sir."

A long arm wrapped around her from the back, followed by a kiss on the cheek. "So pleased to see you, sweetheart."

"Aunt Elena, you too." She turned to face the smiling woman. "You get more beautiful every time I see you."

Elena King batted her hand. "Oh, no, dear, it's you who's grown into a stunning woman. You look so much like your mother. All that exotic beauty."

No one in Virginia ever brought up her mother. The compliment was both kind and uncomfortable. "Thank you."

Elena waved her arm toward the dining room. "Why don't we take our seats at the table? We can continue catching up there."

Lucas took Ramona's hand as they marched to the extravagant room, greetings snuck in on the way, and took their seats around the meticulously set table. She couldn't stop looking at their hostess.

Even as a young girl, Ramona had been awed by Elena King. She was the counterpoint to her sister, Olivia Winston. It was miraculous how siblings could have ended up so differently. Elena King was warm, gracious, devoted to her family, while Olivia was a selfish, power-hungry snob. She'd lashed out at her husband and son until they'd learned to keep an arm's length from her. She had no use whatsoever with Ramona's family - a foreign, outspoken mother and a drunk father.

Elena seemed to master effortless grace without ever giving a hint of subservience to her powerful husband. She was smart - Ivy League educated - and yet had a bunch of kids and what appeared to be a loving marriage. How had she managed all of that? Ramona was at the top of her game, career-wise, but it was at the expense of all her personal relationships. And kids? There was no way she'd be able to handle that. Especially considering what terrible role models she'd been around. Maybe if she'd had more time around Elena King instead of her evil sister, Olivia Winston. Maybe if she'd known it was even possible.

"I'd like to make a toast." Jonathan King stood at the head of the table, shared with his wife, and held his crystal champagne flute aloft. "We are blessed, as always, to be together as a family, and have the special gift of a surprise visit from my dear nephew Lucas, and our wonderful friend Ramona. Cheers!"

Ramona touched her glass to the ones gathering in front of her, keeping a special clink for Lucas. He really couldn't look any happier. Coming to dinner was a great idea. It didn't matter that she was physically exhausted and emotionally tender. The King family, unlike any other family she'd been around, was a safe place to land.

She had just begun the second course of seafood salad when Jonathan broke the silence. "Lucas, my boy, I've heard you got yourself involved in a bit of a scandal."

Ramona swallowed, thankful her mouthful of food went down instead of out.

"Well, Uncle Jonathan, it's true. But you know how life in DC can be. Scandal is-"

"No need to defend yourself, sweetheart," Elena interrupted. "No one here has been immune from a ruckus or two." She turned directly toward her husband. "Isn't that right, darling?"

Jonathan shared a smirk with his wife. "Right as always, my love."

A chuckle passed around the table. There was clearly a story Ramona didn't know. She couldn't imagine how these folks, the most upstanding people she knew, had any scandals of their own.

Lucas rubbed her shoulder. "I'm not sure Ramona knows the story, Aunt Elena."

"What? I was sure my little sister had been blabbing it to anyone who would listen."

"To tell the truth," Lucas admitted, "she did use to talk about it all the time. But Ramona had already left Virginia by then."

Ramona put her fork down. "Okay, will someone please tell me what we're talking about? The mystery is killing me."

Elena, Jonathan, and Lucas all spoke at the same time.

The two men deferred to Elena, who paused, tapping a finger on her upper lip. "Thinking about it, I suppose the *first* scandal was my going up north to go to school. A *Yankee* school. Everything about that was untoward for my very traditional family. My sister was all about being the best southern belle, but I wanted to learn about the world."

Although Elena was speaking, Ramona's attention was on Jonathan who gazed at his wife with such adoration, it almost felt too intimate to watch. It crossed her mind that for the first time in her life, she'd created the possibility of that type of love for herself. Her hand slid down to Lucas' thigh.

"Then I met this young man, who much preferred machines to manners-"

"-and didn't have two nickels to rub together," Jonathan interjected.

Elena shook her head. "Well, as you can imagine, my family was none too pleased."

"That is an extreme understatement, my love. Your brothers threatened me, your sister ignored me, and your father brought out his guns whenever I came to the house. The only one who stood up for me was Lucas' father, Robert. And even then, he hardly had any clout in the family himself."

Knowing Lucas' family, especially the Pembertons - his mother's side - Ramona didn't find any of this hard to believe. In fact, she could nearly see the scene playing itself out in front of her. But instead of the threats and snarls she knew they were capable of, she focused on Jonathan and Elena smiling at each other. Their simple tenderness had her spellbound. "Wow. I can't believe you survived all that pressure pushing you apart."

Elena turned her enormous blue eyes toward Ramona. "When you find the one, my dear, you'd move mountains."

"Hear, hear!" Jackson, who apparently had also found his *one*, raised his glass for another toast that Ramona was quite happy to share.

She caressed Lucas' hand during the entire car ride home. The tickle of nerves that had left her on edge all day had transformed into sheer excitement. Moving to Virginia and being with him were two of the best decisions she'd ever made. Ones where she'd given her heart equal weight to her head.

She gazed at his profile against the dark sky. There was no doubt he was the one. And she didn't even have to move mountains.

CHAPTER TWELVE

*R*amona woke up well before the 3am alarm, bursting with energy. The moving guys had already begun their trek across the country, and she'd be on her way in just a few hours. They had booked the earliest flight out so that Lucas could get back in time for an event at the restaurant. Some sort of annual event, apparently. She'd made coffee and was nearly done cutting fruit for her travel snacks by the time he was out of the shower.

He appeared in the kitchen, still wet, with nothing but the towel he was rubbing through his hair. Good thing she had already put the knife down or else her digits might have ended up on the cutting board. *Damn, that man was nice to look at.*

"Look who's up." He dropped the towel onto his shoulder. "What happened to my bed-loving babe?"

She wondered if they had time for a quickie. It would be a crime to let all that manly goodness go to waste. "Today's a big day. Besides, I always do this before I travel. Have to get all my food prepped."

"Right. I forgot. No eating airplane food. Can I help?"

"Hmmm..." She licked her lips and stared. "Maybe something..."

His mouth opened just enough to let out a surprised sigh. In two long steps, he was behind her, hands on her hips. "Would you like me to take you... here?"

It didn't matter what time it was. The flight could wait. She moved the cutting board away from the edge of the counter and jutted her hips back. "Yes, please."

Her leggings and thong were down in seconds. His erection pressed into her back. Without heels on, she might not have been tall enough for the proportions to work. He'd have to-

He spun her around, dropped to his knees, and bit the top of her mound. She gasped when his tongue slid between her lips. An even better surprise. With a pull of his mouth and a glide of his thumb, perched at her opening, he'd wiped out any thoughts about meals or planes or anything but his face between her legs. His thumb slid inside her, teeth grazing her clit, and Lucas' mighty orgasm-making mouth succeeded again.

Her fingers burrowed into his hair as pulses rippled up her center and a groan escaped her open mouth. Before her breathing had stilled, he was on his feet, picking her up and placing her a few feet away, on an unoccupied stretch of counter.

His lips pressed against hers, coating them with her own scent. His tongue filled her mouth, his fingers sunk into the soft flesh of her hips, and the head of his cock pushed inside her.

Every time, that sensation made her feel like she couldn't take him in. It would be too much. Then he stopped and looked her in the eye. Breathed with her. Whispered his love for her.

"This is my favorite position, you know."

So. Hard. To. Talk. "Why?" It came out more like a breath than a word.

He smiled. "It was our first."

She moaned into the crook of his neck, his strokes lengthening, his pace increasing, her body dissolving into pure pleasure.

His recognizable slowdown, telling her he was close, pushed her to an edge, even higher, even brighter, then-

"Fuuucccckk," he howled as he pushed them together, bone on bone, flesh in flesh, orgasm bounding between them in synchronized bursts.

She held onto him as if she would never let go.

Ramona wasn't even a tiny bit fazed by the flurry to get to the airport on time. Her normal compulsion with never running to catch a plane, born from a lifetime of travel, never kicked in. Riding on a high of Lucas-loving, she arrived in her seat without a smile ever leaving her face.

"So, you always fly in first class?" Lucas fiddled around with the panel of controls between them.

She gave him a face. "Can you imagine flying a few million miles in coach?"

"I can't imagine flying a few million miles, period. I'm a homebody, remember?"

She stroked his beautiful face. "I love that about you, by the way."

"Even though you won't move in with me."

Not that again. "Lucas, it's okay for us not to take everything at hyperspeed."

"What can I get you to drink before we take off?" The

flight attendant startled her, suspending her plans for the perfect next words.

"Water for me, please," Ramona said to the young man.

"Same for me. Thank you." Lucas dropped his head back and closed his eyes.

Maybe he was tired. It had been an emotional time for him, too, which she sometimes forgot. Having to hold the secret of his engagement for so long, the risk of coming to San Francisco to profess his love, the week they spent together negotiating their future. It could take a toll.

She gazed at his profile, the flutter beneath his eyelids, the bobbing of his Adam's apple, the tiny twitch around his lips. There was no question about her commitment. Not wanting to move in with him had nothing to do with that. She wanted to spend more time with her father, certainly, but mostly she wanted to allow some space for her and Lucas to grow into their new relationship. The pressure of too much too soon could go terribly wrong. And that was a risk she wouldn't take.

With a touch of her palm, she brought his face to her for a soft, lingering kiss.

He blinked as the straight line of his lips curved upward. "I know what you're doing is a big deal for you. I'm not taking that for granted." He let out a sigh. "It's just hard for me to imagine you there, minutes away, and not with me."

They'd had a week of being together night and day, and it had been one of the best weeks of her life. She couldn't have asked for more harmony, greater love, or better sex. But it wasn't real life. Neither of them was working, there were no families around. It was different.

"You're going to get sick of seeing me so much."

All the softness disappeared from his face. "There's no possibility of that happening."

The flight attendant brought their glasses of water, once again interrupting the brilliant response Ramona hadn't yet formulated.

Lucas rested his head back again. "I'm going to close my eyes for a few minutes, okay?"

She hated how weary he sounded. "Yes, of course. Sweet dreams."

A couple who looked like they must have been newly-weds sat across the aisle from her. Would that be the next situation they'd have to negotiate? Lucas was definitely the marrying type. She didn't have anything against getting married, per se, but never considered that she would. It just didn't seem necessary in this day and age. She wasn't looking for some man to take care of her or some kind of sanction by a religious organization.

The newlyweds started laughing. Why was she thinking about marriage, anyway? *One step at a time, Ramona.*

Getting some work done would be a good idea. She pulled out her journal and tablet from her bag. There was so much planning to do, not only for the move but also the project with her grandfather's house. She considered herself excellent at organization and prioritizing, but this project was straining her capabilities. Camille, who was providing the bulk of the capital, had even less experience. Top of the list was hiring a project manager who could be the point person for the construction and all the permits she'd have to file. Hopefully, Connor would help with that, considering he was Mayor.

The thought of her brother brought tightness to the back of her jaw. Why couldn't he just be satisfied with being Mayor? He had a great life, plenty of money, enough fame to satisfy his ego. Why step into the cauldron of evil that was national politics? It didn't make any sense, considering all they'd experienced in that world. Maybe being back in Virginia had warped his brain.

She rubbed the sore spot near her ears. Her moving might have yet another benefit, in addition to being with Lucas and spending time with her Dad. Perhaps she could talk Connor out of this crazy idea of running for Senate and spare them all the inevitable suffering should he achieve the impossible and win.

Ramona shook her head at the idea and returned to the nearly blank page of her journal. The act of writing out each task she could think of for the mansion was as soothing as a neck massage. Next - tackling her emails.

One by one, with gratitude for in-air wifi, she dealt with each of those messages cluttering up her normally pristine email program. Things moved too quickly in her world to ever slack off on communication. She could get inundated very fast. Ramona didn't *do* inundated.

Satisfied with her progress, she went back to the to-do list in her notebook, this time focusing on personal items. A growl-like yawn from the next seat stopped her from adding the final dates to her now extensive list. "Hey, lover. Look who's the sleepy one, now."

"Oh, but I was so busy in my dreams," Lucas said, the sleep not yet out of his voice. "And so were you, by the way."

She chuckled. "Really? What was I so busy doing?"

He shut his eyes and filled the rest of his face with the kind of smile she knew how to decipher. "How about I show you later?"

Ramona planted a kiss on his lips. "I'm looking forward to that." And that was the truth.

He blinked down at her tray, covered in papers and devices. "What are you working on?"

"Mostly planning. I want to get everything set up in Virginia before my trip next week."

He nodded. "How can I help?"

"Uhhh..." That was a good question. One she never considered. "Not sure, honey. Keep me well fed?"

He met her shrug with a furrowed brow. "You know, I'm good for more than just grilled cheese sandwiches. I've been running successful businesses for some time now."

That statement made her swoon, nearly as much as that dimple of his. Successful men were a special kind of pleasure. "I know that. You're a damned impressive man, Lucas Winston. And don't even get me started on that ass of yours."

He failed at holding back a smile, instead snuggling over to her side and peering into the page open in her notebook. "So, what's on the list?"

"Remember, it's just a brain dump. Not in order of priority or anything." She'd never shared her personal to-do list with anyone before. At least someone who wasn't on her payroll. This was weird. She cleared her throat. "Let's see... I've got to get a new driver's license, shop for a car-"

"Why don't you use your father's car? He's not driving much."

"Maybe in the short term." She jotted down a note to ask her father.

"Alright, what's next?"

She reluctantly re-directed her thoughts from how fun a make-out session would be and placed them back on the scribbled words below her. "I'd like to find a personal assistant - someone to help with coordinating the moving people and travel plans... that kind of thing. Oh, and I need a new gyno. I'm pretty sure it's time to replace my birth control implant."

He rubbed his chin. "Hmmm... Want me to ask my mother where she goes?"

She could not have rolled her eyes more dramatically. "You're kidding, right? No, that's fine. Maybe I'll ask Leni. Although, I don't think birth control is her concern any longer."

"Probably right on that. But you'd rather ask your father's girlfriend than my Mom, who's known you forever?"

"Asking your mother about a gynecologist will draw her attention to my lady parts and sex, which will draw her attention to *us* having sex. I'm not going there."

Thankfully, the flight attendant interrupted them with a drink order. What Olivia Winston thought about Ramona's involvement with her precious son was pretty close to the bottom of her 'Things I Give a Shit About' list. Even so, the idea of it made her shudder in disgust.

Between working on her lists and sneaking in ample amounts of kissing, Ramona barely noticed the five-hours of the flight. Her bags were the first off the carousel and Connor greeted them at passenger pickup, holding a sign that read 'Scandal Twins'. The big dork thought he was oh so clever. Too bad Lucas encouraged it with that ridiculous back-slapping guy greeting.

Regardless, everything had gone smoothly and Sunday afternoon traffic toward downtown DC was a breeze. Ramona took this all as incontrovertible evidence of the perfection of her decision.

"How was your week in San Fran?" Connor asked.

Lucas squeezed her hand. "Amazing."

"Well, you sure left a big mess here. The phones in my office still haven't stopped ringing, and my email has blown up. All these alleged reporters want a statement about the woman who broke up the wedding of the decade. It's hard to legislate when all anyone cares about is the transgression between my sister and my best friend."

Ramona wasn't going to take any of this. "Oh, is that what you're calling your job now? *Legislating?*"

"Come on, Mo. You know I'm trying to keep things clean for the Senate run."

Lucas reached toward the driver's seat and clasped Connor's shoulder. "Sorry, man. I wasn't trying to sully your reputation. I'm sure it'll blow over soon enough. It's not nearly scandalous enough to linger."

Ramona wasn't feeling nearly as gracious. She would have preferred giving him a smack in the back of the head.

As they waited at the stoplight a few minutes away from home, Connor twisted around to face them in the back seat. "So, where am I headed? Dad's? Lucas'?"

She looked at Lucas. Logistics was her superpower. "Since Luc has to get to the restaurant, why don't we drop him off first, then we can head to Dad's?"

Lucas grabbed her arm, harder than expected. The look on his face didn't bode well.

"Is that alright, honey?"

He shook his head. "I suppose. I'm just having a hard time thinking about going our separate ways."

That man had the ability to dissolve all her logic and level-headedness into pools of fangirl swooning. She threw her arms around him and planted a well-deserved kiss on his mouth. He didn't resist.

"Hey, get a room!" came from the driver's seat.

"Planning on it." Lucas could not grin any wider.

She looked into his eyes. "It'll only be for the night. You're going to be super busy anyway, probably getting home at some crazy hour."

"Are you sure you don't want to come?" Hope glimmered in his eyes.

"Not tonight, love. You can focus on work, and I'll spend some time with Dad. All right?"

Lucas pressed his lips together and gave her a reluctant shrug.

Ramona walked Lucas into his house, an unexpected feeling of desperation keeping her lingering at the door. He was right. The idea of being apart for the first time in a week felt very strange. Shit.

He emerged from the kitchen dangling a tiny retractable tape measure from his hand. Confusion was short-lived as the key attached to it landed in her palm.

"Use this, please."

She nodded as if she'd never been given the key to a man's house before. Because she hadn't.

She got back into the car, face tight with the effort of staying cool and collected. All she wanted to do was get back to her father's, give him a great big hug, and begin the process of settling in. Maybe even sit in the tub for a few hours. The image of a bath brought up Lucas' amazing bathhouse, which didn't help dissolve the lump in her throat. How foolish. She had survived saying goodbye to him weeks ago and was now struggling to keep it together because they'd be apart for a night. Ridiculous.

"You okay there, sis?"

Her brother was weaving his way through some unrecognized neighborhood.

"Yeah, I'm fine. Totally fine."

"Hmmm. Are you sure everything's all right?"

Something in the tone of his voice rubbed her the wrong

way. "Yes, I said everything's fine. Why are you asking me this?"

He stopped at an empty intersection. "I can tell it's a big deal for you."

Those same words. Enough, already. "I wish everyone would stop saying that. It was my idea to move back. It's not like I'm here unwillingly."

"Mo, you're the most commitment phobic person I've ever known. And you swore to everyone that you'd rather die than come back to Virginia. Maybe you should expect that there's some skepticism."

This was the kind of bullshit that made her want to strangle her big brother. Too bad he wasn't a weakling anymore. "Please don't start with me, Con. I just fucking got here."

"I'm not starting with you, Ramona. I'm just saying that I understand. It was different when you thought you couldn't have him. More exciting, probably. Now that you two are settling down, it's natural to have second thoughts."

She closed her eyes and wondered how her brother had become such an asshole. "I'm not sure, but it sounds like you're trying to give me relationship advice. Which is funny, because I don't see a ring on your finger, either."

"Not for lack of trying." A heavy coat of resignation made his words feel like they weighed a hundred pounds.

A series of honks blared from the car behind them. They'd been sitting at the intersection, blocking traffic and fighting.

There was no way she could begin to respond to anything he said - his accusation or his admission. What a sad pair they were. Connor continued driving but stayed silent for the rest of the ride to their father's house. She almost jumped out of the car before it had come to a complete stop in the driveway.

A few quick moves and she'd retrieved her bags. "Thanks for the ride. Later."

His face gave away no emotion. "Later."

Thankfully, her father's warm greeting mostly counteracted the terrible half hour before she'd arrived at his house. He then informed her that he wouldn't be home that night, as he and Leni were headed to the special event at Winston's. A moment of sadness made way to the realization that she'd actually have the house all to herself. She hadn't had alone-time in much too long. This was going to be great.

Ramona got to spend a few hours with him - she made him tea and a snack - before Leni arrived to pick him up.

"You two look amazing." Ramona hardly recognized her frail father. A nice suit and a beautiful woman on his arm made him look strong and healthy, happiness radiating off him. He even had a smudge of red around his lips where Leni had planted an impressive kiss. Although watching her father make out with his girlfriend was as odd as it was foreign, Ramona understood very clearly that this was the kind of moment she had come back for. She ushered them out the door like a mother sending her son off to prom.

She couldn't change into pajamas fast enough, excited about her newfound quiet time. Having Lucas around 24/7 for the previous week had been like heaven, but a bit of solitary recovery was just what she needed. She prepared her favorite TV snack of carrot sticks and sesame dressing, headed to the couch and settled in. It was early, and even earlier on the West Coast, where her body clock was still set.

After too many episodes of her favorite medical drama, she was no closer to being ready for bed. It was eerily quiet, and the house was unfamiliar enough that she felt more like

an intruder than a resident. Much sooner than she anticipated, she found herself uncomfortable with the emptiness. It
pushed her to her feet, pacing through the empty rooms and
corridors.

She ran her hands along the stained cherry molding in the
main hallway. Her father had done a good job maintaining the
old house. She had often wondered how he'd managed to keep
it during all those years of being drunk and out of commission.
Maybe her grandfather had paid for it, the idea of which gave
her the first warm feeling about the Governor in years.

The day of the funeral replayed itself in her head - from
the high of her night with Lucas to the crash of Abigail's
outstretched hand. What an emotional roller coaster it had
been. And less than a month ago. It crossed her mind that
maybe she was moving too fast, not giving herself enough time
to think things through. To be reasonable. To plan appropriately.

There was no solace in reason when it left you alone on
the couch.

Almost without realizing it, she'd slipped on her sneakers
and picked up her purse. She pulled her father's car keys from
the small hook near the kitchen light switch and walked
toward the front door, the tiny tape measure safely in her
pocket.

CHAPTER THIRTEEN

It was strange to be milling around Lucas' house without him there. But there was something comforting about it, too. Ramona had never thought of homey-ness as a quality before, but this house had it. With only the kitchen light on, she walked barefoot around the shadowy house, ducking in and out of rooms, running her hands along anything that looked like it felt nice. It was as if Lucas had actually infused himself - his beauty, his kindness, his creativity - into the walls and floors. She got a sense that every detail had been scrutinized for both precision and pleasure. It was clean and orderly and smelled like fresh wood and cake.

The only thing out of order was his tousled bed, set in the center of a simple room the colors of a tropical beach. She'd been in an orgasm-induced daze her last time in that room and hadn't noticed the blues and tans on the walls and accented throughout. He had great taste.

She picked up a small wooden box and brushed her fingertips across the inlaid pattern. It looked like the type of thing one would keep a small memento, but there were no seams or hinges. Shaking it created a dull rattle. Curious.

She smiled at the disarray. Maybe he'd left the house in such a rush the week before, he hadn't had time to tidy up. Maybe it represented his quest to profess his love, to claim her and rescue her from her mundane existence. That messy bed made her heart beat faster and not only because of everything that had happened on it. Ramona hadn't been the recipient of many grand gestures from men, but she knew that what had happened on that Sunday morning, just over one week ago, was extraordinary.

The sheets were cool under her palm. Soft, inviting, begging for her to enter. She slipped out of her pajamas and into his side of the bed, hoping his pillow would smell of him. Everything that had kept her body from fully relaxing, from surrendering to sleep, from allowing a sense of home, evaporated as she snuggled herself into the space that was his.

Her dreams were particularly vivid. She could hear his whispers, feel his kisses, taste his-

She woke up with a start to find Lucas' face, barely visible in the dark room, inches from hers. "You're home," she mumbled.

"And so are you."

She settled into his arms, cocooned in skin and breath and love. Just before she let herself go, a burst of thought pulled her from the delicious daze of sleep. Connor had gotten it all wrong. The potential issue with her brilliant plan was not her inability to sustain a relationship. It was the loss of her comfort with being alone, the quality she'd spent a lifetime mastering.

As if it had been years since she'd last been with him, she reached her hands and mouth for anything within her grasp. His response was immediate and matched in intensity. She pressed herself on top of him, he entered her in one swift stroke, their limbs in a tangle and their voices free. Ramona lost the ability to tell where she ended and he began. It didn't matter, anyway. All she cared about was having him, taking him, being joined in every possible way. Someone moaned, someone cried out "Fuck!", someone began shaking.

She collapsed on him, breath heaving, brow damp from sweat. His heart pounded through his chest into her own. The slowing beat, the regular rhythm of his breath, was the lullaby she needed.

A full bladder forced her out of bed, the light filling the room the only indicator that time had passed. As she sat on the cold porcelain toilet, he turned and pushed the sheets off his body, erection pronouncing its presence. When would she tire of that sight? Sometime around never.

"Come back to bed, baby. I've got something for you."

Hands washed, she bounded back into the bed to receive her very welcome gift.

They both lay sprawled on the bed, too hot for anything but their fingers to touch.

She turned her head to take in the sight of him, happily spent. "I'm not sure you're going to need any Crossfit today, hot stuff."

Lucas ran his hand across his glistening forehead. "If that's how things are going to be from now on, I'm going to cancel my membership right now."

With great effort, she pressed herself up to sitting, then blew a breath through pursed lips. She was definitely going to be walking funny today. "I'll go get us some water."

By the time she'd returned, he was sitting up in bed, pillows supporting his back and across his thighs. He took the large glass of water she offered and guzzled it.

"Thirsty boy."

"Yes, someone insisted on fucking me to within an inch of my life."

Eyebrows raised and hands on hips, she countered, "Oh, is that what happened?"

"That's my story, and I'm sticking to it. Now, come back to bed. I need to have you within touching distance at all times."

With an easy tug of his arm, she was back on the bed, head in his lap. She adjusted to make sure she wasn't crushing anything... important. "Better?"

"Much." He ran his fingers through her hair.

She looked down at her naked body and up at his bare chest. Any self-consciousness about being naked together had been wiped away during their week in San Francisco. Not that she was necessarily bashful, anyway, but they'd spent much more time unclothed than clothed.

"I've got a question, Mo." He interrupted her recollection of a game of tag that ended on her living room floor. "I'm dying to know... how is it that you came to be here last night?"

Oh, that. She'd almost forgotten about her insistence on staying with her dad. How much vulnerability was the right amount for their new and old and tentative and intense relationship? How much of the truth of her feelings would cause him to flee? She chewed on the corner of her bottom lip and assessed.

"Hmmmm." He caressed her cheek. "Is it a secret?"

Courage, Ramona. Courage. "No, it's not a secret. I just... I missed you. I thought I really needed a night to myself, some solo time, but all I felt was your absence. Like it took up the whole room. I got so uncomfortable over at my dad's, but as soon as I got here, I felt better. Weird because I was just as alone. But I felt you here, and that was enough."

His face lit up as if she had offered him a lifetime supply of blow jobs.

"What are you smiling at?"

"I expected that I would be the one, falling all over myself, jonesing for you like an addict. Which I am. But I didn't expect that you would feel some of that too. It makes me happy."

She placed her hand on his heart. "Lucas..."

"And my offer stands. I'd love to have you here, as much as you want. Or all the time. Whichever works. "

She sat up to kiss him, her lips lingering with a sweetness and softness she hoped made him feel like the most loved man in the world.

He held her gaze. "You're not going to respond to my offer, are you?"

"Nope. I think we both know what's going to happen."

"Hmmm..." He didn't look convinced. "Tell me more about last night, then."

Ramona dropped back onto his pillow-covered lap and drew his hand to her mouth. She loved everything about his hands - how they looked and felt and smelled. "That's about it. I walked around the house and then went to bed."

"No, I mean tell me about what you were feeling. About me."

She lifted her gaze from his broad palm to his open face. Unsure what he was asking, she paused.

"Is it hard to answer?"

"I'm not sure I understand, and it sounds important, so I want to get it right."

He closed his eyes for a breath before speaking. "There's something that I see in you - like now, and like last night, and when we were in San Francisco - and I'm curious about what gets you there."

Her eyes and brows and cheeks all pressed in toward each other.

He tried again. "There are moments when I can really feel you wanting me. Not just sexually, I mean loving me, without any guards or defenses. I want to know what's going on in your head when that's happening."

Ramona knew exactly what he was talking about. Those moments when she forgot who she was supposed to be. When she stopped analyzing her life and just lived it. It was the great emptiness that all her yoga and meditation lessons had pointed her toward, but she'd never realized it would feel just like love.

"I don't like to need anyone. It makes me feel very uncomfortable. But with you, it's sometimes the opposite. Wanting you, and wanting to be with you, makes me *more* comfortable, not less. I'm not sure I can explain it any better than that."

His expression was so hard to decipher. It wasn't at all clear that she was making any sense.

She had one more idea. "Loving you makes me happy."

That combination of words had never formed itself in her head nor come out of her mouth. Apparently, the time had come.

"Now, I want to hear all about your night." She needed to move on to something else. "How was the wine dinner?"

His hand settled on the soft spot just above her navel, his pointer finger drawing a circle around her undersized innie. "We were at a hundred and ten percent capacity. Remember what I said about scandal? Well, we are now booked out for six months. Shelley - she's the house manager - told me that there was some black market trading on seats for the dinner last night. Nuts, right?"

She tried to keep her attention on his words instead of

that pesky finger trying to undo her composure. "That's crazy. How did you manage?"

"Thank God for Luis. He saved the night."

"Luis?"

"Oh, sorry, I forget that I haven't been blabbing about the restaurant endlessly. Everyone else is tired of hearing me talk about it. Luis is my sous-chef. The best sous-chef on the planet. I had to basically drop the restaurant in his hands when I took off. He's brilliant. I'm resigned to the fact that he's going to have a restaurant of his own sooner rather than later. So I'm thankful for every day he sticks with me."

"It's great to have people you trust. I'm sure you're surrounded by loyal, devoted employees. I could see you being a great boss."

"Aren't we full of compliments."

"Well deserved." She ran her hand over the mound of his chest muscle. "Anyway, go on. Tell me about dinner. Any big names show up?"

His shoulder quirked up. "I have my fair share of fans from the Hill."

The Hill. Ramona would have to reorient herself to DC lingo. The Hill - all the politicians, judges, and staff working in Congress and the Supreme Court. The Mall - That would be the stretch of green flanked by the monuments, the White House and the Capitol. "Did you notice anyone talking about your recent... situation?"

He chuckled and patted her belly. "A trail of whispers followed me throughout the kitchen and dining room."

She tried to imagine him strolling through a restaurant bursting with gawkers, dealing with everyone's interest, curiosity, possibly even scorn. "But how did it feel... being the center of attention?"

A laugh burst out of him. "Darling, I'm a chef. Enormous ego is a prerequisite. I have no problem being center stage."

It's not something she would have ever thought of, but it was true. He'd always been so sure of himself. Her confidence was forged out of necessity, but his seemed to have come naturally. She gave him a wink. "That explains a lot, Baloo."

He returned with a shrug. "Everything went as well as could be expected. It was a bit of a shitshow at first, but we found our groove. And it was amazing to see your dad and Leni there. I think they had a great time. Your dad was schmoozing up a storm."

She could hardly picture that. Her father was about as comfortable in that milieu as a canary at a cat show.

A smile, full of child-like exuberance, filled his expression. "When I came out of the kitchen after final service, I got a standing ovation."

My guy. Of course, she could take no credit for his professional successes, but the thought of him kicking ass made her proud to know him. To be with him.

"What's that smile, Mowgli?"

"I'm just so impressed with you, Mr. Chef Lucas."

He tilted his head down to kiss the tip of her nose. "Double back atcha, love."

His circles around her navel had broadened and now skimmed the underside of her breasts and top of her mound. The room was getting warmer by the second.

"What's the plan for today?"

Focusing on anything other than the tickle of his fingertips was Herculean. "What? Today? Oh, I've got to make significant inroads on those lists of mine. I'm going to be running around all day."

His hands flew up to his face, and Ramona's belly contracted with the sharp absence of his touch. "I almost forgot! I have a ton of information for you. I think I've already forwarded a couple emails, and I have notes in my jacket."

She scrunched her eyes in confusion.

"So, Luis' wife was a top aide on the Hill before the kids. She's amazing and would make a great assistant. Would love to work part-time. I have her info." He tilted his head up. "Shelley gave me a couple options for doctors, and it turns out her wife is a yoga teacher. I didn't even know that. Anyway, she sent me a list of all the local studios with some notes on what's good and bad."

Ramona blinked over and over, trying to get her brain to engage enough to process the stream of information. "Can we back up, please? When did you have time to get all this information? Weren't you crazy busy?"

He cocked his head. "Of course I was busy. But priorities, love."

"I can't believe..." She realized something. "How did you know I was looking for a yoga studio?"

"Connor had asked me when you were here, the first time."

Her sneaky brother. Maybe he wasn't a jerk, after all. She sat up and wrapped her arms around Lucas. "You're the best."

He kissed the crook of her neck. "I'm trying."

All the leads Lucas had acquired took enormous pressure off her day. There'd be no reason to feel guilty about the extra hour she'd spent in bed after their conversation. In any case, he had earned all her gratitude, which she chose to offer with her mouth.

By noon, they had gone off to their respective obligations, with a promise to meet later for movie night at her dad's. It occurred to Ramona, while waiting in line at a promising-looking coffee shop, minutes away from Luc's house, that her life might have just taken a big step forward. Her work was going well, the project to convert the Governor's mansion to a children's center was exciting, and she was surrounded by people who loved her. Every day, she could come home to someone thrilled to see her, whether it was her father or her lover. She had to dig way back to childhood to remember the last time when those conditions existed. Truthfully, it might never have been this good.

"Triple Americano, please."

The young barista gave her a perfect, gleaming grin. "Coming up."

Virginia was a different universe, though. Her favorite barista at home had been a pierced, tattooed, dred-locked wisp of a young woman. The one here sported a collared shirt, a military haircut, and the build of a Navy Seal.

She took a look around Brewed Awakening while waiting for her coffee. Modern art on the walls, with hand-written inspirational sayings interspersed throughout the place. A few tables filled with students, what looked like a mom's club, and just a couple guys in suits. If the coffee was any good, this place would be a top choice.

She carried her coffee out into the overcast day and stood outside the door, considering what direction to head. There was enough time before her next meeting that a stroll around the small town was possible. A window display down the block, that might have contained shoes, made the decision easy.

The coffee was good. Not overly roasted like the national chains. And there were so many cute shops, at least four that she would come back to when she had more time. She'd even found a photograph of sea glass that would be perfect in Lucas' bedroom. Framed just right, it would be beautiful.

Ramona was accustomed to being in new places, surrounded by strangers. She prided herself on the ability to slide gracefully around unfamiliar customs and cultures. It confirmed her other-ness, which was strangely comforting. When the faces around her had almost nothing in common with her own, the story she told herself about being different, about not belonging, made sense.

Walking along those few blocks, it wasn't a separateness that she noticed, but a discovery that she was very much not alone.

Her phone buzzed. Unrecognized numbers were never a surprise, but their frequency had increased with all of her recent changes. She paused next to a store with a beautiful miniature house in the window. "Hello."

"Hi, Ramona. It's Abigail."

CHAPTER FOURTEEN

Ramona dropped her phone on the sidewalk, the bright, loud crack causing a gasp somewhere around her. A young boy released his mother's hand and lifted the device to Ramona.

"Thank you," she said while staring through the shattered screen to the phone icon and timer. Unbelievably, the call was still connected.

"Hello? Are you there? Is anyone there?" Abigail's voice, clear as day, came through the speaker.

"Hi. Yes, I'm here. Sorry, I dropped the phone."

During the silence on the other end of her cell, Ramona watched a little girl pull her mother into the store with the miniature house. A bell above the door announced their entry.

"Why are you calling me, Abigail?"

"What? No greeting? No niceties?" Sarcasm seeped through the phone.

Ramona squeezed her eyes shut, trying to make sense of what was happening. "What do you want, Abigail?"

"Right to it, then. I heard you moved back to Virginia."

"Yes." She could have asked how Abigail knew, considering it had been all of two days.

"I wouldn't have expected that."

The phone crackled and went silent. Ramona checked the screen. Still connected. "And?"

"You might want to reconsider." Abigail dragged out every word as if she had a mouth full of cotton balls.

It wouldn't be possible to breathe deeply enough to suppress her growing rage. "I don't know how you got my number, but I'd recommend you lose it."

Ramona tapped the red circle with her shaking finger. "Goodbye, Abigail."

It wasn't until after her next two appointments that she had enough time to deal with her increasingly unusable phone. Thankfully, she'd been able to mostly put the odd conversation out of her mind.

Ramona fiddled with her fingertip, pretty sure there was a sliver of glass in there from trying to swipe across the shattered screen. A young man greeted her at the entrance to the bright white electronics store. Without answering, she showed him her phone and was led inside. Twenty minutes later, she left with a brand new phone and no less confusion about the reappearance of Abigail Langley in her life. A text message hovered on her home screen: *It's best not to ignore me.*

Ramona sat in the car outside her father's house, staring down at the notification. This bitch was threatening her. Unbelievable. As if it wasn't bad enough that she forced Lucas to pull this scam. What could she possibly want that she hadn't already gotten?

Maybe Abigail was jealous, which would be unexpected

but not inconceivable. Maybe she had real feelings for Lucas, and it hadn't all been political theater.

There were too many unknowns and Abigail might be even crazier than Ramona assumed. She didn't know the woman well enough to understand her motives or her limits. Ramona didn't do well with bullies and crazies, and Abigail was turning out to be both.

Ramona wished she knew the extent of the threat. She should have asked Lucas to see the NDA, to understand the penalties. Funny how she hadn't thought of that until that moment. What was Abigail's leverage?

Money didn't make sense. Lucas seemed to be doing well enough. Did she have some dirt on him? Was it blackmail?

Ramona closed her eyes and tried to remember that Sunday morning. Both Lucas and Connor had said *ironclad NDA* or something. What would be so bad that Lucas would let her suffer in ignorance instead of risking that it get out? It had to be really, really bad. And why didn't he trust that she would keep his secret?

Ramona palmed her forehead. Tequila and relief had short-circuited all her logical processes that day. She hadn't paid attention to the right things or asked the right questions. When he had appeared at her door, all reason had walked out of it. Fuck.

In this flurry of unknowns, there was at least one thing that was perfectly clear: she didn't have the whole story, and Lucas was still lying.

She picked up the phone and opened her recent calls. The number she was looking for was still on the top of the screen, a single click placing her exactly where she never wanted to be.

· · ·

The minute Lucas stepped through the door of her father's house, Ramona pulled him into the kitchen. She broke away from the kiss he offered.

He tilted his head. "What's up, baby?"

"Abigail called me."

Eyebrows up, mouth open, body stiffening. "What? What did she say?"

"She thought I should know what was going on with you."

Lucas pushed his palm across his curls, his expression contorting into panic. "What does that mean?"

First things first. "Tell me about the non-disclosure agreement. What were the terms?"

He stepped forward and shook his head. "Don't jump to conclusions, Mo. It can all be explained."

She huffed a laugh. "I think I've heard that before."

"Please-"

The front door opened and closed, followed by Connor's voice. He would be coming into the kitchen any minute, and she definitely didn't want to be talking about this in front of him. He was already claiming that the wedding scandal was reflecting badly on him. Leading people to question the pristine reputation he'd taken a lifetime to create.

"I guess we'll have to finish this later." She walked out of the kitchen.

Throughout the evening, Ramona watched and waited. This was feeling just like the week she'd spent wondering about Lucas' engagement. So much discomfort. Her father looked even more tired than usual and the movie sucked. The dark mess of a film left everyone in an awkward silence.

Lucas reached into the nearly empty popcorn bowl. "Mr.

Barrett, Ambassador Qadir wanted me to let you know how much he enjoyed your company."

Her father slapped his thigh. "What a nice young man. Please tell him we look forward to seeing them again."

"Absolutely."

Her father's secret life kept surprising her. "What's this about, Dad?"

"Oh, at the wine dinner, Lucas introduced us to the ambassador from the UAE. He was holding a private party in the back and invited us to join. It was one of the most extravagant things I've ever seen. So much fun!"

Leni shared a smile with her guy. "Yes, it was a great night."

"Is he still trying to steal you away?" her father asked.

This deepened the frown on Ramona's face. "What?"

Lucas reached over to touch her hand. "The ambassador has been a big supporter since my first restaurant. Keeps trying to convince me to open up a place in the Burj Khalifa."

The name sounded familiar, but not enough. "The what?"

Connor answered. "Tallest building in the world. One of the most exclusive addresses for any business. I keep telling Lucas to go for it. Would vault his career through the roof."

"It's in Dubai," Lucas said. "Not really commuting distance from DC."

"You could make it work. Lots of chefs have places around the world."

Ramona's surly smile pushed against the tightness in her face. "Wow. Everyone knows about this, I see."

Lucas turned toward her. "It's not a big deal, Mo. One of the many crazy offers I get on a regular basis."

One of the many crazy secrets he keeps on a regular basis.

Lucas slapped Connor on the back. "Hey, how's it going with Margo?"

Connor put down his drink and scowled. She'd seen that face many times before. "I had to end it. It just wasn't going to work out."

Ramona rolled her eyes. Another one. "I thought this one was promising. You've been raving about how your overpriced matchmaking service had really nailed it this time."

"Well, she was great on paper. But getting to know her made it clear. And I'm not into blondes."

"Made what clear?" Leni asked.

In unison, Ramona, Lucas, and Connor answered. "She's not White House material."

Their dad's head dropped, Leni gasped. "Connor Barrett! Are you evaluating this woman based on being a suitable First Lady?"

He sighed and put on his 'let me explain it to you' face. Ramona thought she might barf. "Leni," he began, "that's the reality of political life. I know what my target is. I want someone who can go there with me."

Leni's eyes batted from side to side. Must be trying to make sense of the ridiculous statement. "So, you're not interested in love? Just a partnership to further your career?"

Ramona had never liked her father's girlfriend more than in that moment. "Connor doesn't believe in love. Thinks it makes you weak."

All eyes turned to Connor. "Untrue, Ramona. And pretty hypocritical, too. I have practical considerations that you don't understand."

She slid forward in her seat. Game on. "You know who'd make a great First Lady? Abigail Langley. I hear she's available now."

Connor and Lucas both sprung to their feet, but what most got Ramona's attention was the clear, loud laugh coming from her father. The sight nearly made her forget her feelings about the other two men around her. "Don't you agree, Dad?"

"Yes!" His laugh filled the whole room. "Oh my gosh, pumpkin, that was one of the funniest things I've heard in a long time." He brushed a palm across his face and let out a bellow of an exhale. "Thank you for that."

Lucas took two steps away from his chair and stuck his hands in his pockets. Connor also remained standing and cleared his throat. "In any case, I have some news about that." He glared at his sister. "And no, Abigail Langley is not a possibility."

"I don't know, Con. I mean she's beautiful, classy, has that Ivy League pedigree, understands politics, has-"

"Shut the fuck up, Ramona," Connor seethed.

Ramona's scathing response to her brother was halted by one look at Lucas' face. Anger slashed across his features and caused a tremor near his cheek.

"That's enough, you two." Her father had sat forward in his chair, all the humor erased from his expression.

Connor worked his jaw from side to side.

She spoke directly to Lucas. "Oh, is it too soon for jokes?"

Leni stroked Dad's arm. "Tell us your news, Connor."

"I'm announcing my candidacy next week. I've got a tentative agreement from Stanley Grayson to manage the campaign."

Lucas gave his friend a hug. "Congrats, man. I'm so proud of you. Next stop - Senate!"

Ramona watched them with equal parts curiosity and disgust. How could her brother want this, and how could Lucas be happy about it? Incomprehensible. Their generation was supposed to be keeping their hands clean, and her brother was dipping further and further into all of that mess. It felt as if all the garbage from her childhood had been retrieved from the dump and deposited in her lap.

Her father nodded, his lips pressed into a thin line. "You got Stanley Grayson. That's something. He doesn't work with anyone who's not a sure bet."

"Yeah, I was surprised too, Dad. I think Luc's father convinced him."

"Congratulations, Connor," Leni added.

There was not enough paper on the planet for Ramona to start listing everything that was wrong with what had just happened. Her brother had already started contorting himself for this world that had nearly destroyed them all. She shook her head at him but decided to shut the fuck up, as instructed.

When they arrived at Lucas' house, she purposely stopped in the living room and did not follow him toward the bedroom. That wasn't going to solve their problems tonight. She sat on the end of the couch and waited.

He emerged from the hallway and took a seat beside her, the silence between them palpable. "What did she say?"

No. He didn't get his answer before she got hers. "Tell me about the NDA. That's where we're going to start." She folded her hands in her lap to hide the shaking.

"Alright. It was fairly standard, with a few unique constraints."

Interesting. "What was the penalty?"

He looked down. "Half a million plus the Bistro. Pretty exorbitant, I know, but at the time it meant nothing. I agreed to her charade and had no intention of breaking it. I gave her my word."

Ramona shook her head in disbelief. "You agreed to give up your first restaurant?"

"It was ridiculous, Mo. She knows nothing about restaurants. It wasn't like she was really going to take it from me. And even if she's claiming there was a breach, I still don't believe she'd sue." He lifted his gaze from her hands to her eyes.

"If you didn't believe she'd come after you, why did you keep the secret? Why didn't you tell me the truth, from the beginning?"

His swallow was audible. Ramona braced herself.

"There were a couple of things that weren't in the agreement. Things I couldn't..."

"If you didn't care about the money or the restaurant, then what was at stake? I really want to understand what would be so damaging that it was worth what I went through? Did she threaten you? Your family? Who was it?"

"Connor."

She gripped the edge of the couch cushion. "What the fuck does my brother have to do with any of this?"

"That's the question I've been avoiding this whole time."

Of all the questions... "That one? Why?"

"Because I don't know." He brought his hands to his head, pulling on clumps of hair. "She's got something on your brother. I don't know what it is, but she swears it will destroy him."

Disgust curled her lip. "That's it? That's the super intense secret that has caused this mess? And you don't even know what it is?"

The look of control returned to his face. "I didn't want to know. But I know Abby. I could tell she was serious and that was enough for me."

This was getting less intelligible. Not more.

"Here's what I know, Ramona: when I told her about my situation with you, she doubled down. Told me she could make one call that would end your brother's career. He wouldn't even be able to run for school board. That's what she said."

He was protecting Connor. Connecting those dots was like trying to tie a knot with her toes. "I still don't understand why you couldn't tell me."

"Because I knew that the first thing you'd do is try to find out the information about your brother. Then you'd confront Abigail, and maybe even Connor, then the whole thing would blow up."

She evaluated what he'd said as if she was creating a flow-chart. One action leading to another, leading to another. "You think I wouldn't have been able to keep the secret. That's what you're saying?"

He straightened. "What I'm saying is that it might have been even harder for you to deal with if you knew your brother was involved. Between your righteousness and Connor's hot-headedness..."

It dawned on her that Connor was one of the most rule-abiding, straight-laced people she'd ever met. There's no way he would have some skeleton in his closet. No way. All she would have to do is ask him. Then he could clear it up. They'd all have a great big laugh at the misunderstanding.

But there was still the fact that Abigail had made an accu-sation. A threat. He'd definitely go after her for defaming him. Really hard. He didn't like people messing with his reputa-tion. She wouldn't know what was coming. Then...

Lucas had been watching her. Damn. He probably knew she'd get to exactly the same conclusion he already had. It would have blown up if he'd told her the truth. Exactly as Lucas had predicted.

Her lungs emptied. "Was there even an NDA?"

"Yes. It's still in effect, though." His eyes closed for a

second, then opened to take her in. "I was sure you would see right through my explanation. That the questions you asked me today would have come up much sooner. Part of me wanted you to force me to tell you when you were here. Then to call bullshit when I showed up at your house so I could tell you everything. But you didn't, and I rationalized that maybe it was best you didn't know." He took her hand. "It killed me to lie to you. To see you hurting. I just thought…"

She didn't doubt his sincerity, but the story wasn't holding together. The timing didn't line up. She looked around for a pen and paper - plotting it out would help - but there was nothing. Damn Lucas and his tidy house.

She resigned herself to having to make a mental tally.

Point 1: "You told me about your situation on the morning of your wedding."

Point 2: "You had already told Connor before that."

Question: "What made you think that it was no longer a problem for Abigail? Why didn't you worry that Connor would go after her?"

His head bobbed up and down. Thinking, she presumed. "She knew that I was going to tell you and my family on the day of the wedding. In fact, she didn't seem concerned, which was odd." The line between his brows appeared. "I was more worried about Connor's reaction, but he rolled with it. Didn't question any part of my explanation, didn't find any of it unbelievable. Like you, he was more relieved than anything else."

Ramona imagined her brother, still angry with his best friend, finally able to stop biting his tongue. Holding back was not one of Connor's strong suits. She and he had both been so delirious with relief that they'd shut off their brains. Not impressive.

"I know it was wrong that I didn't tell you everything. You

can't imagine how many hours I've spent replaying this story, from start to end, trying to figure out what I could have done differently, how I could have handled it better." He pressed his knuckles to his lips. "How I could have prevented all the pain I caused..."

Just as Ramona's anger and blame began to dissipate, Abigail's voice popped into her head. "I don't think she's done."

"I'm done. She got what she wanted."

"But she didn't."

"Of course she did. The fake wedding went off without a hitch, she's been getting tons of media sympathy, it seems like her campaign has taken off. What else could she want?"

"That's what she called to tell me. She wants you."

Lucas' mouth dropped open before he regained composure. "I don't think that's possible, Mo. She never really wanted me. Just what I could do for her."

"That's what I'm trying to tell you." Ramona's voice was much more wobbly than she liked. "She said that the two of you were going to be together. And I was going to find out soon enough."

He shook his head so hard his curls danced. "It can't be..."

Something in his expression was definitely evaluating the new information. Ramona swallowed a short spike of fear - maybe he wanted her too - and tried to access reason instead. It didn't matter if Abigail wanted him or not. He wasn't interested. She was sure of it. Almost certainly sure of it.

His eyes grew increasingly narrow. "Mo... don't even... you can't start believing her wild claims. I don't know what she's after, but it doesn't matter. You are the one that I want. The one that I love."

She nodded. *Yes, but...*

"Good. Now let me take care of this."

Although the words were supportive enough, something about the way he said them left a wisp of doubt that tainted all that powerful logic of hers.

Thankfully, it didn't last long. Just as abruptly as Abigail appeared, she disappeared. Maybe she just enjoyed messing with people, which Ramona admitted made her divinely suited to politics. Of everyone Ramona knew, Abigail was the most likely to have skeletons. Ramona, conceding her shaky threats couldn't have scared the persistent woman away, considered the possibility that maybe Lucas had done some counter-blackmail.

Either way, the unexplained evaporation of Angry Abigail was highly welcome and allowed Ramona to successfully push all that crazy to the very bottom of her *Things To Worry About* list. There were more important items on there, anyway - her work, her brother, her father, and Lucas.

CHAPTER FIFTEEN

*A*s the weeks passed, Lucas continued working hard to make things up to her, to prove his devotion, to ease her concerns. In fact, she might have even let him grovel. She'd almost forgiven him. Almost.

She believed him when he said there was nothing going on with Abigail.

She believed him when he explained, over and over, why he did what he did.

She believed that he loved her.

She believed he was sorry.

The residual grit in their shiny relationship was a sense of irritation she couldn't shake. Something about the Abigail story felt incomplete, but she didn't know what to ask and Lucas made it clear he didn't want to talk about it. The Connor angle was a sharper barb. Lucas had chosen to let her suffer while he protected her brother. He claimed that although her struggle with his secret had been terrible, destroying Connor's future would be worse.

It didn't land well. Coming in second to her brother was not a position Ramona ever accepted, but she tried to get past it. It was still incomprehensible that her goody-two-shoes brother had done something so bad that it would ruin his career. Despite expectations, she'd succeeded in keeping her mouth shut about it. For the sake of love and family, apparently.

The fact that her brother had been completely wrapped up in his new campaign, and she'd hardly seen him, also helped.

All of that had been rendered meaningless, of course, when her father passed out in the bathroom after family dinner.

Days later, after a flurry of emergency rooms, specialists, and enough medical jargon to scramble her brain, Ramona settled into the faded pink chair that had been designated as hers, set up right next to her sleeping father's bed. Her stomach grumbled with emptiness. It was a good time to step out as Lucas would be returning in a few minutes.

Ramona dragged her achy body to the nearest visitor lounge, a family in various states of waking and sleeping filling up a row of seats. She squinted at the flashing keypad on the vending machine. These hospital fluorescent lights were murder on her eyes. And since when did a tiny bag of pretzels require higher math? After her fourth dollar bill had finally been accepted, she pressed F467 and hoped for the best.

"There you are!"

She looked at her minuscule bag of pretzels, then at the large man walking toward her. He better not want any. "I came to get some food."

Lucas took the bag from her hands. "This isn't food, Ramona. Why don't you go to the cafeteria?"

"I didn't want to go that far. The doctor will be here any

minute." She grabbed her bag back and began the short walk back to her father's room, keeping rhythm with the symphony of growls from her cramping stomach.

"You can't go on like this. I don't think you've eaten in three days."

The idea was shocking enough to prevent her next step, not because of some memory of eating, but because it had been three days. It couldn't be. "Have you seen Connor? He promised he would be here this morning."

Lucas shook his head. Great. Her fucking brother.

"I'm going to get you something nutritious." He stopped her from walking away with a gentle tug on her arm. "Unless you want me to stay and wait for the doctor."

He had dark circles under his eyes. Hadn't left her side. Probably needed a break. "No, you go, honey. I'll be fine."

After a chaste kiss, he disappeared down the hall. She hid the pretzels under her jacket and kept walking toward the nephrology wing.

Ramona hunched down into her chair and evaluated the small brown bag. All that crackling and crunching was sure to wake her father up. The pretzels would have to wait.

She dropped her head onto her hand, as she'd sat, moving only for bathroom breaks, for most of the past few days. Alone, watching her father sleep, she had plenty of time to think. Although thinking would not have been on the top of her list, that's what she was left with.

Her poor, sweet father. They'd come such a long way in those weeks. Almost as if those decades of him being unrecognizably damaged had disappeared. She spent most evenings with him, when Lucas was at the restaurant. He and Leni, and she and Lucas even went on a few double dates. Ramona loved Leni and her dad loved Lucas, and they couldn't have been happier. If only she had more time.

. . .

She'd dozed off when Dr. Fein arrived, flanked by his two assistants. The small man and his burly companions reminded her of a dork mafia.

"Ms. Barrett, you're still here." His nasal voice was not void of care.

"Yes, Dr. Fein. I was waiting for you." She ran a hand over the disaster that must have been her hair. It was no use. "How is he doing?"

The portly man bobbed his balding head. "Much better. His numbers have stabilized. We're going to move him to a general floor today."

She looked at her father, sleeping so soundly he might have even been at peace. Oh, the glory of pharmaceuticals. "But he's barely been awake."

"Yes, we can wean him off the meds now that the blockage is cleared. We just needed him calm to be able to control his blood sugar."

"Now what?" Ramona had no idea how the frail old man in the bed would ever resemble her father again.

"We'll watch him for a few more days. Then he can go home."

"Go home? How can he go home? He nearly..."

Dr. Fein put on his best *I feel your pain* expression. "Ms. Barrett, your father's situation is serious, but manageable. We're doing our best to minimize these crises, but they are inevitable. It's best to understand that so you can be prepared."

He squeezed the smaller IV bag and squinted at the label. "He'll be more awake in the next few hours."

Unintelligible banter passed between the three men.

Without saying goodbye, they marched out in step. So much for the meeting she'd been waiting for.

Hospitals sucked.

Lucas returned with a large plastic bag and a green juice.

"How'd you get that past the nurses' station?" They'd never missed a chance to let her know that no food was allowed.

He shrugged. "Scandal has its privileges."

Jeez.

She took a long pull from the drink and imagined that the sensation of the cool liquid entering her body must mimic what it felt like for a vampire to drink blood. It was liquid life.

He sat in the folding chair on the other side of the bed. "Did the meeting happen?"

"Sort of. Dr. Fein said they're moving him to a regular room, weaning him off the pain meds so he'll wake up, and that this is going to keep happening."

Lucas cinched his eyebrows. "What? He didn't..."

"He did." A tear rolled down her cheek and landed on the lid of her drink.

Lucas walked over to her side and squatted. "Baby, he's a fighter. He'll get back on his feet."

She shook her head, tears and snot flowing across her face. "No, he won't."

Lucas took her face in his hands. "He's been here before, love. I know this was scary for you but he's doing better."

She pulled out of his grasp. "How could you possibly know that?"

Lucas glanced over at her father. "Because we need him to."

Ramona took another sip of her drink, focusing on swallowing between ragged breaths. "I don't know how you're so calm about it. Connor doesn't even think it's important enough to show up at the hospital."

His fingers wove through her hair and squeezed the base of her neck, the move that disabled her defenses and dissolved her tension. "That's because he's used to it, Mo. He's been dealing with this for some time."

With a rush of guilt, she stopped trying to hold back the tears. A million *shoulds* flooded in. She should have come home sooner. And more often. She should have pried deeper when Connor glossed over her father's health issues. She should have pushed for more details. She should have-

He stood and pulled her into his abdomen. "I'm here, Mo. You don't have to hold this up on your own."

She dropped into his body and let her tears soak the middle of his shirt. Her fingers wrapped around the waist of his pants as if she could pull herself so far into him that she could be protected. No matter how close she pulled, it wasn't enough.

She opened her eyes to search for a tissue box and found Leni leaning over her father. "Leni... I didn't know you were here."

"Sorry to startle you." Exhaustion deepened her voice and darkened her eyes. "How is he?"

Ramona repeated what the doctor had said, while Leni stroked his hair. Her position was the one directly across from Ramona's. Together, they had been his constant companions.

"Ramona." Leni's tone shifted, weariness gone. "The doctor is right. These episodes are going to come more and more frequently. His organs are not in good shape. It's important that you don't let yourself be depleted each time. Then you'll be unable to support him."

Ramona heard the words coming out of Leni's mouth, but the big picture remained distant and blurry.

"Do you understand, Ramona? You must take care of yourself. So that you can take care of your father."

There was no question about the look in Leni's deep brown eyes. Message received.

The day they brought her father home there was a huge accident on the highway just before their exit. Connor drove, Lucas joined him up front, and she sat in the back, never taking her eyes off her dad. His discomfort increased as they sat in the unrelenting traffic. He needed to lay down.

Panic made time slow even further. "Why are we sitting here?" Ramona said, a bit too loudly. "Can't we go another way?"

Connor glared at her through the rearview mirror. "We're almost off the highway, Ramona. There's no *other* way."

She'd never been angrier at her brother. He'd been a ghost during this crisis, hardly showing his face at the hospital. And when he deigned to visit, he was on his phone the whole time. Too busy. Critical point in the campaign. Too important. Blah fucking blah.

"There's always another way," she muttered under her breath, then silently held her father's hand for the rest of the trip. Fighting with Connor wasn't worth the upset it would cause her dad.

Ramona filled a pitcher from the fancy new water purifier she had installed and brought it to her father's room with a glass. Leni, who arrived at the house before them, had set up all the pillows to prop him up like he had been at the hospital. He did look better, a smile brightening his pale face.

She handed him a full glass and lightly kissed his forehead. "I love you, Dad."

His trembling fingers wrapped around the glass. "I love you, too, Pumpkin. Thank you for taking such good care of me."

"Of course, Dad. I didn't do anything."

Ramona sat and watched her father as he had the soup Leni made for him. Other than a grimace every now and then, he looked like he was enjoying eating. Now that she was there, she'd make sure he followed doctor's orders for regular, nutritious meals. Had to keep his blood sugar steady. She'd make sure he kept up with his glasses of water, too. Keep those kidneys flushed and he'd be back on his feet in no time.

Connor popped in to say goodbye. He'd been having a heated conversation down the hall for the whole time at the house. She turned her head as he tried to kiss her cheek, with no interest in concealing her scowl.

"Off to do more campaign stuff?" Double helping of sarcasm - done.

The eyes beneath the dark-rimmed glasses narrowed at her. "I have dinner with a large potential donor. It's important, Ramona."

"You bet." She swallowed the rest of her profanity-laden response.

Lucas nearly had to pull her out of the house. She didn't want to leave, but everyone insisted. Even her father told her she needed to go home, get a good night's sleep, and spend some private time with her guy. That's what he said: *private time with her guy.* Not a phrase she ever wanted to hear from her father.

She wasn't sold on the whole thing, anyway. She and Lucas hadn't had *private time* in days, but her father needed her more. And Lucas wasn't acting so interested in her. He hadn't said anything since leaving her father's. Not even glanced at her during the drive to his house.

The line of his mouth and the position of his shoulders indicated something other than fatigue.

"Are you all right?" She regretted the question as soon as it was out.

"It's a rough time, Ramona."

His response could have been called emotionless, but she knew better. The use of her given name was a clear indicator that something wasn't right. "Are you angry about anything?"

"I'm not." His hands tightened around the steering wheel. "But... how you're treating Connor is upsetting."

She pressed back into her seat, mouth agape. "How I'm treating Connor? Did you notice how useless he's been?"

"I know you hate that he wants to be a Senator. Maybe even President. It seethes through every word, every look, every interaction. But I don't see how you have a right to judge him. Just because it's not something you ever wanted doesn't make it wrong that he wants it."

Breathe, Ramona. Breathe. "I'm really surprised to hear you, of all people, saying this."

"Why? Because I didn't choose politics either? Well, it makes no difference. He's my friend. He's my brother, and I'm going to support him. Don't you see how hard this is for him? This is his Everest - conquering every belief and fear he's ever had to go after something that's going to be harder than any of us could imagine. He's trying to climb, and you just keep kicking him in the face."

"I'm not-"

"Can't you see that he's also having a hard time with us? He's been desperate for a relationship for a long time and we just fell into one. Despite ourselves. Add that to the stress about your father and you've got to know it's crushing him. You're showing about as much compassion as an onion."

No matter how many times she blinked, she couldn't erase the look on his face. She certainly couldn't un-hear what he'd just said. "Wow. I see whose side you're on."

They pulled into the garage. "Don't start, Ramona."

Confusion. "Start what?"

"We're not kids anymore." He turned to face her. "You can't make me choose between you and your brother."

The slam of his car door felt like a slap in the face. She sat stunned until the automatic garage lights had gone out and she was in the dark. Resigned that the appropriate response just wasn't coming, she exited the car and entered the house.

It was dark and quiet. Maybe he'd gone straight to bed.

Bedroom - empty. Office - empty. Bathrooms - empty.

It dawned on her as she saw the light outside the kitchen door. She entered the bath house to find him fiddling with the controls under the side panel. He didn't acknowledge her arrival.

"I'm assuming you want to be alone. You don't want me here."

The solid frame of his body drooped. Tired, wide eyes turned to her. "I don't want to be alone. I always want you with me. I wish you'd stop demanding I prove it."

Whoa. It felt like he'd not only undressed her, but taken off all her skin and left her to be assaulted by the cool air. Her breath rattled. "I... I'm..." Shit.

She stepped toward him but stopped, arm's distance away. Having him reject her embrace would be impossible to handle. "I didn't realize that's what I was doing. What I've been doing. I don't..." *Calm breath, Ramona.* "I'm sorry."

"Me too. I shouldn't have lashed out at you. Especially not tonight. We're all raw." He closed the panel. "Will you bathe with me?"

She kept her eyes on him as she undressed, looking for a sign that it was going to be okay. That he would forgive her. Even after entering the warm water, she couldn't shake a cold chill of worry.

He closed his eyes and leaned back. She couldn't remember a time, since their first night, when he hadn't immediately reached for her. His arms hung by his sides, his body still. As if she wasn't even there.

It was so quiet, she could hear crickets. Literally. At least, she guessed they were crickets. The lapping sound of the water, as she stretched her arm toward him, snapped his eyes open. She froze.

He looked down at her hand, then at her face, then at her hand again. "Are you afraid?"

Fuck yes. She nodded, certain her voice wouldn't hold.

"What are you afraid of?"

"This." It was barely a whisper. "Of something coming between us."

"Then why don't you come to me?"

She hadn't even considered the possibility but now that he'd said it, it was the most obvious thing in the world. Instead, she'd been waiting for him, so there would be no chance of rebuff.

She pushed her body through the water toward him. He pulled her the final few inches until their bodies collided.

"I love you, Lucas." Too much, she was now learning.

By the time they headed to bed, some of Ramona's skin had regrown. That raw fright had mostly passed, enough that when he made love to her, there were moments when everything seemed all right. He stroked her face, gazed into her eyes, whispered his words of love.

She watched as his face softened into sleep, his breath growing hushed. Exhausted as she was, there would be no sleep for her anytime soon. Their small fight, inconsequential to some, perhaps, had brought with it a realization she'd never expected.

This was what it felt like to care about someone so much you'd do anything not to lose them. She didn't like it one bit.

CHAPTER SIXTEEN

Two months later

Although Ramona was facing straight ahead, she didn't register anything in front of her. There was nothing to see.

A lovely feminine voice filled her ears, but she didn't make any effort to understand the words that were being said. It made no difference.

Another wave of nausea hit as she tipped her head down to examine the folds on her black skirt.

She closed her eyes and prayed that her mind might wander as far away as possible.

After all, it had been going well. She had embraced her new-again home more than anywhere she'd ever lived. She'd stopped resisting making a home with Lucas and had put her mark on their house, one sparkly pillow at a time.

There were coffee dates with yoga friends, lots of time with her couple besties, Jackson and Camille, parties with Lucas' friends and coworkers, and a general sense of belonging that made her happy to come back after every trip away.

Her relationship with Lucas, after some growing pains, had become a remarkable love story. In such a short time she'd gone from relationship-phobic to a woman who used the word *forever* liberally.

The children's center, which everyone had started calling Barrett's Bambinos, was moving along. Thankfully, she'd been able to find the right people to fill in all the holes in her knowledge and experience.

There were huge swaths of contentment and excitement that she wouldn't have believed existed.

This particular day and the week that preceded it were devoid of any of those good feelings. It might have been mistaken for a similar day, several months prior, when the summer had still been blazing. Now, a few days before Christmas, with the threat of snow looming, nothing was the same at all.

Instead of a cathedral bursting with hundreds of people, there were only a dozen or so in that small, simple room. Instead of an ostentatious casket, a small silver urn sat on a narrow, unfinished table. The unusual wood had caught her eye, blond with huge brown spirals, but she refused to look toward it any more. Best to keep her focus down.

An arm squeezed her shoulders, fingers wrapped around her hand. She was pretty sure one of those belonged to Connor and the other to Lucas, but she didn't particularly care which was which.

What mattered was that instead of her father right next to her, his body leaning into hers, his frail hand resting on her arm, instead of a sense of relief and connection, all she had was a room she couldn't allow herself to see, a devastation that blurred the rest of her senses, and a father in an urn.

Another surge of sickness, much larger this time, caused her to gasp. It might have been that the room went completely quiet, or it might have been that her mind went quiet in a desperate attempt to block out all the thoughts she insisted on ignoring.

The biggest difference between the day of her father's funeral and that of her grandfather, the one that had brought her back to Virginia, where everything went right and wrong at the same time, was a very specific set of sensations. Instead of tenderness between her legs from the most exciting night she'd had in a long time, instead of a smile she couldn't suppress, she swallowed against the unrelenting nausea she was fairly certain signaled the first signs of morning sickness.

Someone helped her stand, although she wasn't quite sure who it was. Then there was a car ride, during which Olivia Winston didn't stop talking, then arrival at the Winston's house. Ramona leaned to the side to ask if she could be taken home, but everyone was already scurrying out.

Masculine voices rumbled around her, but she couldn't focus enough to decipher what was said or who was saying it. She was surprised to find herself on a bed. Laying down sounded like a very good idea.

"Ramona... Mo..."

Something was shaking the bed and calling her name.

"Baby, it's time to go."

And then she was aloft, traveling through the house, back into a car, into another house, back in bed.

Ramona woke up two days after her father's funeral to find that the world had not ceased to exist, no matter how much she wished it had. There was no decrease in her grief or despair - in fact, it might have grown - but whatever psychological mechanism had forced her asleep had stopped. Or malfunctioned.

Her bed was empty, again, Lucas likely outside building something - his version of therapy. Personally, she much preferred a dark bedroom to a cold, sunny day. She took several deep breaths, trying her best to enjoy the act of breathing. Of being alive. It didn't work.

Without changing out of her pajamas, or putting on a coat or shoes, Ramona walked through the empty house to the back door, and then outside. Lucas froze at the sight of her, not trying to hide his surprise.

"You're up," he stuttered.

"I think I'm pregnant."

The piece of wood in his hand clattered onto the pile of tools. "You're... what?"

Assuming he'd heard her, she turned back toward the house, noticing only after stepping inside that the sensation of cold grass on her bare feet had been quite pleasant.

She hadn't made it to the couch before Lucas blew into the room, red-faced, dirt clouding around him. He reminded her of Pigpen, which was almost enough to force a smile on her exhausted face.

"Ramona!" His whole body was shaking, which she found curious. "Why did you walk away?"

Her body dropped onto the soft couch. She didn't try to sit up. "I needed to sit down."

He took two steps closer. "Mo." His voice cracked. "I think you just said you were pregnant."

She took a moment to evaluate whether what he'd said was a statement or question. "Yes."

"Oh, my God."

She looked at him, and then at the expanse of the couch.

Maybe he didn't want to sit down and dirty the couch. But that didn't seem like him. "Why don't you sit with me?"

His body wavered as if it couldn't decide in what direction it wanted to go. She closed her eyes, heavy with the exertion of carrying her unhappy body around those few steps that day.

She opened her eyes at the dip of the cushion to find him staring out the large windows.

"I... I didn't... Fuck!"

Well, that was unexpected. She squinted at his profile which had grown jagged with tension. "Are you angry?"

His head spun, panic shifting the landscape of his face. "God, no, Ramona! How could I be angry? I'm just... just..." His Adam's apple bobbed up and down. "I'm so sorry, babe. I thought you were in bed because of your father. I thought you wanted to be alone. I didn't realize you were..."

Ramona waited for him to finish the sentence, but he never did. "It was both, I guess. But you didn't do anything wrong."

He slid across the couch, closing any distance between them. "I can't believe it, Mo. I mean, I'm really happy about it. Are you happy about it? I mean, I know you're not happy right now... your father... but how do you feel about this? How long have you known? How-"

She reached over and squeezed his forearm. Her head was already spinning. One more question and it would explode. "I'm shocked. I'm disappointed in myself. I forgot to replace my birth control implant, apparently. Other than that, I'm trying really hard not to feel anything."

A tickle on her lip let her know that tears were running down her face. There'd been so many tears, she couldn't even tell anymore.

He ran his hand across her cheek. "Mo, please don't cry, baby. It's going to be okay. I promise. I'm going to make it be okay. I love you so much."

Before she could ask him how this disaster would ever be okay, his body was wrapped around hers, squeezing just past the point of comfort.

On the third day, she ended up in the bathtub without a clear understanding of how, but she was fairly certain she hadn't walked there. He must have carried her. There had been a lot of carrying. Maybe her days in bed, without bathing, had left her repulsive enough to warrant involuntary hygiene.

A stream of water splashed over her forehead and she blinked to keep the water out of her eyes.

"Sorry, love. Sorry. I'm just trying to get the last bit of shampoo out. Can you lean back?"

It was easy to do as she was told. That's what she wanted. Someone just to tell her what to do. To give her simple, clear instructions for moving forward. How to continue on with her father gone, a human being growing inside her body, and in the middle of the largest professional undertaking of her life. None of it was comprehensible at that moment. But the gentle stroke of the soapy cloth along her chest and arms, the warm water on her back, the soothing voice of the man she loved... those were within her ability to process.

During those hours when sleep wouldn't come, but getting out of bed was out of the question, Ramona made mental lists. Her habit since childhood, when she would count how many round items were in her room, or the dates of all the Saturdays until her next birthday. She loved lists and the more complex, the better.

She recited all the countries she'd been to, then all the cities, which was much more difficult. She listed all the addresses she'd had and the make of every car. There was even a cataloging of the full names of all the men she'd slept with, which was challenging, not because of the number, but because of the transience of most of those encounters. It crossed her mind that Lucas could well be the last man she would ever sleep with, the final name on the list. And if things continued the way they were going, she might never sleep with him again, either. On a list of things that sounded appealing to her at that moment, sex would be hovering near the bottom.

As her mind settled enough to make sleep a possibility, all the itemizing temporarily suspended, her mother suddenly entered her thoughts. It was almost as if she felt her entering the house or the room. Their relationship could never be described as affectionate, but Ramona had always felt connected to her distant mother, as if she could track her despite thousands of miles between them. She wondered what her mother would think about this predicament. As if the petite woman, whose waist-length hair would now be streaked with silver, was standing by the side of the bed.

"What should I do, Mom?" Ramona whispered to the empty space.

The imaginary figure took her ever-present stethoscope from the pocket of her white coat and placed the buds in her ears. "Stop being so dramatic, Ramona." The dark eyes examined her. "And take a pregnancy test, for goodness sake."

On the fifth day, a violent heave propelled Ramona out of bed and into the bathroom. When the deep contractions had stilled, the next sensation was of a hunger so intense, it folded her body over itself. Instead of calling out for Lucas, praying that he was within hearing distance, all she could muster was a raspy cry that barely made its way out of the large bathroom.

She slumped onto the floor, chilled by the cold tiles but grateful to be horizontal. If she wasn't pregnant then she must be dying.

A hand stroked her face, called her name. She was so thankful to see him, to feel him lift her and bring her back to bed.

He placed her on top of him and instead of the bed that had become her constant home, his body - warmer, firmer - became her anchor. She slept, her fingers never releasing their grip around his wrist.

It was dark when she next opened her eyes, which made it much easier. The dimness of the room allowed everything to enter much more gently. She watched him sleep until there was no more patience and she touched her lips to his. He pulled her in. God, that feeling. It had been so long.

"Baby... how are you?"

Her mind felt clearer, but her body was ravaged. "I'm hungry."

The movement of his eyebrows, the opening and closing of his eyes, all pointed to some confusion with what she'd said. But it had been so clear.

As if there hadn't just been an enormous pause, he continued. "Are you craving anything in particular?"

Her stomach clenched as if it could reach outside of her body and fill itself. "Something simple. And not too much. I don't know if I'll be able to keep anything down."

He slid himself out of bed, which would have been devastating except for the fact that he'd be returning with food. Glorious food.

Using all the strength she could muster, she pushed herself up to sitting, pillows gathered around her. The scent of bread wafting in from the kitchen nearly made her moan. Maybe this was what people called a foodgasm, which caused the first almost-laugh she'd had in a week.

He returned, set a tray down on her lap, and for a second she thought he'd brought her a children's puzzle. Variously colored rectangles were lined up in perfect precision.

"This," he indicated, "is plain." His finger moved to the next triangle. "This is butter, then cheese, jam, avocado, honey, and peanut butter."

He'd made her a toast buffet. The most brilliant thing she'd ever seen.

"Pick which ones you want, and I'll make more of that. I can take the other ones away."

Her eyes scanned the assortment. There was no hiding her body's reaction. Plain and peanut butter got salivation. Cheese, avocado, and jam elicited a small gag. The rest were somewhere in between.

She pointed. "This and this, please."

He gathered up the unchosen slices and turned to leave.

"Come right back, Baloo. I'm not sure if I'll eat more than two anyway. Maybe leave the buttered one."

The first bite was a symphony of pleasure and pain. She hadn't chewed and swallowed in so long, the muscles of her mouth ached. All that retching had left her throat sore but it didn't matter. This was sublime.

Lucas walked toward her, looked down at the mostly empty tray, up to her face, back down at the tray, then smiled. "I'll go make some more."

How was it possible that one man could be so perfect?

The next time, he brought a small stack of toast, some

slices of Asian pear - her favorite fruit - and a fresh glass of water.

"I read that dehydration makes nausea much worse, so you have to drink all the water."

She took the glass and gulped down as much as she could. It didn't go down as smoothly as she would have wanted. Several more bites of toast helped quell that sense of sloshy fullness.

Lucas barely moved from the edge of the bed, watching her as if something dramatic could happen at any moment. "How are you feeling now?"

She swallowed, the world coming into greater focus. "So much better. Wow."

He shifted a few inches closer to her and touched her cheek. "God, Mo, I've been so worried. I've been Googling if this sort of sickness and fatigue was normal, but there weren't any articles on what happens if at the same time you're grieving a loved one, so I had to extrapolate, and I wasn't sure what to do-"

"It's all right, love." She held his palm over her mouth, inhaling him, then brought it down to her chest. "I'm sorry I was so useless. I didn't want to worry anyone. Especially my Dad. He'll-"

Lucas' grimace preceded her recognition by a fraction of a second. Before the dam of her composure broke, his arms were around her, his hand stroking her hair.

Tears stopped flowing well before the feeling of crying passed. Perhaps she'd overused her crying ability. Running out of tears was poetic. Maybe it really happened.

She lifted her head off his shoulder. "I'm going to lie down, okay?"

"Mo, sweetheart, of course. I'm here if you need anything."

"Will you stay with me?"

He didn't hesitate before crossing over to the other side of the bed and enveloping her in his body. She released herself into his hold, their palms stacked on her belly. Where their baby was busy trying to kill her.

CHAPTER SEVENTEEN

*R*amona looked between Connor and Lucas huddled in the entryway, grumbling in their man voices. She could have tried to discern what they were saying, but that would have required focus. And giving a shit. Whatever it was, she'd find out soon enough.

The change of scenery, from darkened bedroom to bright living room, was pleasant, for the moment. The late afternoon sun streaked pinks and purples across the sky, softening the bare branches of the dark trees. It had been days since she'd left the house and she wondered if it was as cold as it appeared.

She curled her legs underneath her and settled into the corner of the couch. She considered reaching over to the other end to retrieve a blanket, but it was too much effort. Her morning, mostly spent over the toilet, had zapped her energy.

Connor raised his voice. Again, something unintelligible. Had they forgotten that she was sitting just a feet away from them? Maybe they thought she was as delirious as she had been all week. She hadn't quite decided if this newfound awareness was a good thing or not.

She'd agreed that Lucas could tell Connor about the pregnancy. It wasn't her first choice, considering how early it must be. For whatever reason, she knew that announcements weren't supposed to be made until twelve weeks. Too many of those medical shows, probably.

It's not like this was a real announcement, anyway. More like an explanation for her incapacitation. Connor would probably think it was great news, although the scowl on his face didn't quite support that theory.

Something about this supposedly impromptu family meeting had the veneer of an intervention. Less Lucas' posture than her brother's. Connor stood as if he was preparing to deliver a stern lecture. Lucas threw his hands up and turned away from her red-faced brother.

Both of their expressions flipped when they noticed her appraising them. Lucas sat next to her and Connor took the seat on the other side of the coffee table. She took a sip from the lukewarm tea Lucas had made for her. The taste had initially made her gag, but she was used to it now, and it did help with the nausea.

Her brother spoke first. "I'm really worried about you, Mo." He turned toward Lucas. "We both are."

This was not off to a good start. *Worried about you* was her brother's code for *I'm going to tell you what you're doing wrong.* "Really?"

Connor continued. "Yes, really. You need to see a doctor. You've been out of commission for a week. This isn't normal."

She looked over at Lucas to see if he was buying this bullshit. He turned his attention to his lap.

Ramona forced herself to sit up, a defensive posture forming over her weakened body. "I see."

"Lucas told me you haven't even confirmed the pregnancy

yet. I think you need to do that. To know how far along you are. And to rule out anything else."

She glared at her brother. "Anything else? Like what, Connor?"

He cleared his throat. "You've been having a hard time, Mo. You can't deny that. Sometimes the body can play tricks on us-"

"Are you fucking kidding me? Do you think I'm having some hysterical grief pregnancy? Maybe you're the one who's not in their right mind, Con."

Lucas brought his hand to her thigh. "That's not what he meant, Mo. That's-"

"You two have some nerve. While I've been nursing my dying father, you," she turned to Connor, "were pretending to be politician of the century, and you," she turned to Lucas, "were trying to be Bob the Builder. I was the one, day and night, taking care of him, taking care of everyone. And now that I'm legitimately ill, that I'm more exhausted than I've ever been, that I cannot grasp that my father is dead, you think it's okay to tell me that I'm not behaving appropriately? Fuck you. Fuck you both." She would have stood up for dramatic effect, but she was fairly certain her legs wouldn't hold her.

Connor rose and marched toward the door. Ramona was surprised, but not unhappy, that he was ending this discussion so abruptly. When he turned back and walked toward her, she realized he was pacing. The Barrett signature move.

"I'm not sure why you're so angry with me. I'm really trying to be patient with you. I know everything's intense for you right now." Connor stopped, turned his body to face her, but kept his gaze down toward the floor. "Yes, Dad getting sick was the impetus I needed to go after what I wanted. It's my way of making a difference."

She couldn't grimace hard enough. "Yeah, the Barrett political legacy really makes a difference."

"What the fuck, Ramona? You think you've got the monopoly on doing good? Where is all this coming from?" His four paces toward the door didn't fool her this time. She knew he'd be heading right back. "You seem to forget, little sister, that I came back. I've been here, all these years, while you stayed as far away as possible. I'm the one who took care of Dad through every fucking crisis. You come in at the end to make a grand appearance and think that you've got a lock-down on caring? Well, that's just as selfish as you've always been."

Lucas got to his feet. "That's enough, Con."

"Is it? Because you know as well as I do that she didn't even come back for Dad. She came back here for you, so you could shack up and play house, and now she's pregnant, and everyone's acting like it's a huge fucking tragedy."

In two steps, Lucas had placed himself between Connor and a disintegrating Ramona. "You need to stop."

Ramona wished she could say something, but opening her mouth at this moment felt incredibly risky. For many reasons.

Lucas grasped his best friend's shoulder. "Everyone's suffering here. But now is not the time to be-"

Connor jerked out of his grip and glared at Ramona. "I came here today to help. To be there for you. But I see you're still running the same game - run away and condemn. Are you going to shun us all like you did to Dad? Like you did to Lucas? Is it my turn to get the blame for everything?"

Ramona curled into herself as Connor loomed over her. She squeezed her eyes shut but knew exactly what expression had taken hold of his face. Their grandfather's fury in a different voice.

"You need to go."

She didn't understand how Lucas' voice had remained so calm. Grumbling voices, shuffling feet, and a door closing flashed in her awareness, but the shell around her was hardening by the second. The next sensation was Lucas' arms around her, lifting her off the couch.

She held on. "I'm going to be sick. Again."

He walked faster.

After cleaning herself up in the bathroom, Ramona slid into bed. It took several minutes to still the hard beating of her heart. She would have been angry if it didn't take so much damn energy.

Lucas slipped in beside her. "I'm sorry, babe. That went terribly wrong. I didn't know..." He touched her arm so lightly she could hardly feel it. "It wasn't right to do that to you. I was desperate, and Connor convinced me he needed to talk to you." He fiddled with the sheet. "I want you to know that I trust you and I'm here for you. And you need to go to the doctor."

She opened her eyes enough to catch his. "Do you think I'm crazy, too?"

"Absolutely not. But you're suffering and we need to find out... confirm... what's going on."

So many emotions swirled underneath the fixed line of his brow. One day, she'd have to find out what he'd been going through while she was incapacitated. For now, there was one thing she needed from him. "Doctor Sanchez' number is in my phone. Can you call in the morning?"

"Of course."

She fell asleep.

. . .

Something about having to get up and get ready to leave the house filled Ramona with more energy than she'd had in days. Or maybe it was her brother's rage-filled voice, playing on a loop, that electrified every movement. It was as if someone had turned on the power to her brain. Sure, Connor was going to get an earful from her as soon as she had the chance, but in the meantime she let it go. Lashing out was the Barrett way, especially when cornered or frightened. He was hurting, and maybe even felt abandoned. Neither she nor Lucas had been available to him. Ramona, the mediator, might have to make an appearance.

The cold hit her as soon as she stepped out of the house, but it felt glorious, as if she was coming back to life. Lucas wanted to carry her to the car, but she insisted on walking. Every step reinforced her intention to be strong. To be capable. To be the woman who handled whatever came her way.

She stroked his arm while he drove. He'd never mentioned it, but worry was carved into his face. Maybe it wasn't fair to have asked him to hold everything up while she collapsed into a pool of uselessness. He carried his distress so differently than she did. Hers was the armor that either shielded her or weighed so heavily that it dropped her to the ground. His was like a child in his arms who he vowed to protect and yet, touched with unbounded tenderness.

He was going to make an amazing father.

Lucas never let go of her hand during the multiple examinations. He might have even been shaking. But aside from the plastic bucket that never moved a few inches away from her, Ramona felt like herself again. All of this emotional collapse, of this *poor me* nonsense, had to stop.

"Yes, you're about eight weeks pregnant." Dr. Sanchez

smiled and paused. "I'm surprised I haven't seen you sooner. Especially considering the extent of your morning sickness."

"Sorry, doctor. My father just died and I've been having trouble coping."

Lucas squeezed her hand. "It's been a really hard time. I've never seen anyone this sick. Is there anything you can do?"

"There is a condition, called hyperemesis gravidarum, which might be indicated considering the intensity of your sickness. I'm going to hold off on that diagnosis just yet, as there are several other factors at play. Right now, we have to address the dehydration. It's at a dangerous level, Ramona. I'd like to admit you, just for a day or two, to give you IV fluids and nutrients. Will that work?"

She looked up to Lucas' face, concern darkening his eyes. *Don't be scared, Ramona.* "Yes, that's fine."

"Good. I'll call down to get a bed. As for helping with the nausea and vomiting, there are several medicinal interventions. None without risk, unfortunately. We've had great results with a B vitamin regimen. Many women also find relief from natural remedies, like ginger, and slight shifts to their diet. And it all goes away around twelve weeks for many of us. I can prescribe you something, if you need."

Ramona shook her head. "No, that's fine. I'll be fine. I think the combination of things made it much worse for me. I wasn't taking care of myself, but now I will. I promise."

Dr. Sanchez had the best bedside face, all soft and pretty and full of compassion. Ramona thought they might have been good friends if they had met socially. "Ramona, there's one more thing. Grief is a powerful emotion. And it often takes much longer than we expect to work its way out of us. I would recommend getting some support. I can give you a list of referrals for therapy. It's your choice, of course, but you might find it beneficial."

Ramona wasn't quite sure why her breath quickened. It almost felt like fear. "No, thank you. I'm feeling much better." She tried to smile convincingly, but a jumble of anxiety and despair pressed against her cheeks.

"Maybe we could just take the list anyway. In case you change your mind," Lucas said to the doctor.

"Good. Let me put it together." Dr. Sanchez turned back before stepping through the door. "You can get dressed now."

Ramona slid off the vinyl exam table, the crinkly paper sticking to the backs of her legs. Lucas' hand on her back stopped her from reaching toward her clothes, folded on a chair.

The look on his face - watery eyes, a twitch around the edge of his lips - was not at all what she expected. This situation was scary as hell, but at least she didn't have a huge tumor.

"Lucas... what's going on?"

He rubbed a palm up and down his face, then huffed out a few breaths. Someone had turned the fear knob all the way up.

"Say something. Please."

His arm dropped to his side. "We're having a baby."

She nodded, waiting for him to continue. It took an excruciatingly long time.

"You," he pointed to her belly, "are carrying our baby. What I want to do is jump up and down, howling and singing. I want to go hug every nurse, doctor, and patient in this place. I want to run into the street and announce it to the world. This is a day I won't ever forget."

She put her hand on his chest. "Yes, honey, I understand."

He stepped back, out of her reach. "No, I don't think so.

Because I look at your face and what I see is sadness and pain. What I feel is you pushing me away, when all I want is to pull you in as tight and close as I can get you."

"I... I'm not... I'm trying to be strong. To feel okay. To take all of this in and... " The struggle between protecting him and telling the truth stole her words.

"It's fine, Mo. I don't want you to fake happiness. I want you to *be* happy."

She lifted her arms and wrapped them around his neck, dropping her head onto his chest. His ragged breathing was hard enough. She couldn't watch him cry.

The opening door startled her, nearly causing her to lose her balance.

"As soon as you're ready, I have your papers. The bed is waiting. I'll meet you at the hospital."

Ramona dressed without speaking or even looking at Lucas. There was nothing she could say that would convince him that it was going to be okay. Probably because she didn't know if it was.

They walked in silence to the parking lot and drove the short distance to the main part of the hospital campus. Registration was surprisingly smooth, and she was in a small curtained room within a few minutes. Lucas held her hand as the nurse set up the IV.

"I'll be fine here tonight, honey. I know it's a busy night at the restaurant."

The line of his lips hardened before he spoke. "I'm not going anywhere, Ramona. Luis is running things tonight."

"Oh." She shifted in the small bed as he reached back to pull a chair closer to where he stood.

The distance between them created a cavity in the center of her body. "Will you lay down with me?"

"I don't think we'll both fit in that tiny bed."

She slid all the way back to the far edge, back against the guard rail, leaving an open space for him. "Please."

He laid down, careful to avoid the tubes leading from her arm to the hanging IV bag. She curled herself into him and closed her eyes. "I love you, Lucas."

"I know."

It wouldn't have been hard to say to him, "I am happy." To ease his worries of rejection or fatherhood or whatever else it was. She could have done it, but those words wouldn't come.

Ramona bargained and pleaded with the doctors to let her leave the next night. All she wanted was to get home, back to her own bed. Maybe at home, in *their* home, she'd be able to find something to say that would fix all the hurt.

Lucas walked her to their bedroom, tucked her into bed, then excused himself to his office. Paperwork was his reason. She knew better. Although the extreme nausea was gone, and her head was clearer than it had been in weeks, there was no satisfaction in being home. Just like that night, after their argument about Connor, the one she needed closest to her was moving farther and farther away.

The slight jostle of the bed as he got in woke her. She hadn't even realized she'd dozed off, waiting for him.

She snuggled in next to him.

"You're awake." He didn't sound particularly pleased.

"Will you be my awake friend?"

He didn't hesitate to pull her into him, their bodies fitting together as if they were formed that way. "Of course."

"I know you've had to deal with so much. I've been

useless for weeks, and instead of being grateful, I've just been..." There really wasn't a word.

His chest rose and fell with a deep breath.

"I'm sorry that I'm ruining this for you. It's just hard to imagine that this is happening. We just became *us*, and now it's going to be so much more. I'm not sure I'm ready."

His breath caught, tension gripping his abdomen. "What are you saying, Ramona?"

She flashed to what he might have been thinking. "No. I'm not saying I don't want this... pregnancy."

An exhale preceded the press of a kiss into her hair.

"I'm more scared than I've ever been. People don't stick around in my life. My Dad ran to the bottle, my Mom ran to the jungle, Connor is running toward the life he knows I can't tolerate. I won't be able to do it on my own. It's too much." The tears fell hard and fast, her body finally hydrated enough to cry.

"How about me, Mo? I've never run away from you."

"I know, but..."

"But what?"

There was no use in holding anything back. Her silencing her true feelings was not protecting him. "How could you possibly want all this? A woman who's not even happy to be pregnant with your child? I saw the look of disgust on your face. I know it's going to be too much for you, too."

His grip tightened around her back as she coughed and sputtered the final words.

He didn't speak until she'd settled back into stillness. "I'm not going anywhere. And this... you... our child... is everything I've ever wanted. There's nothing you could do that could change that."

"I'm so scared, Luc. What if-"

"That's not what we're doing right now. Tonight is for you

to remember how much I love you and that I'm here. I've got you."

It did not take long for Ramona's exhaustion to push her into a deep sleep. She dreamed of being eaten alive by piranha.

CHAPTER EIGHTEEN

*R*amona untangled herself from Lucas' arms and nearly didn't make it to the bathroom in time. Her hopes that all the vomiting would disappear after her stay in the hospital were dashed. Maybe the doctor was right and it was just a matter of time before it went away. At least she could hope.

She crawled into the open space left by his curled body, letting herself be spooned.

A moan resounded from his body to hers. "How are you, love?"

"It's not as bad, I think."

"Can I do anything for you? Would you like me to make you some tea? Get you a green juice?"

Just the thought of the sharp, pungent drink that used to be a daily staple caused her to grit her teeth. Her body definitely didn't want a green juice. "I'm okay for now."

They snuggled in silence. Ramona couldn't get back to sleep. "Thanks for listening to me last night."

"I'm always here to listen."

"I said some pretty awful things."

His arms tightened around her. "I wish you'd talk to me more. I know it frightens you to say some of the things you're thinking. But you need to remember that it's me. You can't scare me away."

She hadn't ever been that honest with another person. "Nothing's coming out right. Like my brain is scrambled or something."

"Grief and severe dehydration will do that to you. But you don't have to make sense. That's not who we are."

She pressed herself into him and for the first time in a long time, a swell of desire filled the center of her body. Nearly as violent and consuming as the waves of nausea had been. She needed him. Now.

Ramona spun herself around to plant a kiss on his mouth and grab a handful of his ass. His shock and resistance passed quickly and he was on top of her, pressing her knees open, before she caught her breath. He pushed into her, their groans matching the fever pitch of desire. And then everything stopped.

"Why are you stopping?" she panted.

"I... You're so fragile, Mo. I don't want to hurt you."

"I need you to fuck me. Please. Like it's just you and me again." She pawed at him, but he wouldn't let himself go. "Please, Lucas."

The entire spectrum of emotion appeared across his face. He held himself up on stiff arms while she pulled him to her. She tried to relax, to slow her breathing, to connect with his panicked eyes. "It's okay, Lucas." She stroked his cheek. "It's me."

He closed his eyes and dropped a bit of his weight down. She wrapped her arms around his back, using all her self-control to touch him gently. Her hips softly pulsed and within a few breaths, he matched her movements.

"God, Mo, I've missed you so much."

She caressed his broad, strong back, his powerful legs, his carved arms. The bristle of his beard rubbed against her cheek as the vibration of his breath penetrated her. Each stroke deepened the tremor in his body. This tower of muscle and mettle was crumbling in her arms.

It didn't matter that this wasn't what she had in mind. She'd wanted to lose herself in the type of passionate claiming that made her knees buckle. But this - holding her guy as he released all he'd been protecting her from - was exactly what they both needed.

As carefully as Ramona could, she crawled out of bed for another trip to the bathroom, which, surprisingly did not end up with her face-down over the toilet. Maybe the hydration and the vitamins were working. Maybe.

She splashed her face with cool water and took an unwavering look in the mirror for the first time in a long time. It was not a great sight. Sunken eyes, gaunt cheeks, none of that tawny glow she'd inherited from her mother. A month of not eating had taken its toll. It would be some time to get back to normal, and maybe by then, the whole pregnancy glow would kick in. The thought made her gasp. She was pregnant. Officially. Fuck.

Thankfully, Lucas was still asleep as she slipped back into bed. *Deep breaths, Ramona. Don't panic.* She closed her eyes and soothed herself with the most complicated list she could think of: the master list of parenting dos and don'ts.

It wasn't nearly as complex as she hoped, primarily because of her complete ignorance. How the hell were they going to manage?

The sight of Lucas, so peaceful, helped her release some

of the tension building up around her chest. He needed the sleep. He'd been going nonstop, taking care of her and the restaurant and everyone who needed anything. Maybe they would spend the day in bed together. And maybe she would convince him to have another round of sexy time. Her way, this time.

His mouth opened wide in a yawn while his hands rubbed the sleep from his eyes. He lifted his head up, as if to look for her, then put it down on her chest. One hand cupped her breast.

"Good morning," he said between kisses to her chest and belly.

She smoothed the hair from his face. "Good morning, love."

"How are you feeling?"

"Mmmm... so much better. Maybe Dr. Sanchez was right, and I don't have the hyper gravy thing."

His hand skimmed over the top of her concave belly. So empty. But strangely full. His fingers continued downward, curling into the space between her legs. She stopped, mid-breath.

With the heel of his hand pressing on her mound, he spread her open. The first stroke of his finger along her slit emptied the breath she was holding. The graze of his teeth on her breast elicited the first moan. When he gave her clit a light smack with several fingers - just once - she yelped.

She closed her eyes as the sharp, hot sensation dulled. "Do that again."

He slapped, just a tiny bit harder this time, her wetness creating a wonderful snap to accompany the nearly involuntary squeal.

"More?" he growled before biting harder.

"Yes."

Three more times, until she could have sworn the bed had started vibrating. Maybe the entire room. Then, instead of the piercing pleasure, he took a single fingertip and circled her. Slowly, with each cycle, the pressure increased. Her fingers burrowed into his scalp and wove through handfuls of curls.

Just as she thought she might crack from the pressure, his finger circling and circling, his thumb swiped across her clit, fingers plunged inside her, and her orgasm exploded around him.

She was hardly aware of the lift of his body and the turn of hers so she was on her stomach instead of her back. He slid his hand into the space between her and the bed, one finger pressing on her while he thrust so hard, she went sliding up toward the headboard.

He dipped his head down to her ear and whispered, "Hold on."

Any worries about Lucas' previous tentativeness vanished as she braced herself, fingers gripping the bed frame, and got wonderfully, gloriously, mind-blowingly fucked.

Ramona evaluated the bits of egg on the side of her plate. She had agreed, under duress, to try to eat something other than toast or pear slices. The first few bites of egg were fine. Lucas had cooked it perfectly, as expected. But something about the current state of her stomach was guiding her to stop. Best not to push it and ruin what had turned out to be the best morning she'd had in a really long time.

He squeezed her shoulder. "You did great, baby."

What a silly thing to smile about - the fact that she'd partially eaten a tiny meal - but it didn't stop the smile spreading across her face. "Although I'm not taking advantage of your culinary range, I'm infinitely grateful for your help."

"My help?" He shook his head. "Nothing means more than feeding the two most important people in my life."

"Two?" Oh. She patted her belly. "Winny says thanks."

He froze. "Did you just call the baby, Winny?"

Couldn't deny it. "I guess so. I've been thinking Baby Winston, and it just got shortened on the way out."

Her awkward self-consciousness sent heat to her cheeks. Before her hand had risen to cover her face, his mouth was on hers, fingers tangled in her hair, not giving her an inch. She gasped as he pulled away, just as dramatically.

His eyes blazed. "Is it weird that I thought that was one of the sexiest things I've ever heard?"

Probably, but it didn't matter. If giving their poppy seed of a baby a silly name meant kisses like that, she was all in.

The stun slowly wore off, allowing Ramona to speak again. "Do you have anything going on today?"

"I hate to leave you, love, but I have to go to work. We've got a high profile event and I'm expected to be there. It's for the ambassador. I think I had mentioned him."

Yes. *With my Dad.* "I understand." She tried not to let disappointment seep into her expression.

"If there was any way I could get out of it..."

Don't be a baby, Ramona. "Oh, sweetie, it's okay. Of course you have to work. I'll be fine."

"The ambassador has been a major supporter. He's basically my sole advertising on The Hill. I need to make an appearance."

She hated that he felt he had to justify his doing something other than waiting on her, hand and foot. "It really is alright." She wove her fingers through his. "Isn't this the same guy that Connor said was trying to steal you away?"

His face tightened. "It doesn't mean anything, Mo. It's just an offer."

"It doesn't sound like nothing. How many American chefs get this kind of offer?"

Lucas swallowed. "Well, only one other, as far as I know."

Her mouth dropped open. "Holy shit! This is a really big deal." She shook her head. "Why aren't you even considering it?"

"There's nothing to consider." He stood up. "You... our family... my life... it's all here. I'm not going to spend weeks or months away building a restaurant on the other side of the planet."

He picked up her plate and brought it over to the sink. His discomfort was palpable, but she couldn't let it go. "I'm going to ask you something, and you have to promise to not get mad."

He turned with a frown. "Mo..."

"If I wasn't here, and... pregnant... would you be taking this more seriously? It sounds like a once-in-a-lifetime offer."

He dropped the plate, which clattered loudly. "Business comes and goes. Love and family are my priorities. I thought you knew that."

Guilt pushed on her partially full belly. She should have known. This discussion wasn't worth ruining the wonderful morning they'd had. "I *do* know. And I love that about you."

His frown turned into a smile, but her concern didn't dissipate quite so easily. The last thing she wanted was for him to feel tied down, unable to pursue his heart's desire. If it wasn't for her, he would go after this amazing offer. She was sure of it.

"You remembered that Camille and Jackson are in town, right?"

The abrupt change of topic made her head spin. "Wait! It's the thirtieth? Today is December thirtieth?" It couldn't be.

He laughed. "Yes, love. We've been living time-free for a while. Pretty much missed Christmas."

She scrunched her face. "Shit. What a mess. I'll have to make it up to you soon. But today, I'm pretty sure I'm supposed to be meeting with Camille about the bambinos."

"If you're not up to it, I'm sure she would understand. I can give them a call and-"

"No. It's fine. It'll be nice to wrap my brain around something that's not..." She couldn't get herself to actually say it, the topics that had hijacked her life: her father's death, her pregnancy, and now the fact that she had become the proverbial ball and chain.

By the time the doorbell rang, Ramona could almost be mistaken for someone who hadn't spent the past ten days in bed. Hair tied back, clean clothes, smile on her face.

She had hardly opened the door before Camille was wrapped around her. Ramona wasn't even able to hug back, her arms pinned to her sides in her friend's unrelenting grip.

"It's so good to see you," Camille said as she finally loosened her grasp.

Ramona stepped aside. "Come in."

"I've been thinking about you so much." Camille paused before sitting down.

"You have?" Ramona hadn't meant for that to come out sounding quite so dumbfounded.

"I'm so sorry about your father. We didn't get to see you at the funeral and I was so worried."

Ramona rubbed her forehead, trying to piece together the

sparse memories from that day. "You were here for the funeral?"

Camille's brows lifted. "Of course. Lucas told us you were really ill, so we didn't want to intrude."

Ramona shook off the memory and remembered her manners instead. "What can I get you? Coffee? Tea? Something to eat?" Thankfully, her amazing guy had set up some snacks.

"I'm fine for now, thanks." Camille nodded.

The compassion coming off of her friend reached right into the center of Ramona's chest. Camille had experienced one of the worst tragedies imaginable - both parents murdered when she was a teenager. But now, she was one of the most together people in Ramona's life. So smart, recently engaged to Jackson, and not at all scarred or broken. This woman was like a rare bird.

Camille tilted her head. "I really want to know how you're doing."

"But we're supposed to be meeting about the mansion. Next steps and such."

Ramona picked up the glass of water she'd left on the side table and took a sip. Camille gazed at her, eyes so soft and warm, a smile lifting her lips. If ever there was a moment to come clean, to say everything she'd been holding in for fear of hurting Lucas, this was the moment. Especially with Connor mastering his assholery, she might never have as receptive an audience again.

"Come sit down, Ramona." Camille patted the couch. "We can talk business afterward. First, I want to hear about you."

The tears began as soon as her bottom hit the cushion, as if they'd been lying in wait. Camille slid over and took her hand.

"Not that great, Cam. Actually, not great at all."

Camille's arm moved around her shoulders as she sobbed.

The burst of emotion passed quickly. "Wow, I'm always surprised to have any more tears left. I think I've used a few lifetimes' worth."

Camille handed her a tissue. "I'm here, Mo. You can talk or you can cry or whatever you need. I know there comes a time, much too soon, when people expect you to be normal again even when you're feeling anything but. You don't have to pretend that everything's okay. I get it."

Of course she did. She'd been through much worse than this.

The urge to speak supplanted her tears. "I don't even know where to start. You wouldn't believe all the drama that's happened in the past few months. Like all of a sudden, my life has become a soap opera, complete with dead fathers, crazy exes, blackmail schemes, power-hungry brothers, and an accidental pregnancy."

Surprise overtook Camille's normally composed face. "Oh... that's... uh..."

Ramona laughed. "Sorry, I didn't mean to vomit it all out at once." She flitted eyes at Camille's open mouth. "I've gotten really good at that, lately. Vomiting."

"Oh?"

"I know I'm not supposed to tell anyone - it's pretty early - but I'm pregnant. How crazy, right? In the middle of all of this, adding a baby into the mix." She dropped her head in her hands.

Camille's hand brushed across her back. "Congratulations."

The sweetness of the word forced Ramona to look up. Camille was the first person she'd told and had no idea what to expect. How do people usually react to unplanned pregnancies? That expression on Camille's face looked a lot like happiness.

"Thanks. I'm as scared as I've ever been, but also..." Happy? Excited? "Hopeful. Is that insane? I've got this brand new relationship, this brand new life, and I'm almost excited about having a baby."

"It makes total sense to me."

Ramona wanted to ask how and why and what could possibly make sense about all that, but instead hugged her friend.

"I'm sure Lucas is thrilled, right?"

Thrilled didn't begin to describe it. "When I look at him, I feel like this is his fairy tale. He built this house for a wife and whole bunch of kids and then made it happen."

Another vault of Camille's eyebrows. "Wife? Are you two...?"

Ramona shook her head. "Oh, no. Not that. He knows better than to ask, I think. It's all happened too fast, as it is. And then there's the lingering scandal with his fake wedding."

Ramona's hand flew up to her mouth. Shit. Giddy on honesty, she'd forgotten where the lines were. "I wasn't supposed to say that."

Camille bit her lip. "And I'm not supposed to know. But I do."

"Jackson?"

"Yeah. They talked about it during the move. Jackson swore me to secrecy, so you're not the only one who wasn't supposed to say anything."

Instead of worry, Ramona was filled with relief. She hadn't realized how difficult keeping everything bottled up had been. And how good it would feel to let it all out.

"Did something else happen with Abigail?"

Ramona considered how much to divulge. Best to tread

carefully. "She started calling me. Claiming that I was getting in the way of her being with Lucas."

"Holy shit! Did she threaten you?"

"Not directly, no. She made some claims about damaging information about someone in the family, but mostly she was trying to convince me that Lucas was lying to me. That our relationship was just a continuation of the scam."

Camille scrunched up her face. "That's really frightening, Mo. What did you do?"

"I ignored her, and she stopped. Then my dad got sick and it didn't matter."

"Did that cause any trouble with Lucas?"

"Yes. I was angry. The whole situation was so ridiculous, it was hard for me to understand how he could have gotten involved in the first place. It's taken a while for me to feel comfortable... to trust him."

Camille kept shaking her head as if the thoughts wouldn't settle enough to make sense. "You're not kidding about having a lot going on."

Ramona wanted to add that there was still more, but held back. It would be impossible to explain all the issues with Connor.

Camille sat back on the couch with a sigh. Ramona gave her a minute to process. "Can I get you something now?"

"Coffee would be great if you have it. Otherwise a glass of water."

Ramona smirked. "Our coffee machine could launch a space shuttle. Come look."

She grabbed Camille's hand and led her into the kitchen.

The glint of an enormous diamond nearly blinded Ramona as Camille took a sip of her espresso.

"Cam! Oh, my God. I completely forgot to congratulate you on your engagement."

Camille put down her cup and looked down at her hand. She failed at holding back a huge smile. "Thanks. It's been, well, Jackson's been like *my* fairy tale. He proposed the day we moved back into the house. It was a complete disaster, boxes everywhere, a layer of construction dust that would take days to clean. I mean, not some exotic setting. But it was the most romantic thing that's ever happened to me." She beamed at the ring again. "Sometimes, I still can't believe it."

Ramona swallowed, the tiniest hint of envy bubbling up from her empty stomach. "You two are perfect for each other. If you've been able to tolerate Jackson for all these years, I think you have an amazing future ahead."

They shared a laugh. "You know, even though we were best friends for so many years, it's different now. More pressure, which I didn't expect. Before, I was able to mostly stay hidden, away from his celebrity life, but now it's me on his arm, with all the cameras flashing. There was a time when I started to feel myself disappear, like all my work and my dreams would just be consumed by his bigger ones. It's hard to go from a woman who's basically taken care of herself to the one who only matters in relation to someone or something else."

Ramona dropped her glass, which surprisingly, didn't spill. It made no sense that her jumble of emotions had just been summed up more eloquently than she ever could. "How did you manage?"

"It's a constant dance to get everyone's needs met. When they conflict, we work it out. Jackson has always made it clear that I come first. I think that's what makes it work."

Unbelievable that the exact person who had experience with the issue she'd just had with Lucas was sitting in her living room. "How about if something that would be amazing for him would be terrible for the relationship? What do you do?"

Camille lifted her cup, then put it down. "We haven't had to deal with that, thankfully. I'm not sure what would happen. But I know that when I decided to work with you on the children's center, he started turning down clients on the west coast and trying to build more of a base around here. He wanted to make it easier for me to come here as much as I could and for him to come with me."

This type of relationship was incomprehensible. Not two people having to compromise what they wanted for the sake of a relationship, but two people wanting the best for each other. Trippy.

"You look confused, Mo." Camille's sweet face held back a smirk.

"Oh, Cam, I'm way out of my depth here. From free and single to shacking up and *family*." That word was so loaded, it made her voice crack. "I haven't felt this incompetent... ever."

The doorbell startled her out of the next thought. It was probably a package delivery service.

Ramona opened the door and froze. The petite woman who'd been filling her thoughts was standing in her doorway, complete with silver-streaked hair and eyes the color of night.

"Mom..."

CHAPTER NINETEEN

octor Cecilia di Falco Barrett hadn't aged one bit. Her skin was a bit more tanned, her frame a bit more slight, but otherwise, she looked almost exactly like the woman Ramona had last seen five years before.

"Cariña, are you going to invite me in?"

Ramona nearly tripped over her own feet moving out of the way to let her mother in. "Mom, what are you doing here?"

Cecilia put down her bags and took her daughter's face into her hands. With a kiss on each cheek, then on the tip of her nose, their special greeting was complete. Something they'd shared since before her mother had enough with civilization and ran to the Amazon. "You are looking too thin, Ramona. I can see all your bones."

Ramona ran a hand over her belly, then felt self-conscious and dropped it to her side. "Mom, why are you here? Is everything alright?"

Cecilia walked a slow circle around the room, looking, touching, making small noises of approval. Ramona was about to blow when her mother finally decided to speak.

"I tried to get here for your father's funeral, but I couldn't extract myself quickly enough." She picked up a small wooden carving of a meditating monk. "I came to see you, of course. Connor told me you've been having a hard time."

"Connor? You talked to Connor?"

Cecilia's brows drew together. "Of course, dear. I talk to both of you. He is in a meeting right now, so he told me to come here. I think he will be along later."

Ramona could not get a grasp on her scrambled thoughts.

Cecilia peered toward the entrance to the kitchen. "Oh, hello!"

Camille had stepped into the room, eyes darting from one of them to the other.

"Cam, this is my mother, Cecilia."

The two women embraced while Ramona tried to figure out what was happening.

"Nice to meet you, Camille," said Cecilia.

"And you."

"You remember Jackson, Mom? Lucas' cousin? Camille is his fiancée."

Cecilia's face lit up. "Oh, wonderful! Congratulations." She turned her attention to her daughter. "It seems all you young people are settling down."

This was too much. "What can I get for you, Mom?"

"It has taken nearly three days to get here, so I would love to lie down for a bit."

"Of course. Let me take you to the guest room." Ramona picked up her mother's bags and headed down the hallway.

When Ramona returned, Camille hadn't moved. She might have not even blinked.

"Uh... were you expecting your mother?"

"Ha! One never expects my mother. She comes and goes as she pleases." Her appearance, at this time, with everything going on, felt more than coincidental. And frankly, unwanted. There wasn't a single thing about Ramona's new life that her mother would approve of. Or agree with.

Camille crossed her arms. "Maybe I should go." Her eyes flitted down the hallway. "So you can have some time with your mother."

Time with her mother was the last thing Ramona wanted. "No, please stay. It's been so nice having you here. She'll probably sleep for a while. And I clearly need to be picking your brain about how to not ruin a relationship."

Camille laughed, then caught herself. "Sorry, I didn't mean to be so loud. Anyhow, I'm not sure why you're worried about your relationship, Mo. You and Lucas are so well suited, and clearly in love. I imagine it all feels too fast, especially since something like this is new to you, but trust yourself. Trust that you're going to do what's best for you and your family."

Ramona's eyes dampened. *Don't start crying, Ramona. Again.* "You are amazing, Cam. Why didn't I meet you years ago? Maybe I wouldn't be so relationship stunted."

Camille hooked her arm through Ramona's and walked them back to the couch. "Don't forget what a smart, strong, capable woman you are. You got this."

With a high five that felt great and ridiculous in equal parts, Ramona settled back and smiled.

After an afternoon of laughing, planning, and even eating a bit, Ramona found herself in an silent house once again. Camille had headed off to meet Jackson and Mom was still sleeping. Might as well see if she could sneak in a little nap.

Sleep did not last long, as Ramona's thoughts filled with all the dangling threads around her. It was time for serious list-making. There was Lucas and his Dubai offer. There was Connor and his run for Senate. There was Abigail, whose sudden silence had begun feeling less and less settled. And there was her mother, whose reproach was imminent.

Each would require their own set of options and tasks. There had to be a logical way to handle all of this, while still managing the children's center project, keeping her man happy, and growing a human being in her body. A rush of terror forced the air from her lungs. The ever-present option, of course, was to run. Nothing was irreversible, and she had mastered the art of the exit. Getting out would solve most of those problems.

Ramona was forced to abandon her plotting and panicking as loud noises emanated from the kitchen. She found her mother puttering around, opening and closing cabinets, stirring something on the stovetop.

Cecilia lifted a white ceramic bowl from a neat stack and set it on the counter. "Not working today, dear?"

It hadn't taken long for the judgy questions to start. "I'm just taking a break, Mom. I've been very tired lately."

Dark eyes scanned her from head to toe. "Yes, I can see that. You don't look as well as I would have thought, considering."

"Considering?"

"Well, your life has slowed down quite a bit, hasn't it?" Cecilia turned off a burner and slowly poured a thick saffron-colored soup into her bowl. Ramona wasn't aware they had soup in the house.

"Actually, Mom, I've been working on the biggest project of my career." Ramona reminded herself that she had no reason to get defensive. "Dad's death hit me hard. I'm still reeling."

Cecilia brought the bowl to the table and sat down. "I'm sorry I wasn't able to be here for you." She blew on the spoon and looked up. "I hope I'm not too late."

Ramona's stomach growled, but it wasn't clear whether from hunger or frustration. Her mother's ability to see right through her had not lessened one bit.

Cecilia put down her spoon. "Would you like me to heat up some soup for you? I'd love for you to sit and eat with me."

"No, I can do it. Please start. You must be starving."

The only sounds in the kitchen as she heated up more soup were the clang of pots and utensils, as well as a soft hum from her mother. Ramona thought of Leni, singing along to her music while cooking. Under different circumstances, the two women might have gotten along very well, but Ramona wasn't about to test out that possibility. There was already enough conflict in the house.

She took the seat next to her mother and swirled her spoon through the thick soup. She had no idea when Lucas had made a batch of her favorite coconut curry soup, but there it was, in the fridge. It would be impossible for him to be any more thoughtful. If only she could figure out how to do the same.

The two women sipped their soup.

"Are you going to tell me why you're really here, Mom?"

Cecilia crinkled the corners of her eyes in an expression that made her look even more like a devilish pixie. "I told you, Cariña, I came for you."

Ramona groaned. "Please, Mom."

"You've become so cynical, sweetheart. I don't understand why you doubt me. You know that I can *feel* you. And what I felt told me you were in trouble. Of course, I was not sure until I saw you."

"I'm not in trouble, Mom." The double entendre of those words did not go lost on Ramona, but she let it pass. "I'm grieving my father. I'm adjusting to a new life. I'm embarking on a challenging phase of my professional life. That's all."

Cecilia gave her a half-smile. "Hmmm. This soup is wonderful, by the way. You're lucky to find a man who will always keep you well fed."

Ramona resigned herself that she'd get nothing more from her mother. Demanding an explanation from the woman who never explained herself was futile. "Yes, I am very lucky. Lucas is the most wonderful man I've ever known."

"I heard that he left some woman at the altar." An eyebrow rose. "For you."

Ramona swallowed the story that wanted to come out. "Yes, it was a difficult situation."

Her mother burst out laughing. "You must think that I've gone daft in the jungle. Quite the opposite, my dear daughter. Regardless, I won't force you to talk about it." Cecilia spun in her chair and bore her ebony eyes into Ramona's. "There is something I need to tell you. More importantly, you need to hear it."

Ramona tipped back in her chair, an involuntary fear response creating a tightening in the center of her chest. The confrontation she knew was coming had arrived.

"I know I've always told you to fight your own battles. What matters is being able to stand on your own two feet. Don't depend on any man. And, dear daughter, you've excelled. You've kept yourself clear of any of that nonsense that took me down and has destroyed many women before you. But-"

"Hey there! Anybody home?"

Both women jumped up at the unexpected sound of Connor's voice.

He appeared in the kitchen, picked up his mother, and spun her around. "So sorry I'm late, Mom." He put her down and stroked her hair. "I'm so glad you're here."

"I had a good rest and have been spending time with your sister. No trouble at all."

Connor tipped his head toward Ramona. "Hey."

Her mouth set in a hard line. "Hey."

He turned back to his mother. "Are you ready?"

"Yes, sure. All my things are in the guest-room."

Ramona pushed down the urge to cross her arms and get into fighting stance. "Ready for what?"

"Bringing her to my house. She's staying with me." He turned to his mother. "I'll go get your bags."

Ramona blinked at the sight of him heading toward the bedroom. Those two together, like a flashback to childhood. Connor and Mom, as it had always been.

Her mother clutched her arm. Not gently, either. "We'll continue our conversation another time, sweetheart. Maybe I'll come over tomorrow morning." She kissed her on each cheek, then on the tip of her nose. "I love you."

Ramona stood at the front door well after Connor's car had driven away. The whole thing felt like a prank. He probably knew their mother was coming and never said. She wondered what they were up to, the winter air adding a shiver to the growing anger rippling through her.

Ramona crossed and uncrossed her hands. Perhaps she should have taken her mother's comment the day before about coming over more seriously.

Since her mother walked in the door that morning, she wouldn't stop staring, as if she was looking straight into her soul. Ramona blinked. There was nothing there she wanted her mother to see.

"Are you sure you don't want to eat, Mom? You know Lucas always has something delicious in the house."

"No, dear. I don't want to ruin my appetite for Connor's luncheon. It's a special occasion, you know."

Ramona bit her tongue to not start railing against her brother, who'd neglected to extend her an invitation to his *special occasion*. Even Lucas hadn't mentioned that her brother was holding a party at the restaurant. In any case, complaining about her brother to her mother was a lost cause. Everyone knew which child was her favorite.

"I was hoping we'd have a chance to finish the conversation we started yesterday, but I don't want to be late."

"Don't worry, Mom. Winston's is only a few minutes away from here. We have plenty of time." Which Ramona didn't actually want.

"Ramona, I'm worried about you. Your brother has been telling me that you haven't been yourself, and now that I see it with my own eyes, I think it's even worse than he described."

"Worse? Wha-"

"You're bone thin and your eyes are dark. Like you haven't been sleeping or eating. And there's the fact that you seemed to have thrown away the entirety of your hard-won success and independence to come back to this evil place and play house with Lucas, of all people."

Ramona prepared several responses in her head, but none made any sense. It was impossible to know where to start in that ridiculousness her mother was spewing.

But she couldn't stay quiet. "I just lost my father, so, yes, I haven't been sleeping or eating as well as I could have, but I'm getting better every day. I haven't thrown away my career. The children's center is the culmination of everything I've done. The first thing that will have my name on it. I couldn't be more proud of it, Mom. As far as Lucas, I don't understand what your issue is. You know him. He's the best man I've known, since childhood. What could you possibly have against him?"

Cecilia's face contorted in an exaggerated scowl. "You can't be serious, Ramona. Your relationship with him began with a scandal. Do you think it's going to be any different with time? And how can you even trust anything he's told you? These schemes always weave their way into your life, and when you least expect it, bite you in the ass. I pulled you away from all of this, and I don't think you understand the extent of the indecency of this place. And these people. Instead of shielding yourself from it, you've placed yourself right in the middle of it."

Ramona sat stunned, unable to swallow. It was even worse than she expected.

"And what about this Abigail woman? If she was able to coordinate this masquerade, how do you know she won't try again? Create more chaos in your life? And are you sure she isn't still... associated... with Lucas? These situations can be quite deceiving."

Ramona's breath came in short, sharp bursts, nausea pushing against her throat.

Cecilia didn't relent. "I hear you've been attacking your brother. I don't understand that at all."

She had a response for that. "Why is it okay for Connor to be here, to be in the political game, but it's not okay for me to be outside of it?"

"Because you and Connor are not the same. His convictions are much stronger than yours. Someone like him will be able to dismantle the system from the inside. Someone like you will be crushed by it."

Ramona pushed to her feet and felt immediately woozy. Fuck. She sat back down.

Her mother took her hands. "Ramona, it's not too late to get your life back. Maybe after you're done with the center, you can reclaim your life. For goodness sakes, please don't do anything that would force you to stay here. I know you're high on this relationship, but don't tie yourself down. You-"

"That's enough! You're in my house now, Mom, and I won't have you speaking to me like this." Ramona put on her best glare.

"This isn't *your* house. This is Lucas' house. Which supports my point, completely. Where are you in all this Ramona? Why have you let yourself disappear?"

Ramona attempted to stand up once again, this time taking it more slowly. She blinked away the dizziness before speaking. "I haven't disappeared. I'm right here. You seem unable to see me."

"But-"

"It's time to go. I'll take you to Connor's party now."

CHAPTER TWENTY

*R*amona turned the volume on the car radio well past comfort to prevent any more conversation. Ignoring her mother's comments would have been great except they were all too familiar. Like a crappy song that got stuck in her head and wouldn't go away. She also couldn't get herself to say all the hateful things she wanted to. Distant politeness had been a fine strategy with her mother all these years, but silence seemed to be the current best option.

She pulled up to the entrance to Winston's and stopped the car, with no intention of going in. Her mother fussed with her purse, then the seatbelt, then the door handle, giving Ramona plenty of time to change her mind. Lucas would probably be busy, but maybe she could sneak in for a hug and kiss. He would know exactly what to say to help her feel better.

Connor's large party was evident as soon as they entered the restaurant. Congressman Winston, Lucas' father, along with one of her uncles, and twenty or so people she'd never seen before filled the space next to a wall of windows. An eccentric-looking man in a purple jacket and bowtie held up a skinny glass and spoke to the crowd. That must be the inimitable Stanley Grayson, who everyone referred to as the Kingmaker. He was the one who was going to take Connor all the way to the White House, apparently.

Ramona seethed with anger. Even if it wasn't a social event, it was downright rude to invite their mother, hold it in her boyfriend's restaurant, and not even mention it. She longed for the days when her brother was a dorky bag of bones.

Connor pulled away from the crowd and embraced their mother. "You made it!"

He looked back at Ramona with a polite smile. "Thanks for bringing her."

She forced herself to smile back. "Yeah. So, what's this about?"

"I'm congratulating the team for all their hard work. We've got our most important rally in a few days and they've been working their butts off. And, of course, it's New Year's Eve, so..."

A loud laugh drew her attention away from her brother. She grimaced at their pervy uncle looking down a young woman's blouse.

Connor cleared his throat. "If you're done judging me now, Ramona, I'm going to head back to my party."

"What the f-" Someone grabbed her hand while she glared at her brother.

"Stanley Grayson here. You must be the famous little sister!" Stanley pumped her hand up and down.

She looked down at the shiny little man. "Yes, nice to meet you."

"And you. I'm a huge fan of the Barrett family. Your grandfather was one of my heroes."

Ramona caught herself mid-eyeroll. "Thank you. Well, I've got to get going now."

She tried to yank her hand out of his grip, but instead, he pulled her in, even closer. "Congratulations on your *situation*, by the way."

Her stomach lurched, not only at the words he said but how he said them. In full voice.

"I'm hoping you won't add an illegitimate child to your brother's morality-based campaign. I know you have a willing man, and a ring on that finger should clear that right up."

Ramona's attention darted from her mother's shocked face to her brother's shame, to the crowd's horror, and finally back to Stanley's sneering smile.

She stepped back and gripped her stomach as if she could protect her baby from all the evil she saw in that room. Three long breaths later, she answered the still smirking man. "Well, Stanley, I see you and my brother are a perfect match."

As she turned on her heel and headed toward the exit, the bellows of her brother and cries of her mother merged and faded into an unrecognized jumble behind her. Halfway there, Ramona was stopped by the sight of a tall, thin brunette wearing a cream suit that must have been sewn around her, sauntering out of the kitchen and brushing a palm across her tightly bound hair.

"Abigail," fell off of a breath.

The woman's gaze flitted from the dining room to Ramona, who expected shock and was greeted instead with a self-satisfied grin. Then, she waved as if in a parade and continued walking toward Connor's party.

Ramona stood frozen long enough, staring in the direction of the kitchen to then see Lucas emerge, steps behind Abigail. Her eyes slid to his hands, tightening the strings of his apron around his waist.

The world screeched to a halt, and Ramona was power-less to keep her body from turning around and striding toward the front door. Accompanying her was a small number of distinct voices calling after her in the restaurant. The rush of blood and the pounding of her heart did nothing to drown out the cacophony of voices in her head.

From Stanley: "Don't degrade your brother's moral standing."
From Connor: "You're still running your same game - run away and condemn."
From her mother: "This place will never be home for you. It's full of liars, cheaters, and criminals. Don't let yourself get used, destroyed. Don't trust that anyone has your best inter-ests at heart."
From Lucas: "Abigail is out of our lives. She means nothing to me."

Like a series of waves crashing against the shore, all these thoughts caused her legs to give way, and she stumbled into the door with a loud thud. Arms she recognized caught her, pushed open the door and then she was outside, cold air whip-ping against her face. Lucas' repeated calls of her name even-tually registered, followed by her mother. "Cariña! Is it true you're pregnant?"

Then Connor. "Mo, are you all right? Mo?"

She pushed out of Lucas' arms and found her legs again. As soon as she was upright, dizziness grayed out her vision before she doubled over and threw up all over the front entrance to Winston's. Despite the collective gasp, Ramona felt better, as if all those terrible thoughts she'd been holding in were now out.

She stood up, caught her breath, and turned toward her car. Heavy footsteps trailed behind her.

"Mo, please say something. Where are you going?" His voice was compelling, but not enough to slow her down.

She held on to the car door as she addressed Lucas. "I'm going home now. I know it's your house, but it's also my home. And you're not welcome there until you're ready to tell me the whole fucking truth about Abigail."

He staggered back as she peeled out of the parking lot.

She drove with an unexpected calm and a noticeable absence of fear. It's not that she didn't care about the scene she'd left - the hurt on her mother's face, the concern from Connor, and the pain from Lucas. It was that it suddenly felt very funny.

She'd just thrown up in front of a large crowd of people at a very fancy restaurant. Her pregnancy had been announced to a group of strangers. She'd just threatened her boyfriend that he wasn't allowed back into his own house.

The humor of it all bubbled up to the degree that she laughed hysterically for the first several minutes of the typically short ride. The third time she passed the same drugstore, she knew something was wrong. Getting between the restaurant and the house was second nature at this point. She could do it without much thought, but as she stopped in front of a fast food restaurant she'd never seen before, Ramona had to admit she was utterly and completely lost.

The situation could be rectified by retrieving her phone and using her navigation app. But her phone was likely full of messages she had no interest in seeing. And what would she put into the GPS, anyway? Where the hell was she trying to go?

Ramona dropped her head onto the steering wheel and sobbed. Old Ramona would have pointed the car toward the airport and gotten the hell out of there. Maybe even just headed west and kept driving until she was back in California. The realization that there was nothing for her there brought another surge of tears.

She'd lived this grand life - traveling the world, doing great things - but hadn't left a single trail. Even her father, whose footprint had been so faint to have been nearly invisible, had always had somewhere he could point to and say, "This is home."

Hell, even her mother, while fighting against any sort of label, had settled down. Her home was in those villages, with those people as her new family. People found their places, built their nests, created something to hold them.

Ramona blinked away the last of the tears and retrieved her phone from the bottom of her purse. Maybe she could just stop fighting, stop driving around in circles, stop all of it. Maybe she could finally stop letting all those other voices pull her from where she knew she wanted to be.

It didn't need to be hard or fraught or painful. It could be as easy as opening up her navigation app and tapping on the top listing, the one with a bright red star next to it. *Home*.

Ramona walked around the house to the back, destination beyond question. Lucas would probably be at the restaurant for hours, which was fine. A good, long soak, accompanied only by her own thoughts, was exactly what she needed. There was a lot to parse: choices, actions, declarations.

She stepped into the tub, the lists already forming in her busy mind. Even before she'd submerged herself, the first level of decisions had been made, answers obvious:

Stay vs. Go.

Punish Lucas vs. Give him a chance.

Kill Connor vs. Let him live.

Her fucking brother. He'd been coming between her and

Lucas since the beginning. That had to end, even if it meant making a stand. In so many ways, she'd mothered him. They all had. But the Connor issue was not going to be solved by either her coddling or her silent anger. A hard talk was in their future.

She sank down to the tip of her chin, warmth finally penetrating her body. She'd sat across from Lucas in this tub, not too long ago, scared to death. She was convinced that her actions had made her un-wantable. Had made her undeserving of love and care and belonging. Prepared that all her comfort would be suddenly ripped out from under her as he forced her out of his life.

How foolish.

She didn't have to protect herself from being evicted. Hell, she'd evicted herself her whole life. Not anymore. This was her home. So much so that she was going to be adding another human being to it. Ramona's hand skimmed over the skin of her belly. If she looked at it just right, she could see the beginnings of a bump. Her bump. That baby sure didn't have any problems claiming where it belonged and to whom.

Sudden pressure on her bladder reminded Ramona of baby Winny's ownership. Ramona stepped out of the tub and paused under the warming lamps. The door to the bathhouse swung open. Lucas' panicked expression had not left his face, but on it was added the surprise of finding her naked and wet.

"Ramona, baby, I'm sorry. I-"

She held her hand up, and he scurried to the cabinet to retrieve a towel. She wrapped it around herself while keeping both eyes on him, chest rising and falling with increasing upset. "What are you doing here? It's New Year's Eve, the busiest night of the year. The restaurant must be-"

"I don't care about any of that." His voice cracked. "The only thing that matters is you."

She let that statement sink in and be absorbed into her skin, into her mind, into her heart. This was what commitment looked like. *Take note, Ramona.*

He swallowed. "I had no idea Abigail was in town or going to show up at the restaurant. I swear - nothing is going on between us. You have to believe-"

"I know."

"You - Wait. What?"

"I know nothing is going on between you and Abigail."

It was as if all the parts of his face shifted position. "Oh."

She walked over to the bench and sat down. This conversation was going to take a while. "I'd like to start from the beginning. What was the deal with her threatening me when I first got here?"

He stepped toward her. "She was scared that being cut off from my family would tank her campaign. She needed my dad's Congressional connections, but he stopped talking to her. She thought if you were out of the picture, she could ingratiate herself with him again."

Now, that made much more sense than the ridiculous story Abigail told her about wanting Lucas back. But still, it wasn't as if Ramona was the Winston's favorite person. Moving on. "Why did she stop?"

"At the funeral, Tyler told me about their... activities."

She hadn't known that Tyler was there. It was still such a blur.

"I threatened her. Told her it would be hard to hold on to any of what remained of her sympathy votes if everyone knew about her *extracurriculars*. It worked. But then she found out Connor had hired Stanley Grayson. She wanted Grayson for herself. He would be her only hope in saving her shot."

"So she came to the restaurant to see Grayson?"

He knelt in front of her. "She came to see me, force me to

pressure Connor. Of course, I wouldn't, so she was going to confront him herself. That's when you..." He dropped his head.

She ran her thumb across his brow, and he looked up with love and hurt and determination all flashing across his eyes. "After you left, things got even messier. She made a scene and I threw her out. I can't guarantee she won't come after us again, but I can guarantee that I will protect you. Even if that means your brother has to deal with the consequences."

The force of that statement sent her arm out to the edge of her seat for balance. "You are not allowed to protect me by keeping things from me."

"I understand. And I regret ever thinking that. It's just I never know what's going to..."

She waited for him to finish. And waited some more. "What's going to what?"

He cinched his eyebrows together. "Everything I do, I worry that you already have one foot out the door. One more step and you'll be gone."

That statement felt like an electric jolt. One foot out the door was how she'd been leading her whole life. Pretty successfully, too. But all those paths had led her to this bench, across from the man who'd brought her back. "Is that why you won't consider the Dubai offer? Because you don't trust I'll stick around?"

An exasperated sigh filled the quiet space. "No. But I wonder why it's so important to you. Is it because you want me to have it or you want to test if I would go?"

Any chill from her damp skin dissipated under the heat of her discomfort. She loved and hated his ability to see all the stuff she preferred to hide. "I don't want you to ever feel like I held you back. Like I messed up and you had to pay the price."

"Please hear me, Ramona." He waited until his silence forced her to look at him. "Being with you is the reward, not the price. Another fancy restaurant would be the poor consolation prize. I really need you to believe me when I say that."

She closed her eyes and nodded. It wasn't that different from the offer she'd gotten to go to London. It would have never crossed her mind to think that Lucas had held her back from that opportunity. Compared to being with him, that project, great as it might have been, was inconsequential.

Suddenly, his reasoning made total sense. "I do."

Relief softened the line between his brows. "Why would you ever think that you messed up, anyway?"

That was easy, although explaining it would be challenging. "Everyone kept reminding me what a big deal it was that I had moved back. You, Connor, even Dad and Camille. I wouldn't hear it. In my mind, I was doing this for my father and for the children's center and being with you was going to be a fun and sexy side project. I thought it would be easy."

He flinched as if she had struck him.

"Sorry, I know that sounded bad."

An audible swallow preceded a slow bob of his head. "I want you to be able to tell me the truth. Please go on."

She wished she had a better plan for what she was going to say. A framework or bullet points, at least.

He wrapped his hands around hers. "Please, Mo. I need to hear this."

Here goes. "When I got here, I had no idea about family, and now I'm making my own. I'd just begun to wrap my head around this thing called *home* and now I have one. I don't like not having a plan or not knowing what's next, but nothing that's happened here was in my control. It's wonderful and terrifying, and I have to admit I had no idea what I was getting into. Or what I'm doing. I feel dumb and powerless. And always afraid."

Sadness clouded his features. "I know that's hard for you. It always has been. Even when we were kids, and there was nothing you could do about your parents, you took charge of us. Con and I joke about it all the time." The dimple appeared. "Actually, we kind of liked it. You were the only one parenting us, sometimes."

Parenting. That idea brought a tremor to her breath. "I want to be good at this. I want to be a good mom."

He dropped his head onto her lap, broad shoulders wrapping around her legs. She ran her fingers through his soft, sandy curls.

"I'm scared too, Mo." His whisper was barely audible.

Her breath caught. "What scares you?"

He looked up at her, eyes glistening. "What if it's not enough for you? This simple life in the quiet suburbs, with me and our child. It's a far cry from jet-setting from one glamorous city to another. Or what if it's too much for you? What if I hold you so tightly that I force you to run? What if you do what your mother did and..."

"That's not going to happen." She was relieved he didn't finish his sentence. As horrifying as the thought might have been, it was not unfamiliar. Convincing them both that she was not her mother vaulted to the top of her list.

CHAPTER TWENTY-ONE

*D*espite an intention to stay up until midnight, to celebrate crossing over into a new year, Ramona woke up with a start at 12:43. She'd missed it.

One of many things she'd missed over the past few months. Thanksgiving, Christmas, and now New Year's. Not that anyone would confuse her for a traditionalist, but the holidays were predictable markers for the passing of time. She needed them to remind her to pause the fast-moving current of her life and take note.

She studied the slumbering man next to her. The beautiful, wonderful, loving man who'd brought her a new life to go with her new year. She had heard, on numerous occasions, the adage that how you spent the first day of the year would determine the rest of it. She'd never paid it any mind, not only because she didn't believe in that degree of determinism but also because by the first of January, her whole year had been mapped out. Nearly to the minute.

For the first time in her adult life, she had no idea what the year would bring. It was as if she'd crossed into unknown territory and would be forced to navigate without a map. Her plans and lists would be of little use. She'd have to figure out how to enjoy the surprises as much as she did the schedules.

But there was quite a bit to sort out and maybe, just for one day, she could write it out.

She reached for the small notepad on the bedside table, careful not to disturb Lucas. After making a short list of hard conversations, she tucked herself into the spaces of his body and breathed him in, the familiar and the new mingling into sweet excitement. It was scary to be this trusting of and connected to another person, to remain open to him, their life, their future. The fear, the discomfort, the worry, abated with each breath, with each reminder of her commitment. What mattered, more than the fact that she was afraid, was that she was going to stay. That she wanted to stay. Physically *and* emotionally.

Lucas shuddered awake and pulled her into him.

"Happy New Year, Baloo," she whispered.

He started, quick blinks trying to shift the sleep from his eyes. "Oh, no! Did we miss it?"

"It's okay, darling. It's going to be the new year all year."

"I look forward to another year of your jokes, Mowgli." He gave her that smile - bright and crooked and nearly her favorite thing in the whole world.

"Me too." She kissed him as she might have had they been at a fancy party, drinking champagne, watching fireworks. "I want you to know how much I love you. And how happy you make me."

All the sleepiness fell away from his face before he pressed in for another kiss.

"What should we do today?" he spoke into the top of her head as she ran her fingers across the ripples of his abdomen.

"Well, you're going to work out with Connor in the morning."

"Really? Don't you want to stay in bed all morning?"

"I know your Crossfit is important to you, so I think you should go." She looked up with a grin. "I'll be waiting for you."

He gave her a sly knowing smile. "I like the sound of that."

"And there's something else I'd like to do."

He waggled his brows. "Anything. Tell me."

"I want to have some people over. Our families, maybe Jackson and Camille if they're free. Leni, too." She looked for a change in his expression. "I know you were probably hoping for a day off, not having to be in the kitchen, but I hope it's okay."

His gaze melted into hers. "I can't think of any better way to spend the day than cooking for the people we love, in our home. And it's about time we had a proper party."

Which was exactly what she had in mind.

Ramona kept herself busy tidying up while Lucas was out, waiting for a reasonable hour to begin her calls. Connor had agreed to come over after the guys were done with their workout, so she got to cross him off the short list. With only two more names remaining, it was easy to decide where to start.

Her mother picked up the call before the first full ring. Even though it wasn't even eight am, Ramona knew her mother would be up. "Hi, Mom. Happy New-"

"Ramona! Oh my God, I'm so glad to hear from you. I've been so worried."

"Mom." She closed her eyes and tried to relax. "I'm fine. No need to worry."

"Is it true, sweetheart? You're pregnant?"

"Yes, it's true. I'm sorry you had to find out the way you did, but I hadn't planned on telling anyone for a few more weeks. It was-"

"Oh, Ramona, I can't believe it. This news is-"

"Mom. I need you to stop interrupting me. I called because there are several things I want to tell you." After a reasonable stretch of silence on the other end, she continued. "I know that this place holds a lot of bad memories for you. For me, too. But I've made a different choice and even if you don't agree with it, it's what I want. I'm creating a home here with the man I love and our child. I'm building a center that speaks to everything I've dreamed of, professionally. It's a big change, I know. But I'm happy, Mom. Can you understand that?"

Several sighs came through the phone line. "All I want is for you to be happy, Cariña."

"I know, Mom. I'm just going to do it differently than you." She gathered herself. "I called to invite you over this afternoon. We're having an impromptu celebration and I would love for you to be here."

"Of course I will be there, Ramona. I love you, sweetheart."

"Love you too, Mom. See you later."

Ramona tapped the red icon to close the call and continued staring at the phone. The conversation had gone as well as expected. Ramona knew her mother's experiences had indelibly etched themselves into her personality. She was scarred, but had salvaged a pretty amazing life out of it. Her mother might never agree with Ramona's choices and that had to be okay. It was time to stop avoiding these conflicts and holding her tongue, activities she had reserved only for her personal relationships. She took a deep breath. This whole adulting thing might just work out.

The next call required scrolling through pages of previous calls on her phone. As soon as Ramona saw the number, even though she'd never put a name in the contact, she knew it was the right one. After four rings, Ramona prepared for voicemail to click in. She stood, ready to deliver an extended message when Abigail's voice came through the line.

"Hello."

"Hi Abigail, it's Ramona. Do you have a minute?"

Pausing just a tick longer than what would have been natural, she answered. "Sure."

"Great. There are a couple of things I'd like you to know. First, I am not your enemy, and I am not interested in doing anything to thwart your career. It has nothing to do with me. I won't get in your way or intrude into any of the relationships you think are necessary for you to achieve your goal. However..." Ramona paused to collect her thoughts, find the precise words. "Please know that I have zero tolerance for threats against my family, which includes all of my relatives, Lucas, and the Winstons. If you decide to continue your manipulations and attempts at blackmail, I will marshal the full force of any power I have access to and direct it to your utter and complete destruction."

Ramona gave the other woman a moment to feel the weight of her statement.

"That's quite a threat, Ramona. I didn't picture you as the type."

"You're right. This is not my playing field, and I have no taste for the game. But it isn't about that for me. It's about the people I love and protecting them from harm."

Abigail responded with a high-pitched grunt and Ramona

could almost feel disdain coming through the line. "I don't think you know what you're up against. Getting pregnant to trap Lucas was an amateur move."

Now, that was almost funny. "Ha! Abigail, you're becoming a caricature of yourself. Lucas is free to choose whatever and whomever he wants. No one has given him more opportunity to flee than I have. But it's clear, as enticing as your *offers* might have been, he's here, with me, in *our* home. That's pretty simple, don't you think?"

Ramona waited for some other reaction. Maybe even another round of threats. There was nothing but silence. "As for my brother, no one believes your story. I'd worry about all you have to hide, instead of some nonsense about Connor."

"You have no idea."

Like a flipped switch, all that worry about Abigail turned into boredom with a splash of pity. "Happy New Year, Abigail. Good luck."

That call was neither better nor worse than what Ramona imagined. And also both of those things at the same time. Maybe Abigail would come tearing through her life again. Maybe, between Lucas and Connor, there might always be more drama than she'd gotten used to. In the scheme of things, it didn't matter. When you chose a place, or when it chose you, you took the good and the bad. The beautiful and the crazy.

Ramona put her phone down and walked outside, a cold wind whipping her hair across her face. There she stood, in a beam of sunlight, getting batted around by currents of air. She imagined her yoga teacher creating a whole lesson about that moment. The unpredictability of the wind, the warmth of the sun, the intention of her holding her ground. In other words, everything she needed to know.

Maybe she'd roll out her yoga mat for a few minutes before Lucas returned. But not yet. The sun on her face felt like heaven.

Ramona had already finished showering and dressing when Lucas and Connor blew into the house, arms loaded with grocery bags. She should have known. Lucas was going to create a feast. The guys stopped their boisterous conversation when Ramona walked into the kitchen.

"Looks like you bought out the supermarket, honey."

Lucas dropped his bags and wrapped his arms around her. "You know how I don't like to leave people hungry."

Her face lit up. "Yes, you know exactly how to satisfy."

"Okay, you two." Connor covered his ears. "It's a bit early for all that, don't you think?"

"Hey, Con."

He bowed his head. "Mo."

"I'll take care of this stuff," Lucas said. "Why don't the two of you go chat in the living room? I'll bring coffee."

"How was your New Year's Eve?" Ramona asked her brother.

"Not my best." He tugged at the sleeve of his sweatshirt. "I'm really sorry about what happened at the restaurant. I had no idea Stanley was going to... well... what he did was totally inappropriate. I wish I could take it back."

Her brother's expression was believably remorseful. "It wasn't great, Con. Not really how I pictured my pregnancy announcement would go." She smoothed back the hair falling in her eyes. "But it's done. I need to move on."

"What can I do?"

"Actually, there is something. I need an invitation to the big event you've been talking about. The rally next week at the Mellon Auditorium."

He fiddled with his glasses. "Mo, I know you hate what I'm doing. I don't like that you feel that way, but I understand. So, I don't think it's necessary for you to force yourself to go to my events. You don't need to torture yourself. Or me."

"I'm your little sister. I was *born* to torture you. Thought you would have figured that out by now. And anyway, who's going to woo all the big donors? You think Sleek Stanley is up to it?" The look on her face communicated *definitely not*.

His forehead creased. "You really want to go?"

"Yes, you dummy. You're right, I don't love what you're doing. But you're my big brother and I love you. That's not going to change. Me and my illegitimate baby are going to your rally. Whether you like it or not."

His whole face puckered. "Yuck. I'm so sorry. You know I don't believe any of that stuff Stanley said, right?"

"You better not."

"It's part of what I'm trying to do. Get out from all this hypocrisy in politics. Everybody twisted up about who's having sex with whom when all these kids in Virginia are literally starving. We can do better."

For just a moment, she saw her dorky brother on a grand stage delivering a rousing speech to a rapt audience. She knew he had a good heart, that he cared about the same issues she did. Maybe he could be the exception, the one who wouldn't get destroyed by the toxicity of it. "I believe you."

His long arms were around her before she could formulate her next thought. "I can't stand fighting with you, Mo. I'm sorry I haven't been there for you. I know it's been rough."

She squeezed him back. "Love you, Con."

"Hey!" Lucas' voice startled them both. "Now that's more like it."

They each took a large mug from his hands.

"Thanks for the coffee, man. That ridiculously fancy machine actually makes a great cup."

Ramona shook her head. "Please don't encourage him. He's already having a special accessory custom made in Italy. It has gotten completely out of hand."

"Sis, there are no limits when coffee is concerned."

A high five sealed the agreement between the men. Those two were going to keep her in chuckles and eye-rolls all year long.

"So, Con, can you stick around? I want to move some things around in the dining room. We need to fit a lot of people in there."

"Happy to help."

Ramona put her hand on her hip. "What am I, chopped liver? I can move furniture, too."

The men answered in unison. "No!"

"Mo," Connor continued, "it's bad enough that Lucas knocked you up. At least he can spare you from manual labor."

Ramona was the first to burst out laughing, followed closely by the two men in rounds of hysterics that lasted for minutes.

Decorating the dining room, setting the table, putting personal touches on the already beautiful house, kept Ramona smiling the whole afternoon. She'd never lived somewhere that she was interested in making her own but this was fun.

Actual fun. She popped into the kitchen as often as she could while Lucas rocked out on his five-course gourmet extravaganza. There were dance breaks, kissing breaks, and more than occasional butt slaps.

By early-afternoon, Connor headed home, leaving the couple to survey all their hard work. Lucas kissed the back of her neck while she adjusted the napkins on the table.

"Everything looks beautiful, baby. The house, the dinner table, you even did that cool thing with the flowers by the front door. Will you get mad if I compliment your domestic skills?"

She chuckled. "Why don't we lay down for a minute and I'll show you?"

"Absolutely," he growled in just the way that brought a tingle to all her important places.

She lay on the bed, catching her breath and wondering if the reward for months of debilitating nausea was the ability to orgasm at the snap of a finger. The whole pregnancy thing had taken a delightful turn. She rolled into Lucas' side. Taking a courageous breath, she stroked along his collarbone. "Hey, did you really tell Grayson or Connor that you were willing to marry me?"

His breath stopped and his body stiffened. She waited. He tilted her chin up and pressed his lips to hers.

"Yes. One of the oddest conversations I've ever had with a stranger. Connor had no right to tell Grayson about the baby, but I told them I wanted to marry you as soon as you were ready. I certainly wasn't going to do it for him and his campaign. And I wasn't going to even bring it up to you." He ran his thumb over her cheek. "Does it surprise you that I'd want something as mundane as getting married?"

Surprise wasn't the right word. "No. I've always known that's what you wanted. I didn't know you wanted it with *me*."

"Oh, Mowgli, you are everything to me. You've always been. If I thought for one second you'd want to marry me, I'd whisk you off to a Justice of the Peace before you could finish saying yes."

Ramona imagined the scene in her head: them running down the street, then up the steps of a grand building, hand in hand, like some TV version of a City Hall wedding. Then she added in a baby in her arms. Or maybe in one of those cute baby backpacks. Or maybe she was hugely pregnant and toddling down the sidewalk instead of running. Or maybe she was just a little bit pregnant. Or maybe...

"What are you plotting, my darling?"

Busted. "I'm imagining what that would look like."

He pulled her into him. "I know this has been a hard year for you, but it's been a dream come true for me. I'm going to do everything in my power to give you the life you've always dreamed of."

She couldn't have imagined anything like the life she was living or the life she could so clearly see in her future. But she knew it was exactly what she wanted. "I think that, just for planning purposes, of course, if you thought about making our arrangement official, I could guarantee you better than fifty-fifty odds of success."

His smile reached well past those gleaming eyes. "Fifty-fifty? Not even seventy-thirty? Or sixty-forty?"

"Okay. I'll give you a solid sixty-forty."

Eyebrows rose. "In the project plan I'm sure you've created, is there a timing element I should know about?"

"There's always a timing element, darling."

"Fair enough." His fingers threaded through her hair. "So, if there should happen to be a gathering of all of our loved ones in our home, celebrating the start of a new year, would that be a good time?"

That assessment wouldn't require a single list. No pros, cons, or research. No checking her calendar or weighing options. Nothing could have been more clear or right. "I'd say your chances are quite good, Baloo."

ear Reader,

I hope you enjoyed Lucas and Ramona's remarkable love story. If you'd like to share your thoughts about the book with others, I'd be delighted for your review at your preferred book retailer. Reviews support independent authors!

For all the perks of being a cherished reader (which you are), and be the first to know about new releases, sign up to be part of the Smart & Sexy Reader Team. I regularly send out book bonuses, audio clips, playlists and other goodies to make the wild ride even more fun. Get on the list at http:// bit.ly/PEKSignup.

If you can't wait to find out what happens next, just turn the page to find an excerpt to Claiming Power, which features Connor and Jenna!

Thank you again, and I hope to see you soon between the pages of my steamy love stories.

Excerpt from CLAIMING POWER
Book Three of the Friends & Lovers Series

*C*ONNOR

Connor adjusted himself while waiting for Stanley to get off the phone. They'd been sitting in the limo for long enough that things were getting uncomfortable down there. But it didn't look like Stanley was going to stop screaming into his cell anytime soon.

Maybe he could just step out for a second, stretch his legs, air out his parts, maybe even clear his head before going back to get the scolding he knew was coming. His reach for the door was stopped by the firm grip of Stanley's hand. Connor could have punched him in the face. Who did this guy think he was?

A twist of the wrist freed him from the hold, a kick of the door freed him from the stifling car.

Connor slammed the door, shutting off the string of profanities coming from inside the sleek black Towncar. He looked up to find himself at a rather seedy-looking loading dock, swarmed with young people in uniforms unloading three white panel trucks. Must be the caterers and he must be in the back of Mellon Auditorium, the location for his next political rally.

Connor matched his breaths to each long stride. This was a big night. When his campaign for Senate became real. He'd be asking people for money and votes. Asking for them to trust him.

A cold sweat broke out across his forehead. What was he thinking? He wasn't ready for this. He was a small-town

Mayor. Sure, he had a political legacy, and yes, he'd done great things for his community, but this... This was another league entirely.

He paused at his reflection in the blackened car windows and ran a hand over his hair. No reason, as he was always perfectly groomed. Just to make sure his head was still screwed on, perhaps.

"Dad," he whispered. "I need your help, here. I might have gotten myself into something way over my head."

He didn't expect a response, considering his father had died three weeks before. But what he saw in the reflection looked more like his long-gone grandfather, the one the streets and buildings were named after. The one who'd terrorized his childhood.

"Grow a set! You're not just any boy," he would say. "You're Connor Barrett. Eldest grandson of Virginia's most beloved Governor and the face of a new generation of leadership. So stop acting like a pussy and go out there and show them what a leader looks like!"

Connor shook out his head, desperately wanting the image to dissolve in the cold day. Except for the fact that the man he'd hired as his campaign manager, the inimitable Stanley Grayson, known in political circles as the Kingmaker, was more like his grandfather than Connor would ever be.

It was an honor that Stanley agreed to work with him. Certainly, his best friend's dad, Congressman Winston, had called in some big favors to make it happen. But only two weeks into the campaign and they were already butting heads. Stanley wanted to run things old school - and by old school, he meant wheeling, dealing, and dirty - while Connor wanted to do it better. He wanted to show all the people disillusioned by politics and their leaders that someone would have their back.

It wasn't working. Maybe he wasn't cut out for this after all.

The door to the limo swung open. The man wasn't visible but his voice boomed across the lot. "Get your ass back in here!"

Connor paused before sauntering back to the car.

"I was just waiting for you to finish your phone call, Stanley. No need to speak to me that way."

"You better get your head in the game, Barrett! I was on the phone with the morning show, arguing for you to get top billing. This is NOT the time to be checking out."

Connor exhaled, praying for patience. "I'm not checking out."

Stanley tightened his lips to a nearly invisible line. "Could have fooled me... Anyway. Tonight is extremely important. Many of the critical influencers will be here, deciding whether you're going to be their chosen horse in this race."

Connor flinched at being referred to as a horse. This guy was disgusting. "I understand that."

"Do you? Because you've turned it into a family party. This is not the time to socialize with your buddies. This is the time to make an impression on the power players with deep pockets. They are going to determine whether you even make it to the primaries, much less the main election."

No shit. It was exhausting having this conversation over and over. "That's clear. And that's why Ramona is here. She-"

"Your knocked up sister? She's the problem, not the solution, Barrett. No one wants to see a woman flaunting her promiscuity around like that. As if the scandal with the Winston boy wasn't bad enough..."

Connor slid forward in his seat, fist clenched against his side. It had been decades since he'd hit someone but it might not be much longer. "Don't you fucking dare talk about my sister that way! You and I both know she is the most talented fundraiser on this planet. I'm lucky she agreed to do anything for me, after the stunt you pulled on New Year's Eve. You," he pointed right in the man's face, "are not allowed within ten feet of her. Understood?"

The older man slid back in his seat, that self-satisfied smirk on his face. Again. "Now, that's more like it. That's the kind of fire people are waiting to see in you. That's the stuff that's going to get you a seat in that very impressive building down the street."

And this was how it went. Stanley got to be as offensive as he wanted to be, then shrugged it off as part of the plan. Connor pulled off his glasses and rubbed his eyes, working to manage the rage that brought a twitch around his temples. If this was the price he had to pay to get elected, he would have to pay it. There just didn't seem like another option.

The caterers were scurrying as he wound his way through the prep kitchen. Only a few stopped what they were doing to stare and whisper. He walked a little taller and put on his 'future Senator' face. Looking the part was half the game.

Stanley walked him into the green room, where he'd wait until it was time for him to speak. He wasn't allowed out until that point. He assumed it was because Stanley didn't trust him to not say something wrong. As if. Connor didn't say the wrong thing. Ever.

Connor was grateful Stanley had to step out to deal with some emergency or another. A minute away from that man was good for his mental health. Congressman Winston arrived a few minutes later. During all those hard years when his family was shredded - Mom fleeing to California, Dad lost in the bottle, Grandfather on the war path - he'd depended more and more on his best friend's family. Lucas Winston was more like a brother than a friend and his dad, longtime Congressman, had been the one to support Connor in his political journey. He'd done so much to make this evening happen and would be giving the opening speech.

"Uncle Robert. So glad to see you."

The man put his palm on Connor's face. "Lookin' good, kid. Are you excited?"

Excited? Terrified, more like it. "Yes, I am. We've got a full house and-."

"You know, I remember my first big rally, when I decided to leave my position in the State Senate and run for the House. I don't think I stopped shaking for days. I get what a big deal this is. But your time has come. Virginia needs you. Our government needs you."

The two men hugged briefly before Robert pulled away. "Now, who do I have to fuck to get a drink around here?"

Two young women carried trays into the room minutes after Connor's call down to the kitchen. He was surprised Stanley didn't breeze in after them, admonishing him about the food they'd requested.

"Never eat before a speech," he'd say. "It makes you look fat and lazy. You want to look hungry. That's what sells."

The women set up the table in the center of the room with the bottle of Scotch, several bottles of water, and an assortment of the appetizers he assumed were being served to the guests. He caught Robert enjoying the view, a bit too much. A pat on the back pulled his attention from an admittedly fine derriere back to Connor.

"Did you get the draft of my speech?"

"Sure did. Looks good." A quick glance back over at the

women. "I'd say it's better to err on the side of too little than too much. These folks won't be lingering over their decisions. And our speeches are just going to get in the way of them eating, drinking, and talking about themselves."

He was probably right. You didn't get to be a Congressman for so many decades if you didn't know what to do in these situations. "Okay, maybe I'll cut some from the middle."

Robert slapped him on the back. "Just be yourself, Connor. Have a conversation with the crowd. You're naturally charismatic. Use it. The women will be swooning, the men will remember when they were as young and handsome as you. It'll be fine. Just fine."

The two women snuck a look before disappearing out the door. He could have sworn the blonde actually winked at him.

Robert smirked. "It's good we got some nice looking waitresses, too. That always helps. Especially, if you're looking for some company tonight." He winked. "After the rally."

Not going to happen. By the time the private after-party was done, it was going to be late. Then he had his Crossfit workout first thing in the morning and a day full of appointments. Although it had been so long since he'd had another outlet for all that energy. Young and single was not necessarily a kiss of death for a male Senator, but it rarely helped. He had to make sure he wasn't coming across as a player. Gotta promote those conservative values, as Stanley reminded him. Frequently.

He pulled out his phone and jotted down a note to talk to Lorena, his matchmaker, the next day. So far, all her offerings had been duds. Too boring. Too chatty. Too wild. Too power hungry. Dating, when you were on a fast track to a serious political position, was much more complicated than finding someone to warm your bed. He needed a woman who was smart, serious, and driven, but not too much of either. Someone who understood the life of a political wife and wanted all that came with it. A tall, leggy brunette would be great. One would have thought in this part of the world, streets would be teeming with that type of woman. So far, no luck. Especially since Lorena kept insisting on sending him blondes, who were almost always an immediate *no*.

This woman, wherever she was, had to be White House ready.

JENNA

Jenna fought her way through the crowd like a salmon swimming upstream. She had no interest in following everyone toward the stage, where an older man was droning on. With everyone's attention on Mr. Boring Pants, it was a perfect time to head toward the now empty bar.

Not bad. Off to one side of the enormous event space, that setup could rival any of the fanciest bars she'd seen. Not that she liked fancy bars. Dark and dirty was more her speed. This being her very first political rally, she wasn't aware of the high caliber alcohol they would serve. Her favorite Tequila, in fact.

She eyed the young bartender. Also not bad. Maybe she could rescue this ultra-dull evening after all.

"A shot of Patron platinum, please."

He nodded and turned to retrieve the recognizable bottle. "Aren't you interested in hearing the candidate speak?"

"Not even a little bit."

"Then why are you here?" he asked with a smirk.

She preferred her bartenders hot and silent, and this one was only fulfilling one of those requirements. "He's a friend of the family, supposedly. And they're all here to support him.

But we don't even live in this state and can't vote for him. I don't see the point, honestly."

The crowd burst into applause as the generous shot slid down her grateful throat. The opening act must have finished and the main guy - aka the candidate - would be speaking next. Oh, yay. More political speeches about governing this tiny, inconsequential state.

The huddled bodies separated just enough for her to see the tall, dark-haired man stride across the stage. Her eyes followed his every move as she became aware of three things.

He had terrible taste in clothes.

She remembered him from old family photos, running circles in their backyard wearing thick glasses and a bright red cape.

That swagger communicated something to her body that she would never have expected.

She turned away, slightly disturbed. That guy was not her type at all. Unless of course underneath that dull blue suit and nerdy glasses was a wild streak and a back full of tattoos. But the way he owned the stage and captured the crowd was impressive. She ended up listening, rapt, to his thankfully brief speech about his candidacy for Senate. People were excited. I guess having a young, almost-hot Senator might not be so bad if you were forced to live there.

The applause continued long after he'd walked off the stage. Maybe he was even making his way around the crowd. She couldn't tell.

She'd need to find the rest of her family at some point. Almost certainly, there would be some other event right after this one. More schmoozing, smiling, and hopefully high quality booze.

A run to the bathroom might work before the crowd's attention moved off the stage. She spun around and bumped directly into the center of a broad chest. Boring blue filled her vision. It was him.

"Oh, sorry, I didn't know you were right behind me."

A squint was followed by one of the goofiest smiles she'd ever seen. All loopy and happy, with no smolder whatsoever. "Jenna King, right? Wow, you look so much like your mom. And your Aunt Olivia. It's uncanny."

Right. Olivia Winston was his best friend's mom. Resident bitch of Virginia, far as Jenna could tell. She ran her hand over the mass of her hair currently contained in a low bun. The only similarity she had with those two women was the platinum blonde hair no one ever believed was real.

"I'm Connor Barrett. Thanks so much for coming. Your family has been amazingly supportive."

"Hey." She returned his handshake. "Oh, and congratulations on the... running for office."

He laughed. "Thanks. What are you drinking?"

"Oh, you did well with the bar selection. Patron platinum. Yumm. Way to schmooze the voters."

He put up two fingers for the bartender who was standing at attention, and had finally figured out how to keep his mouth shut.

Two overfull shot glasses appeared on the bar.

He tipped his head toward her. "Cheers."

Even though it hadn't even been minutes since her last shot, it went down oh, so smoothly. She licked a drop of tequila from her top lip and grinned.

He threw his down and instead of the flinch and gag she expected, he smiled right back at her. "Only the best for my supporters."

That look was so hard to decipher. And it was impossible to see his eyes behind those thick, dark frames. "I think we met when we were kids. I don't really remember it, though."

"Me neither. But I remember your brother."

Of course. Her superstar brother. "Yeah, Jackson's pretty memorable. I was really little and probably inconsequential."

"I can't imagine that ever being true, but I'm glad to meet you again."

Jenna shifted her weight from one foot to the other, remembering about her interrupted trip to the bathroom. He wasn't speaking. Or moving out of her way.

"So, tell me something about yourself. What do you do?"

She looked around at the line forming behind him. Wow, what an orderly group of people, patiently waiting their turn to talk to the man of the day. "I'm a schoolteacher. Middle school history."

"Tell me about middle school history. I'm kind of a history buff myself."

The warm tingle of alcohol entering her bloodstream sent a flush to her cheeks. At least, she thought it was the alcohol. "You know, I really thought it was going to work. I thought, if I get them young enough, if I show them the lessons we've learned, over and over, then maybe they would think differently. Act differently. I was top of my class in school – sociology and political science double major. I know stuff that can help them make a difference in the world. Make better choices. Understand the patterns and cycles that are fairly predictable and consistent."

Had he moved even closer to her? It felt like all she could see was blue.

"I'm getting that it's not quite working out that way."

"Well, the first problem is that I'm working in an elite private school. I'm basically a servant to the tyrannical parents and their little despots-in-training. I have absolutely no power, no influence, no impact."

"That sounds pretty shitty."

The tequila was loosening her inhibitions and her lips. "Yeah. I really wanted to make a difference. Bring forth a new way of leading people, of being benevolent stewards of our communities, maybe of this country."

"Why not go into politics yourself?"

"It's not for me. I'm not interested in putting up with what a woman like me would have to put up with just to be heard. I think politics used to be the meeting ground for grand ideas and high ideals. Now it's the last stop for the greedy, power-hungry, and ignorant."

She didn't understand the shocked look on his face at first. Then it dawned on her that she was attending a political rally. His political rally.

Her hand flew up to cover her mouth. Too bad all that nonsense had already slipped out. "Holy shit! I'm so sorry."

He burst out laughing. "Jenna King, you are the most interesting person I've encountered in this whole room. No one talks like that anymore, which I think is part of the problem. We're not addressing the reality of the matter. We're just tap-dancing around all of it."

Relief returned in the form of a deep breath. She had to learn how to hold her tongue at some point. Maybe less tequila too. "I meant no offense. Maybe you're the exception."

"I want to be."

Something about how he said that made her believe him. Wow. This guy knew something about wielding power.

"I've got a funny proposition."

She grimaced.

He grinned. "No, not like that. Come work with me. I'm putting together my team and someone like you would make a great addition. I want the truth, as blunt and inappropriate as it may be. I haven't yet met someone I trusted to give it to me."

Well, that was exciting. "I don't live here, Connor. I live in California."

"Doesn't matter. Come here for the next ten months, assuming I make it through the primaries. Then you can go back to your bratty students in California."

He touched her arm, which would normally have sent off alarms, but there was nothing sexual or predatory about that touch. Interesting.

"I have to tell you, Connor, that's one of the most interesting propositions I've gotten in a long time. You seem like a good guy. I know my family thinks so. But I can't leave my life, move across the country and learn everything about political campaigns. Thanks, but no."

Besides politics is boring.

Someone tapped Connor on the shoulder. Before turning to acknowledge Mrs. Tappy Hands, he looked Jenna in the eye. Yeah, those big brown eyes were something. "Thanks for chatting with me, Jenna."

The couple behind him beamed as he gave them his attention. "Hello. I so appreciate your support."

Jenna snuck past them and made her way toward the bathroom, running into her best friend and soon to be sister-in-law on the way.

"Jenna! Where've you been? We thought maybe you snuck out and headed out to a biker bar." Camille's typical composure had left the building.

"I wish. No, I was chatting up the candidate, if you must know."

"Really? I am actually surprised. But he was so inspiring. I almost wish I lived here, because he'd definitely have my vote." Camille stared up, all dreamy eyes.

Geez. Jenna knew it wasn't the hots. Camille had had it bad for Jenna's brother Jackson forever. And they'd just gotten engaged. So, that look on her face was, like, inspiration, or something. Weird. "Hmmm. So, what's next?"

"We're going back to the house. For a more intimate get together."

Camille had been friends with Connor's sister, Ramona, for a few months and had given Jenna the scoop. The Barretts were an old school southern political dynasty, apparently. Hopefully more stately mansion than plantation. Either way, a definite snooze-fest.

Jenna pretended to yawn. "Yeah. Soooo exciting."

Her best friend jabbed her in the ribs. "Can you stop being such a pain? I'm sure it won't last long, then you can make your way to the seediest, smelliest bar you can find, and go find some leather-clad unshaven dude to grind up on."

Jenna threaded her arm through Camille's and pulled her toward the bathroom. "Now, you're talking."

* * *

Want to find out what happens next? Sign up on the notification list at https://page.co/ww70.

GRATITUDES

As with most of the stories that consume me, this one held a firm grip. Lucas, Ramona, their families and friends fought for my attention, resulting in the first three books of the Friends & Lovers Series. They are characters who've succeeded and failed in equal measure, and whose yearning to be seen and heard and loved stole my own heart.

There are always so many to thank...

The intrepid readers undaunted by the story in its clunky, messy beginnings and who helped me excavate the most gleaming story I could write. Special thanks to my beloved Scribophile groups.

My darling, the Latin hottie who tells me how wonderful all my writing is (even when it isn't) and is always hungry for more.

My girl, who isn't strictly allowed to read my books, but always has a remarkably helpful opinion to share about human behavior, fonts, and Photoshop.

And you. Of course, you, who chose to come along on the wild adventure with me. We've got so much more fun in store for us.

ABOUT THE AUTHOR

I believe that everything we experience exists as a story within us.

My journey as a writer includes the award-winning poem I penned at the ripe old age of seven, decades of hiding and doubt, and then finally... finally!... realizing that art needs to be shared. Storytelling is part of my heritage, even though I denied it for so long. The stories I created - true and imaginary - have saved me numerous times.

> *My characters come to me,*
> *like old friends excited to tell me what's new.*
> *They represent the world I see*
> *and the world I want to see.*

More than anything, I care about recovery from life's setbacks... getting back on your feet after life has brought you to your knees... and my characters fight the hard fight for the lives they know are waiting for them.

I've drawn my inspiration from the many flavors of my life experience. Once a sad, shy girl, I've also been an MIT-trained engineer, biotech executive, professional dancer, yoga teacher and business owner, school founder, spiritual counselor, entrepreneur, and author.

And I own a magic wand that I'm certain will work one day.

When I'm not typing furiously trying to capture the stories that pour from me, you can find me loving my people to excess, globe-trotting to the next great adventure, and sporting bright red lips as a tango diva. And of course on my digital homes: pekavanagh.com and boldsoulcoaching.com.